# RAGTIME DUDES MEET A PARIS FLAPPER

# Ragtime Dudes Meet a Paris Flapper

## Richard Gartee

Lake and Emerald Publications

Books by Richard Gartee
—Fiction—
Lancelot's Grail
Lancelot's Disciple
Ragtime Dudes at the World's Fair
Ragtime Dudes in a Thin Place
Ragtime Dudes Meet a Paris Flapper
—Poetry—
Mountain Breathing
Watching Waves
Canyon Falls
—Non-Fiction—
Skating on Skim Ice

A complete list of currently available titles by the author can be found at www.gartee.com



Published by Lake & Emerald Publications, LLC
Gainesville, FL
www.lepublications.com

Library of Congress Control Number: 2020904303

ISBN 978-0-9906768-8-1

This is a work of fiction. Names, characters, places, and incidents either are the product of the author's imagination or are historical references used fictitiously, and any other resemblance to living persons, or actual businesses, companies, or events is entirely coincidental.

Typesetting services by BOOKOW.COM

*To Dad
who asked me to write a sequel about the Ragtime Dudes*

# CHAPTER 1

New York City, 1922

The man chatting her up evidently thought he was the cat's pajamas.

Cherie drained the last of her champagne and wiggled her glass in his face. They were in an upper Fifth Avenue apartment owned by a minor relation of the Van Dusen family. Not him, he was a guest, like her.

He stopped a passing servant and took two fresh glasses from the tray, offering one to her.

She accepted it. "Thank you . . . um. . ." She'd already forgotten his name.

"Biff," he reminded her.

That's right. A ridiculous name—undoubtedly not his given one. And he was trying too hard to make a fashion statement. His evening jacket, tight, with sloping shoulders, gave him a slim, boyish look. His two-tone wing-tip shoes were the newest style. But a bow tie? For Heaven's sake! Coco would have shredded him. Then, again, Coco would never meet him because she never left Paris.

Cherie preferred Paris, yet here she was in the States again, with its stupid prohibition laws. Still, there was no shortage of champagne and liquor if you chose your party well. New York's upper set had cellars full of it, all predating the Volstead Act, and properly aged. Even if you weren't invited to soirees at homes like the Van Dusen's, she'd heard the city had thirty-thousand speakeasies. She knew more than a few of them. Jazz clubs in old warehouses with hot music and plenty of booze were her preference. No reason to settle for some dark hole where all people did was drink. She'd rather dance.

Of course, none of this was a problem in Paris where you could have wine with your meal at an outdoor café right on the Champ de Elysees without the Keystone Kops showing up to spoil the fun.

A Victrola at the far end of the room playing a record of Caruso reminded her of the first time she saw a Gramophone, way back when she was fifteen. Bryce Holloway had brought three of them to sell in the emporium he, Jack Diamond, and Morgan Silver had opened in Taos. The Gramophone was a wonder, but not as exciting as the three men, who lodged in her mother's boardinghouse. They were the most thrilling thing to come into her young life.

Biff was talking louder now. She took another sip of the surprisingly good champagne and continued to pretend to listen. He seemed less interested in listening to her than in being seen talking to her.

Cherie was the epitome of flapper vogue. Her shapeless dress, with a dropped waist, was scandalously short, displaying her supple calf for all to see. The skirt lengths of her dresses were designed to give the illusion of being, at first, long, and then shorter with dipping, scalloped, and handkerchief hemlines in floating fabrics. The looser, more shapeless fit almost emphasized the feminine woman beneath. And a good thing, too. In Paris, flattened chests and narrow boyish hips were en mode. Her body was anything but flat. Still, the flapper look made men think she was twenty-five.

Biff seemed to think so. After his fifth glass, he'd asked Cherie to take off her slipper because he wished to drink champagne from it.

"Don't be a fool," she said. "First, these are my best Mary Janes. Second, I can't imagine why you would want champagne to taste like feet. Third, I certainly wouldn't put my foot back into a sticky shoe."

Another flapper, her mouth an exaggerated red cupid's bow on a face powdered white and adorned with pencil-lined eyebrows, approached them swirling a pink concoction in a cocktail glass. A New York City girl, Cherie thought. She put her hand on Biff's shoulder, spun him toward the other woman, and nudged his back with her elbow. He fell in line and began chatting up the new fish. Cherie made good her escape by pretending serious study of the wall of art on the opposite side of the room.

The wall art actually did catch her attention. Their hostess evidenced a fondness for Southwestern impressionist painters, something she knew all too well.

The woman herself came over and stood next to her. "I see you're admiring my collection." She steered Cherie further down the wall. "Now, I just got this one, *Taos Mountain, Trail Home* by Cordelia Wilson. Isn't it lovely?"

Truthfully, it reminded her of where she grew up. Just looking at it made her stomach muscles tighten.

"I have a source at the Washington Square Southwest Gallery who specializes in American Impressionism. She frequently exhibits members of the Taos Art Society and other southwest painters." Mrs. Van Dusen hooked her arm in Cherie's elbow and walked her to the next picture. "They're not all landscapes, of course. Here is an early work by Morgan Silver, *Frontier Newlywed*, painted about 1905, I think."

Cherie recognized the painting at once. The woman in it was her sister, Peaches, wearing one of their mother's dresses, standing next to a kitchen stove, spoon in hand, a strainer of vegetables on the counter next to her. Water flowed from a hand pump on the sink behind her. Cherie smiled at the image of an earnest young frontier wife cooking supper. Peaches couldn't cook water—at least back then, she wasn't sure about now. But Morgan had done good work, portraying the fresh-faced glow of a new bride, her lips slightly pursed, like a woman married barely a week, anticipating her husband's arrival.

Cherie felt a pang of guilt. She'd been in New York a week and had yet to visit her sister. In her defense, the Algonquin had been a whirlwind. Poetry readings, afternoon cafés, and early suppers filled her days. Speakeasies and soirees such as this one consumed her nights. Mornings she slept.

"And this one . . ." Mrs. Van Dusen said, dragging Cherie from her reverie, ". . . is a later Silver, painted last year."

Cherie read the brass plate set in the bottom of the frame: *Auburn-Haired Beauty with Flowers*. A woman in the garden of a large Victorian-style house held a basket of freshly cut irises with one hand while tucking a loose strand of hair behind her ear with her other. Cherie knew this place, too. She stepped closer and studied the woman's face. Abigail Diamond, she was certain. Older and more matronly, but still unmistakable. Nostalgia engulfed her.

Cherie shook it off. "Have you seen what the Parisian artists are doing?"

"Not lately. There was a touring exhibit of work by Metzinger and Henri Le Fauconnier a couple of years ago. But I didn't care for all the sharp angles. I prefer the softness of Monet, Renoir, and Pissarro, but who can afford them now?"

"True, but you can find their imitators up and down the cobblestone alleyways of Montmartre."

Mrs. Van Dusen straightened the frame a smidge. "No, it's America's Southwest Impressionists for me."

Great. Cherie had escaped the backwards New Mexico she grew up in for fashionable Paris. And damn if New Mexico hadn't found her in New York.

# CHAPTER 2

**Taos, New Mexico**

Abigail Diamond worked the hand pump on her kitchen sink until the vase was about a third full. She arranged the flowers she'd cut from her garden and carried them out to the studio Jack had built for Morgan behind their house. The building, originally her conservatory, was well lit, having windows on all four sides. Open, the windows caught a good cross draft, no matter which direction a breeze chose to blow.

Morgan was lying on the daybed with his right arm folded across his eyes. Abigail entered the studio and set the vase on a small table near Morgan. "I brought you fresh flowers."

He moved his arm, looked the flowers, smiled, nodded, and covered his eyes again. Abigail picked up a pitcher of water from the table and poured it into his empty water glass. She slipped her hand behind his head, held the glass to his lips, and tilted his head to meet it.

He took a few sips, then sat up. "I'm not helpless."

She handed him the glass. "The pitcher's still full from yesterday. You're not drinking enough water."

He took another swallow, set the glass on the table, and lay back down.

"How about something to eat?" Abigail said.

He shook his head.

"Coffee?"

"No, thanks. I'm just going to rest a bit longer and then finish that painting."

Abigail glanced at his easel. The mostly bare canvas, unchanged for weeks, had an ochre stripe across it, the upper edge of which had a shadow of black and gray paint—the beginnings of a canyon rim. "I wonder if you have Peaches' address in New York."

"157 West Seventeenth . . . No, wait . . . 177 West Fifteenth . . . Oh, that's not right. Look in my secretary, there should be sale receipts from the Washington Square Southwest Gallery. That's her place."

Abigail went to the small desk in the corner and folded down the hinged writing surface. An avalanche of papers spewed out. She picked up those that had fallen on the floor, and sorted through the mess until she spotted a bill of sale from the gallery. "I found one."

"Good."

Abigail restacked the papers neatly and closed the secretary. She ran her finger over the top of the desk. The path of her finger left a visible gray line. "When Maria comes on Thursday, I'm going to have her clean your studio."

"Not necessary."

"The fresh air is nice, but it leaves a lot of dust." She crossed to Morgan and stroked his cheek with the back of her fingers. "When Jack gets back, I'm going to make us all supper. I'll send him to fetch you when it's ready." She leaned down, kissed him softly on the lips, and left to find her son, Cyrus.

He wasn't difficult to locate. Cyrus was sitting on the ground under the tall cottonwood that grew in front of their two-story Victorian house. The twenty-five-year-old house was older than he was, having been built for her by Cyrus's father before she divorced him. Despite its age, the house was in excellent condition, kept that way by Jack and Morgan's efforts.

The cottonwood was even older than the house. She'd had the house built where it benefited from the tree's shade. Cyrus had grown up playing under that tree.

Now he lazed against it, throwing his hunting knife into the dirt between his outstretched legs. Pretty much the same thing he'd done every day since returning from the war.

"Cyrus, I want you to go the telegraph office for me."

He pulled the knife out and flung it again.

"Cyrus?"

"I heard you."

"Well, come along, then."

"Why don't you send Jack?"

*Because I'm trying to help you.* "Jack's not around. He's tending his beer."

"Have him do it when he gets back."

"That'll be too late. There's a time difference in New York, you know."

"Then, you go."

"I'm about to start supper. Come in the house. I'll give you the money, and you can take my car."

She turned and started up the steps. When she reached the wide porch that spanned the front of the house, she paused and looked back at him. Four years since the war ended, and he still hadn't found his way back to anything like a normal life. How much longer would it take?

She reached for the handle on the screen door. "Cyrus."

He pulled his knife out of the ground, wiped the blade on his pants and put it in a sheath on his belt. "Oh, why not?"

# CHAPTER 3

The next day, Cherie slept until noon, bathed, dressed, and ate a light fare of orange juice, coffee, and rolls in the hotel restaurant—her usual routine since arriving in New York.

Now, it was time to do her sisterly duty. No, that wasn't really fair. She loved her sister. It was just that seeing Peaches reminded her of provincial Taos.

She rode the subway from Times Square to Greenwich Village and then walked to Peaches' gallery. The door was unlocked, so she entered, but the place seemed deserted. The room was long and narrow, with electric lights strung along the ceiling illuminating mostly American Impressionist paintings of the Southwest. Some of the works she recognized as Morgan's. The back corner was devoted to a different style—five modernist paintings, two featuring blocky representations of automobiles. In the first, a man stood with his foot on the running board of a large sedan, his forearm resting on the car door. She noticed the headlights blending into the fenders and recognized it as a Pierce-Arrow. She stepped closer for a better look. That fellow certainly could have been Jack Diamond, or how she remembered him.

She moved on to the next, a portrait of a flapper at the wheel of an automobile. Not enough of the car was in the picture to tell if it was the same car, but the painting had bands of flowing colors, giving it a sense of motion as if the car were being driven off the canvas. The model could have been Peaches, but if so, her sister had grown angular and gaunt since she'd last seen her. Or else this painter had cubist leanings. Cherie looked at the lower corner of the canvas for the artist's name.

Morgan? Well, certainly a new genre for him.

An inconsequential clerk in a gray blazer and a bow tie, wearing pince-nez glasses, came from the back. She wondered about all these New York men wearing bow ties. Didn't they know how out-of-date it made them look?

"Guy DePoe." He offered his hand. She touched his fingers, and he gave her a half-handed shake. "Looking for something modernist?"

"No, I'm looking for the owner."

"I'm sorry, she won't be in today. She's left me in charge. I'm sure I can find something to your taste."

She looked around at Taos depicted in all its various hues of ochre and sage. "I doubt that." It wasn't worth explaining.

Cherie left and walked to Peaches' apartment building. The manager there shook his head. "Moved, must be two years ago."

Had it really been that long since she'd last visited? It must have been when, 1919? Yes, after the war. "Do you know where she's gone?"

"Sorry, I don't keep forwarding addresses more than a year." He scratched his head. "Somewhere in Greenwich Village, as I recall."

Oh, dear. Now what? They'd written each other of course, but she'd always used the gallery address. She guessed she'd have to deal with Guy. At least it wasn't that far of a walk back.

Cherie entered the gallery and found him sitting at an ornate reception desk. "Guy, is it? I need the address of Peaches' new apartment."

"I'm not at liberty to give out her home address. Men and women alike come here thinking the sensual paintings she posed for when she was young are an invitation to carnality."

"Listen, I'm not a sapphist. I'm her sister."

"Well I don't know that, or if she even has a sister."

"Look at my face, my figure, you can see the resemblance."

"Not really."

"Then clean your glasses."

"Madam, if you're not interested in buying—"

Madam? That was too much. "Listen, you vapid little man, I sailed all the way from Paris to visit my sister, so find a piece of paper and write down her address before I undo that insipid excuse for a tie and strangle you with it." Sometimes you had to come on strong. That's the way Gertrude would have handled him.

Guy's eyes widened. He stared at her for a long beat, then made a wise decision and reached for the phone. "I'll just call and see if you are who you say." He turned his back on her and mumbled into the mouthpiece.

Too bad she hadn't thought of calling instead of running around the city. Of course, Peaches didn't have a phone last time she was here.

After hanging up, Guy handed Cherie a slip of paper, refusing to meet her eyes. "My apologies."

Cherie glanced at it, nodded, and left the gallery. She hadn't meant to sound so harsh, but a man in a bow tie shouldn't get between her and her sister.

The address, only a few blocks away, was on a side street of old houses— two- and three-story red brick remnants from the days when Greenwich Village was a residential suburb. It had long since been swallowed by the city. Peaches' house appeared to have recently been made over with freshly painted shutters and a sturdy new door. The entryway had iconic door posts and a fanlight window above the door frame. Nice. Cherie rang the bell.

The door opened. "Quicker than I expected—Oh, it's you."

"Lovely to see you too, Sis."

"Sorry, I thought you were the boy from the laundry."

Cherie stepped inside. "Give us a kiss, then."

Peaches hugged her and they kissed. "Where's your luggage?"

"At the Algonquin."

"You could have stayed here."

"Not really. I came with someone."

"Oh?"

"Nothing serious, just free passage. He's a writer—came to meet with his publisher. You'd like him, though. We should all go out one night. You'll like his friends, too."

Peaches closed the door. "Come on in. I'm packing, but I'll make you a coffee if you like."

"No, thanks. I had *la petit déjeuner* at the hotel."

"Come into my bedroom then. We can talk while I pack."

"You're leaving?"

"Yes, a sudden thing. I'd just called the Chinaman and told him I needed my laundry back today. That's why I thought you were his boy."

Cherie stuck out her lip. "I just got here."

Peaches led her into a bedroom that was larger than she expected, given the size of Cherie's typical Paris apartments. "Really?"

How well Peaches knew her. "Okay, not really, but it's been a mad scene ever since I arrived and now we're finally together . . . don't leave. Let's spend this afternoon catching up, have a nice dinner, and go dancing. I've found a speakeasy with hot jazz. We can get zozzled."

"No, I want to catch the afternoon train."

"I'm sure there's another train in the morning."

Peaches bit her lip.

"Come on, Sis. Nothing can be that urgent."

Peaches shook her head. "It's Morgan. He's dying."

Cherie's mouth dropped open. How was that . . . she'd been of an age where she felt romantically attracted to Morgan. He was . . . she thought of him as her own age. Which meant . . . "He's too young to die."

"Apparently not. Cancer. The doctors operated on him a couple of years ago, but it came back. Abigail's telegram said come at once. She didn't think he had long."

"Telegram?"

"Arrived this morning. I put Guy in charge of the gallery and started packing right away. I just need my clothes from the Chinaman and I'll be ready to go."

"If it's so urgent why didn't she telephone?"

"Long distance?"

"She's rich. Or have they run out of money?"

"I doubt it was the cost of the call. I think she didn't want to talk about it on the phone—or maybe couldn't." Peaches took a jersey and two sweaters from a bureau drawer and placed them in her trunk. "You should come with me."

"To Taos? Never. A hick place I left seventeen years ago and never looked back."

"It's not like when we grew up. It's become a nice little colony of artists. I go there every year."

"Little is right. Even New York is too blue-nosed for my taste. As soon as I find a jelly bean with a cabin to France, I'm his Jane."

"So, you don't actually have a return passage booked? Then you have no excuse for not coming with me."

Oh, damn. She'd walked into that. "Except that I don't share your nostalgia for New Mexico."

"This isn't about us. We owe Abigail and Morgan everything. He helped me establish the gallery and arranged for you to tour Europe. The least we can do is thank him before he dies."

Cherie picked up a hand mirror, licked her fingertip, and shaped her eyebrows.

Peaches exhaled loudly. "All right, let me make you a deal. I'll hold off on leaving until morning, and take you out on the town tonight, if you agree to go with me to see Morgan."

Cherie laid down the mirror, turned toward Peaches, and saw that determined look. But on no account was she going west.

"We can call the hotel and have your trunk sent to the station," Peaches said.

"My trunk isn't packed. Besides, I'll need a different dress for tonight."

"You can wear something of mine."

Cherie made a face. Peaches' dresses would fit, but weren't the latest style. "No thanks. Finish your packing and then we'll go to the Algonquin. I can change, and we'll have cocktails before dinner."

"Good, that's settled—except the cocktails. Prohibition, remember?"

"Not if you know whose suite to visit. And you can meet my writer. He's interesting."

The bell rang and Peaches went to the door. This time it *was* the boy with her laundry. She paid him, finished packing, and phoned the ticket office at Grand Central Station. "I have a reservation on a Pullman sleeper to Santa Fe, New Mexico, leaving this afternoon. I'd like to change that to tomorrow morning's train, please. It's under the name P. T. Romero." Peaches drummed her fingernails on her desk. "That will be fine, thank you. Now, I'd also like to reserve a berth in the same car for a second passenger."

"Now hang on—" Cherie said.

"You can put both tickets under my name. Yes, two First Class to Santa Fe tomorrow."

"Peaches, I didn't say—"

"What time does it leave? All right, thank you very much. Goodbye." Peaches placed the receiver back on the hook.

Cherie was leaning against the door to Peaches' study. "I didn't realize the gallery was doing so well you could afford to waste a first-class fare to New Mexico."

"It is. But what do you mean waste?"

"I never agreed to go."

"Don't be ridiculous. You're going." Peaches brushed by her and returned to the bedroom. "Come. Help me choose what to wear tonight."

# CHAPTER 4

When they got to the Algonquin, they learned at the front desk that Cherie's writer was out and hadn't left a note. She had no idea where he had gone, with whom, or what time he'd be back. They proceeded to her room where she stripped to her camisole and began trying on dresses.

"Your hair's shorter than I remember," Peaches said.

"No shorter than the last time I was here."

"I guess I forgot. Of course, now we see flappers everywhere. Shop girls from across the Hudson are bobbing their hair, shortening their skirts, painting their lips, and moving to the city."

Cherie made a face. "It's the same in Paris. Provincial girls wearing cheap knock-offs of Coco's designs." She stepped into a Nile green sleeveless dress, slipped her hands through the armholes and pulled it the rest of the way on. It had a drop waist with a long sash that tied below the hips and hung down. She looked in the mirror, shook her head, and took it off. Too last year.

After trying on two more, she finally settled on a slim white silk number, loose, with straight lines from shoulder to a hemline ending in long fringe, which made the dress appear shorter than it was. It was just coming into vogue before she left, and it hadn't hit these shores yet.

Her sister began folding the cast-off dresses and laying them in the trunk while Cherie applied rouge and freshened her lipstick.

Cherie slipped a half-dozen bangles over her wrist and held a sparkly headpiece over her hair. "Hat or no hat?"

Peaches touched the rim of her own cloche hat. "Definitely a hat—we'll be dining out."

Cherie selected a stylish beret and set it at a rakish angle. She considered her reflection in the mirror and then put on a long beaded necklace that hung to her waist. The bedside clock caught her eye. "It's half-past five. Are you ready to go?"

Peaches laughed. "I was ready when we got here."

Cherie removed her bangles and slipped them over Peaches' wrists and then handed her a pair of dangly beryl earrings that matched the bangles. "Here, wear these." On her own arm, she slid a bejeweled amulet armband over her bicep. "Now, aren't we the berries?"

* * *

The elevator operator let them off on an upper floor. Peaches hung back to thank him as Cherie strode down the carpeted hallway toward a noisy suite at the far end. Cherie rapped twice in quick succession, and they were admitted. The room was crowded with flappers flaunting long cigarette holders and men smoking pipes or cigarettes. Cherie, who didn't smoke, took it upon herself to open a window. As she'd promised, drinks were plentiful and every hand held a martini glass. A handsome couple in the corner was making a fresh batch. The woman poured vermouth into a pitcher of gin and ice while the man stirred it with a long-stem spoon.

Peaches finally joined her.

"That couple in the corner," Cherie said. "Recognize them?"

"Only from the papers," Peaches said. "That's Scott and Zelda, isn't it?"

"In the slightly pickled flesh. Let's get a drink."

"Hello, Scott," Cherie said. "Are you pouring?"

"I am." Scott filled his wife's glass, poured two more for the newcomers, and then left with the pitcher, carrying it over to a trio of men seated in a semi-circle.

The woman touched her glass to theirs. "Zelda."

"Cherie. We met the other night. This is my sister, Peaches."

"Did we? Sorry, I forget names sometimes." Zelda nodded toward the men with her husband. "That's Robert Benchley, a former editor of *Vanity Fair*, a parting he wears like a badge of honor. He currently writes theater reviews for *Life* magazine. The man next to him is Bob Sherwood. I don't know the third. Shall we find out who he is?"

The women ambled over and stood listening to the men, none of whom offered their chairs. The two Roberts had mustaches and wore bow-ties, unfortunately. Fitzgerald and the other man were clean-shaven. Scott had a standard necktie, but the other man wore an ascot. He left without intro-ducing himself, and Zelda followed him. Peaches and Cherie both eyed the empty chair. Scott offered his and retrieved another from across the room. By the time he returned, the sisters had introduced themselves to the men and refilled everyone's glass from the Martini pitcher.

It turned out that both Roberts were Harvard alumni and had been teas-ing Scott about his alma mater, Princeton. "But Bob, it could be worse," Benchley said. "At least he's not a Yale man."

Sherwood nodded. "Say what you will about Scott's Princeton education, he somehow got *This Side of Paradise* from it."

"Now hold on, Bob," Scott said. "H. L Mencken called it the best American novel he had seen of late."

"Mencken's opinion only counts in Baltimore," Benchley said.

Peaches smiled at Scott. "I understand you had a new novel published this spring."

"*The Beautiful and Damned*—came out in March." Scott grinned. "Twenty-thousand copies in the first print run. What do you say to that, Benchley?"

"I'd say you're buying us dinner."

"Oh?" Cherie said. "Peaches and I are dining out when we leave here. Shall we eat together?"

"Not unless you can wait until after the show," Benchley said.

"Show?" Peaches said.

"Benchley performs his parody 'The Treasurer's Report' nightly at Irving Berlin's Music Box Theater," Scott said. "He can probably get you tickets if you want to go. Zelda and I have already been."

"Thanks, no," Peaches said. "I don't want to eat that late. We're traveling tomorrow."

Zelda returned. The men stood. "I'm feeling ignored." She kissed Scott on the mouth in front of everyone and pulled him away by his necktie, like a dog on a leash.

"Zelda," Cherie called after them, "we have a reservation at Keens Steakhouse for supper. Would you and Scott care to join us?"

"We'd love to," Scott said.

"Don't count on it," Sherwood said. "Zelda prefers to be the sole woman in a party of men."

Peaches looked up at the two Roberts. Benchley was tall enough—at least six feet—but Sherwood looked to be at least eight inches taller. "Is Harvard where you two met?"

Benchley stood on the seat of his chair and extended his arm overhead. "Nah, I knew Bob Sherwood back when he was only this tall."

The sisters chuckled.

Howls of laughter drew their attention to the center of the room where Zelda was turning cartwheels. The two Roberts left to watch. Soon Zelda had all the men in the room around her.

"Let's go," Peaches said. "We don't want to miss our reservation."

Cherie wormed her way into the throng surrounding Zelda and tugged on Scott's sleeve. "We're going to the restaurant now."

"Okay," he said. "We're staying at the Plaza. We'll go there to change and then be right along."

# CHAPTER 5

At Keens, after waiting over an hour for the Fitzgeralds, with nothing but bread and water, both sisters were peckish. Peaches complained the aroma of steaks and chops being carried past their table was torture, while Cherie pontificated on how uncivilized it was not to serve wine at suppertime.

Seven large oil paintings in gold frames hung on the restaurant's dark wood-paneled walls. Heavy burgundy-colored drapes braced the windows, and the head of an eight-point buck adorned the brick fireplace chimney. But the rows and rows of long-stem clay smoking pipes hanging around the room mystified Cherie. While they awaited the tardy Fitzgeralds, their waiter explained. The hard clay pipes were imported from the Netherlands. A pipe warden at the restaurant registered and stored the pipes for members of Keens pipe club, whose membership included illustrious patrons such as Teddy Roosevelt, J. P. Morgan, and Buffalo Bill Cody.

Thrice, the waiter returned to take their order, finally sending the maître d' who stiffly informed them that other customers wanted their table. Peaches greased his palm and reminded him they were waiting on Scott and Zelda Fitzgerald. He pocketed the cash and said, "I wish you luck in your wait, but it's unlikely they'll make it."

Peaches looked at Cherie. "He's right. Let's order."

Cherie shrugged. "May as well."

The maître d' signaled the waiter, who came at once.

"We'll each have the filet mignon," Peaches said.

"Very good." He turned and left.

While they waited for their steaks, Cherie toyed with the fine silverware arrayed on the white linen tablecloth, thinking how little this resembled her first trip to New York. Their mother had died that year, and she and her sister had traveled east with Morgan and Rebecca Sullivan, a woman minister who had just lost her job in Taos. Morgan came for an art show and to help Peaches find work modeling for artists he knew here. Cherie was to be a lady's companion to Reverend Sullivan on a trip to Ireland in pursuit of a Celtic myth—it was Rebecca's first trip abroad, and she hadn't wanted to travel alone.

At that point in their lives, New York had taken on mythic proportions. It was a hub of culture, entertainment, and artists, where Broadway and Tin Pan Alley and Greenwich Village were not addresses, but the stuff of Bryce and Morgan's stories. She and Rebecca only stayed in the city for two days before sailing, and money had been if not tight, then a little snug. They'd eaten in diners and sandwich shops—clean but unpretentious—and travelled the city by subway and bus, but it had all seemed miraculous to Cherie. And then steamship passage to Europe! It was almost more than she could take in.

To her credit, Rebecca had never treated Cherie as a maid, but more like a younger sister. That was a role Cherie had learned well, being two years younger than Peaches. Rebecca's Boston heritage was Irish on both sides of her family. Raised on her grandfather's Celtic stories, she had a particular interest in the notion that in certain wild places in nature the distance between heaven and earth narrowed. Her ancestors called them Thin Places. For an entire year Cherie and Rebecca had tramped around the Emerald Isle meditating on misty heaths, rugged peaks, and jagged cliffs, seeking ephemeral experiences.

At the time Cherie had thought the whole thing a lark. Aboard ship, she had spent her time rubbing elbows with the other passengers, learning how to move in high society. Now, here she was, in one of New York's premier restaurants with her sister, a leading dealer in impressionist art, waiting for one of the most celebrated writers of the new century. Yet, she was bored. How had she reached this point?

Rebecca had never seemed bored. As she sat cross-legged on various crags and poked through crevices, she seemed to find what she was looking for. She was getting in touch with something beyond herself, something . . . authentic. Suddenly, the idea of Zelda turning drunken cartwheels to make herself the center of attention to a roomful of drunken socialites seemed . . . small.

Their steaks arrived. The piece of meat, wide and thick as her closed fist, bled when she cut it. Keens was actually more famous for its thick lamb chops, but Cherie was glad to have steak. Her year in Ireland, she'd eaten enough mutton to last a lifetime.

"I hope we get there in time," Peaches said.

"Don't worry. This speakeasy I found is open all night."

"No, I mean Taos. You know, before Morgan passes."

"That again? Let's talk about tonight. You'll love The Jungle Club. Fancier than this place—waiters in white tails, and a live jazz band."

Peaches ate another bite of steak. "Sure, sure, but let's not stay out too late. The trip takes a week, and the train ride can be grueling."

"You keep talking as if it is fait acommpli, I never agreed to go."

"Of course you're going. You owe it to Morgan. Admit it."

"Taos is a hick place that has no appeal to me." It sounded hollow even as she said it.

"Taos has changed, become quite sophisticated since we were girls. About seven years ago, six local painters formed the Taos Society of Artists. You might remember Bert Phillips, but I think the others moved to Taos after we left. About 1915, the Society began sending exhibitions of their paintings across the country. Morgan helped me land several of their shows."

"Yes, I saw Southwestern landscapes in your gallery this morning. They did not make me nostalgic."

"It's more than just art. You've never met Mabel Dodge. She only moved there about five years ago, but she's turned Taos into a literary center. You two have a lot in common. Before the war she lived in Paris and entertained authors such as Gertrude Stein and novelist Andre Gide."

Cherie looked up from her steak. "I've met Miss Stein, had tea at her Paris apartment."

"Good. When we get to Taos, you and Mabel will know someone in common."

"Did I mention I was at a party in a Fifth Avenue apartment last night and saw that painting Morgan did of you posing as a pioneer housewife?"

"So that's where it ended up. I knew it was someplace in the city, but I lost track of who bought it last. Never one of my favorites—I'd just turned eighteen and Morgan put me in one of Mother's dresses. Made me feel like an old lady."

"That's not how you come off. He made you look fresh, almost virginal. Though we both know that just proves how good an artist he is."

Peaches laughed. "See? Our times in Taos weren't all bad."

"I didn't say anything bad happened there. For me, it's like that song, 'How Ya Gonna Keep 'em Down on the Farm After They've Seen Paree?' I have no interest in desert dust and pueblos. And the prospect of watching Morgan die does not increase its appeal."

"Everything we do can't be limited to what appeals to us. Sometimes we have to do something for those who helped us get where we are."

The dark paneled walls, haughty patrons, and stiff waiters suddenly seemed stifling and old fashion to Cherie. "Pay our bill and let's get out. I want to feel the roar of the city."

Yet, somewhere in the back of her mind, she remembered. There were supposed to be thin places in Taos.

# CHAPTER 6

The Jungle Club was loud. Horns and saxes wailed, the piano hammered, and the drummer beat a steady rhythm that was easy to dance to. Twelve musicians played jazz loud enough to be heard over shouted conversations and screams of hilarity. A continuous flow of alcohol delivered by waiters in white tuxes loosened everyone's inhibitions. Flappers and smooth cats put silver spoons of cocaine to their noses and then jumped wildly into the fray of naked arms and silk stockings, flinging about dancing the Shimmy, Bunny Hug and Black Bottom.

This was more like it.

A clarinet blew a long blue note, and the drummer applied his sticks to the cymbals in two/four time. He shifted onto the snare drum, and the piano player added bass notes in stride. The trumpeter blew four bars of the melody, and the whole band joined in a ragtime piece the audience knew.

"That's an old one," Cherie said.

"Reminds me of Bryce playing ragtime on Abigail's piano."

Cherie grinned. "Remember the day Mother caught you dancing with him?"

"Oh, was she pissed!"

A sheik in a silk serge suit pulled Cherie into the melee. She grabbed Peaches' hand and brought her with them. "In Paris, girls dance with girls."

He was a good sport and tried to dance with both women. When the song ended, he bought them each drinks. "Stevie," he said by way of introduction, opening a silver cigarette case and offering them one. "Butt?"

They shook their heads.

He put a cigarette between his lips, put the case away, pulled out a silver Ronson Wonderlite, and lit his cig. He took a drag and then plucked a loose shred of tobacco from his lip. "Your names?" he said exhaling a stream of smoke.

"Peaches."

"Cherie."

He smiled and his eyes crinkled. "Isn't this place the cat's meow?"

Stevie had even, white teeth. Cherie liked that in a man. "Love it."

"Have you been here long?"

The sisters glanced at each other. "A couple of hours," Peaches shouted.

Cherie finished her drink and set her glass on the bar. She squeezed Stevie's bicep. "Dance?"

He nodded emphatically, drained his glass, and dropped his cigarette in it.

Cherie pulled on Peaches' hand. Peaches wiggled free. "You two go ahead while I finish my drink."

Cherie stole the glass from Peaches and drank it in a single gulp. "Come. There's no telling when we'll be out together again."

Peaches shook her head. "Enjoy your dance without me."

Stevie whistled to a man further down the bar. "Tom."

Tom came at once. He looked exceedingly acceptable—new suit, nice cut, expensive tailoring, two-tone wingtips.

"Peaches, Tom," Stevie said. "Tom's a very good dancer."

Both couples stayed near each other on the dance floor for the next several songs, then the band eased into a slow tune. Peaches and Tom went to the bar. Cherie snuggled into Stevie's arms, molding her soft curves against him. They moved as one, and through her dress, she could feel him growing firm.

"It was nice of you to find someone for Peaches."

"Stevie's rule of two."

She leaned back enough to look into his face. "What's that?"

"Men have this fantasy that when they pick up two women, the night will end in a ménage à trois. My rule is, when two women out on the town meet one man, he won't get either of them. You need a second man."

"Divide and conquer?"

"No, more like making sure each gets the attention she deserves."

"And now you think you've got your rule resolved."

He pressed himself into her a bit more. Not exactly subtle. "Don't we?"

"Afraid not. Peaches is leaving town in a few hours."

"And you?"

"I wouldn't mind. You're cute, but not now. I need to stick with my sister tonight."

He backed off a little. "Will I see you again?"

"Can't say. I'm returning to France soon. Give me your address and I'll let you know."

The song ended. They embraced and then joined Tom and Peaches at the bar. Stevie ordered another round of drinks.

"Ready?" Cherie said.

"To go?"

"No. To dance." The band started their next number. "Just us girls this time, boys." Cherie pulled her sister onto the dance floor.

Peaches yielded. "After this one we go, all right? It's getting late."

"Stevie just bought us drinks."

"Okay, we finish this drink, and that's it."

Cherie shimmied her hips. The stories of New York she'd heard as a girl came to mind. "Do you think this is what it was like when Morgan, Jack and Bryce grew up here?"

"No, they didn't have prohibition."

"But they had ragtime."

"Still, something made them want to go west," Peaches said.

"The St. Louis World's Fair as I recall." Cherie dimpled. "God, do you remember the day they showed up at Mama's boarding house? They were so handsome."

"Still are."

"Yeah?"

"Well, Jack and Morgan are. I haven't seen Bryce in years. No one has."

"Peaches?"

"Yes."

"You said that over the years Morgan's come to New York for art shows and to bring paintings for your gallery."

"Sure, and I've traveled to Taos, too."

"So, have you and he . . ."

"No. Never."

"Where does he stay when he's here?"

"With me—at my house, I mean. Not *with* me."

"Why not?"

"It would have been fine with me. You remember how randy I used to be. But Morgan had some kind of rule about it—or maybe it was because of Abigail."

"Abigail? Isn't she still married to Jack?"

The song ended and people stopped dancing. Cherie and Peaches remained on the dance floor.

"Yes. But I think they have an open mind about sharing. You know, after they got married, Abigail had Jack convert her conservatory into a studio for Morgan. They've all been living in the same house ever since."

Cherie's eyes widened. "You mean Abigail has two husbands? In Taos?"

Peaches shrugged. "No one says one way or the other."

Cherie laughed. "When we get rid of Tom and Stevie, remind me to tell you about his rule of two—hilarious."

"Let go, now."

"What about the drinks?"

"They can drink ours." Peaches hooked her by the elbow and headed for the door. "It's not like they're getting anything else from us tonight."

# CHAPTER 7

The doorman for the day shift had just come on duty when the sisters arrived at the Algonquin. Peaches followed Cherie to her room where Cherie promptly fell on the bed. Peaches began emptying drawers and packing the contents in Cherie's trunk. She knew her sister well enough to know she was coming to Taos. She would complain just about every step of the way, but she would be there. "What do you want to wear on the train? You'll also need nightgowns and enough clothes for a week. Do you have a suitcase as well, or just this trunk? If not, I've got an extra bag at my house. We have to go there, anyway."

"Oh, leave me alone. It's my bedtime."

"We have to board the train before we can sleep." Peaches took a glassine envelope from her bra and poured the white powder out into four lines on the surface of Cherie's hand mirror. She had expected this kind of problem and got prepared, thanks to the barman at the Jungle Club. She inhaled two of them and then pulled her sister upright. "Sit up." She held the mirror for Cherie. "Snort these."

Cherie did as she was told and suddenly came awake. "Yowzer. Where did you get that?"

"Never mind. Now, listen to me. Finish packing. You'll want a bath too. It'll be a week before we get another." Algonquin rooms had private baths. Peaches turned on the water and began filling the tub. "I'm going to my house to change and get my luggage. I'll be back to pick you up in one hour."

"You sound just like Mama, hustling us to get ready for Mass."

"Good, then I'm doing it right. Don't go back to sleep."

"No danger of that." Cherie stripped off her clothes and stepped into the tub.

Peaches returned an hour later carrying a floral pattern carpetbag. Cherie opened the door, dressed and ready, wonder of wonders. She had chosen a calf-length periwinkle-blue skirt with a ruffle hem and a matching sweater that extended below her hips. She was wearing stylish shoes with one inch heels and a turban that complimented the color of her outfit. Her trunk was strapped shut and her cosmetics and traveling clothes were in a neat pile on the bed.

"Peaches, about my dividend from the gallery—"

"Haven't got time to stop there this morning. Don't worry. I've enough to get us to Taos and back."

"It's just the man I came with—"

"The writer?"

"Yeah. Writers are always struggling. I thought I'd pay up the hotel tab through today."

"Generous gesture."

Cherie shrugged.

"I can write the hotel a check."

"Thanks, Sis. Take it out of my stipend."

While Cherie packed the carpetbag, Peaches went to registration, settled Cherie's bill, and sent a bellman to fetch the trunk. They made it to Grand Central Terminal with time to spare. Peaches picked up their tickets and arranged for their trunks to be taken to the baggage car.

Assured that they still had time, they took a seat at a café table off the main concourse and ordered breakfast. Cherie gazed up at the lofty arches and elegant marble walls trimmed with decorative flourishes and ornamental inscriptions. Throughout the station were stone carvings and bronze figures. "I've never been here before. This is magnificent."

"It hadn't been built when we came to New York in aught-five."

Cherie gawked like a tourist. "This is like a palace or museum in Europe. And it's a train station?"

Peaches sipped her coffee. "Eat your breakfast. We're boarding soon."

Pullman sleepers had names instead of numbers. A conductor checked their tickets and helped them locate their coach, the *Catania*. He called out, "George!" and a Negro porter, wearing a smart cap and a blue jacket with brass buttons, led them to their seats. The interior of the car had twelve sections containing facing pairs of upholstered sofa-style seats. Theirs was the third from the front.

George pointed out the lavatory and changing room at one end of the car, and helped them unpack, hanging their clothing in a wardrobe. When he'd finished, he touched the bill of his cap. "Just call on me if you should need anything, ladies."

The sisters sat facing each other, but once they were underway, Cherie didn't like riding backwards, so she came over and sat next to Peaches. By midday, the cocaine had worn off and Cherie fell asleep on her sister's shoulder. Peaches was tired too, but the sleeping berths wouldn't be made up until evening, and her sister drooling on her shoulder wasn't exactly dignified. She decided they should go to the dining car and roused Cherie.

* * *

The dining car had tables for two persons and four, but they learned they were supposed to ask their porter to reserve a seating time, and all the tables were taken. Two businessmen were sitting at a table for four. Cherie walked past them, then came back to where Peaches waited. "Come with me."

Cherie slid into the chair next to the man with a mustache. The other was clean shaven. "I hope you don't mind some company." She laid her hand on his forearm. "George forgot to reserve us a table."

"Who?" the man said.

"Our porter."

He laughed. "All Pullman porters are called George, whether that's their name or not."

His partner knitted his eyebrows. "He could get fired for that."

"Oh, no. I just made that up. It wasn't his mistake. We never told him. By the way, I'm Cherie, this is my sister Peaches."

The clean shaven man stood and offered Peaches the seat near the window. "Yes, please join us. We haven't ordered yet. I'm Bill."

"Frank," said Cherie's fellow. "Are you traveling alone?"

"Together," Peaches said.

"I meant just the two of you?"

And so the dance began. Well, it was a long trip with little to occupy it.

A waiter took their orders and Cherie forgot her sleepiness as she flirted over lunch. Both men wore wedding rings and when pressed for their surnames, both claimed they were named Smith, but unrelated. Not newcomers to the dance, then.

After the meal, the men invited them to their car for a game of cards. It was a pleasant way to pass the afternoon, but the sisters eventually got bored with teasing them and grew fatigued. They returned to their own car and asked George how soon he could make up their beds. George set to it like his job depended on it, directing them to the changing room. It was tight, but they changed together. When they returned, George had fresh linens on the beds and the privacy curtains in place. Cherie took the upper berth, and both women fell asleep to the rhythmic clack of the wheels.

They slept straight through several stops at cities in New York state and Erie, Pennsylvania. It was morning when George called softly through the privacy curtain, "Miss Romero?"

Peaches rubbed her eyes. "Yes?"

"Two businessmen in the dining car have asked if you will join them for breakfast."

"Uh . . ." She threw off the covers and kicked the upper bunk. "Cherie, are you awake?"

"What?"

"Those two would-be philanderers from yesterday want to know if we want to have breakfast with them."

"Let's not. They weren't *that* interesting."

"Did you hear that, George? Give them our regrets."

"Very good, Miss Romero. Would you like me to put up your beds now? We'll be in Toledo soon."

"Cherie, are you ready to get up? Ohio awaits."

Cherie yawned. "I guess so."

"Just give us a minute, George," Peaches said.

"Certainly."

"Oh, George?"

"Yes, Miss."

"We didn't tell them our last names. How did you know they asked for us?"

"By your descriptions. You two do stand out a bit."

Cherie giggled. Peaches kicked her bunk again.

"One more thing, George, can you bring our breakfast here?"

"Of course. What would you like?"

"Two poached eggs, bacon, toast, and coffee. Cherie, what would you like?"

"Does the Pullman have croissants?"

"I'm afraid I don't know what that is, Miss."

"That's not surprising," Cherie said. "I'll have a three-minute egg, orange juice, coffee, and a pastry—any kind."

"I'll put in your order and be right back to stow your beds."

"Don't forget to tell the Smiths we decline," Cherie said.

"Who?" George said.

"The two businessmen."

"I didn't know that was their names."

Cherie chuckled. "It isn't."

* * *

In the afternoon there was much jostling of *Catania* as other cars were uncoupled and additional cars coupled to their train. This involved repeatedly going backward, then a short distance forward, before reversing again, punctuated with the *bang* of a coupling.

"Where are we?" Cherie said.

George, standing attentively at the end or their car, replied, "Chicago, Miss. Our car is being switched onto the Atchison, Topeka and Santa Fe."

"So we don't have to change trains?"

"Not for days," Peaches said. "When we're almost to Albuquerque, we'll get off at Lamy and take a different train into Santa Fe."

"Wouldn't it be quicker if we got off in Tres Piedras?"

"Not for Jack. He runs a trucking service transporting supplies from Santa Fe to merchants in Taos. Abigail's telegram said Jack will meet our train if I wire her the date and time it's supposed to arrive." Peaches motioned for George who came to their seat at once. "We're going to Santa Fe. Would you know when the train from Lamy will get us there?"

"We'll be in New Mexico on Thursday. I'll find the departure and arrival times of your connecting train."

"Thank you, George. I'll need to send a wire, too."

"I can take care of that for you, Miss, whenever you're ready."

# CHAPTER 8

Abigail tipped the Western Union messenger a nickel and tore open the yellow envelope. Good. Peaches would arrive in Santa Fe before the end of the week. She'd tell Jack when he got home. Morgan, she'd tell right now.

She laid the telegram on the foyer table and weighed it down with a small bronze statue of Diana that Jack and Morgan had given her for their tenth anniversary.

She pushed open the screen door, hurried down the steps and across the lawn to Morgan's studio. He was lying on the chaise lounge on his side, gazing at a canvas on the easel across the room. On it was sketched a canyon that didn't seem to have any more paint on it than before.

Abigail bent down and kissed him. She glanced at the full pitcher. "You haven't touched your water."

"Uh-huh."

"You're not a camel, Morgan. You need to drink."

"Uh-huh."

She handed him his glass. He sat up, took a sip, and returned it to the table.

"Good news! Peaches is coming from New York."

Morgan's face momentarily lit up, then the corners of his mouth turned down. "I haven't anything new to show her."

"She's not coming to buy art. She's coming to see you."

"That's very kind of her. Too bad I won't ever see her sister again. Is Cherry still in Paris?"

"Last I heard. But please don't say things like that around Jack. He's not . . . dealing well with the idea you don't have much time left."

"Well, a fact is a fact. They don't change because we don't like them."

"Yes, but reminding him isn't making him feel any better." Or her, for that matter. She couldn't understand how Morgan could be so matter-of-fact about it all. "I don't know what I'm going to do with him when you . . ." Abigail wiped her eyes. "What kind of pie would you like for dessert tonight?"

"Aren't peaches in season?"

"They are. Peach sounds good. I'll send Cyrus out to Octaviano's."

She left and found Cyrus sitting on the back stoop, whittling a stick of wood into no particular shape.

"I need you to drive down to Octaviano's Orchard and buy me two bushels of peaches."

"Come on, Mom. Octaviano's is halfway to Santa Fe. Can't Jack stop there on his next trip?"

"No. Morgan wants peach pie tonight, and pie is about the only thing he's eating lately, so I need those peaches today."

"Two bushels is too much for one pie."

"Of course it is. But I'll can the rest for later."

Cyrus continued to whittle.

"You need to get on the road now, so you'll be back in time for me to bake," she said, gently enough not to spark one of his sudden mood swings.

Wood shavings continued to fly from the stick.

Abigail stepped around him, entered the house, and returned with money and the car key. "Make sure there's enough gas before you leave. Oh, and stop at Maria's and tell her I'll need her tomorrow to help with the canning."

Cyrus stood up, squeezed his eyes shut, and shook his head. When he opened his eyes, he held out a hand. It was trembling slightly. She put the money and key in his hand, folded his fingers closed, and hugged him. "I know it's hard. But it's time you started venturing further from home."

Cyrus clamped his lips together and nodded.

At least he was still in control. She gave him a gentle nudge toward the garage and went back in the kitchen intending to plan what she'd make for dinner. But once there, she collapsed in a chair and put her head in her hands. Her three men, her three problems, her burden, and no one to ease it.

The throaty rumble of the Pierce-Arrow engine came through the open window. Jack was a whiz with mechanics and kept their vehicles well-tuned. The sound faded as Cyrus pulled away.

She picked up a basket and went out to the garden. Cyrus would be all right. He hated leaving their property. Said he just wanted to be left alone. Four years now. How much longer could she let that go on?

She insisted he drive her places, not because she needed a driver, but to get him out in public again. Never at night, though. He was given to sudden nightmare-like terrors even when he wasn't sleeping. She thought being out of the army, being back home where things were familiar, would have cured him. It hadn't.

When she and Jack had taken Morgan to Denver for his surgery, they tried to bring Cyrus with them. He wouldn't go. But he loved Morgan more than his father and worried the whole week. She could hear frantic panic in his voice every time she called home to report Morgan's progress. It wrenched her apart, needing to be in two places at once for two different men.

She remembered Cyrus's relief when they'd brought a cured Morgan home. That was a happy day. Maybe the best day since the one when she and Jack and Morgan had picked up Cyrus at the station after his discharge from the Army. An excitement like nothing before, their son alive instead of a casualty. That must have been how Cyrus felt seeing Morgan return from the hospital.

She bent down and pulled onions and carrots from the ocher soil, dropping them into the basket. Of course, neither of those days of elation lasted, had they? Worst of them was the day when Morgan sat them down and said, "I thought I'd gotten away clean, but . . ." Abigail dropped the vegetable basket and ran into Morgan's studio. He was snoozing peacefully. She hesitated to disturb him.

But she needed to just spend a moment with him.

She sat on the edge of his bed and stroked his cheek. He turned his head in his sleep. She slipped her fingers through his brown curls. Just a few threads of gray now.

*Damn it, Morgan, don't die. Not, yet. None of us are ready to let go, even if you are.*

She leaned down and pressed her lips to his forehead.

His arm moved, falling onto her thigh. His hand briefly squeezed her leg, his mind never quite waking up. But she knew he knew she was there. And for now, that would have to be enough.

# CHAPTER 9

Jack, wearing a blue chambray work shirt, leaned against the adobe wall of the train station watching the locomotive and coal car roll past. Steam hissed out the valve as the wheels reversed and the rails screeched in protest. As soon as the train was fully stopped, a man in a railroad uniform came from the depot and slid wooden platforms under the steps of the passenger cars. The conductor stood by the steps of First Class and helped women disembark. Up and down the platform, relatives and friends greeted the new arrivals. A Mexican family standing next to Jack anxiously scanned the disembarking passengers, finally rushing off to surround an old man walking with a cane.

Then, Peaches appeared as the top of the step looking like a houri in an Arabian story. She accepted the conductor's hand and descended. Once she was safely on the platform, he offered assistance to the woman behind her. Jack pushed himself away from the wall and ambled toward her. She smiled broadly and quickened her pace.

A local man further down the platform gave a loud wolf whistle. Jack whirled toward him. "Hey, bud, stow it!"

The man, probably twenty years Jack's junior, held up his hands in surrender. "Mister, I wasn't whistling at your lady, honest. Check out the flapper."

A few yards behind Peaches, a younger woman with kohl-rimmed eyes, wearing a beaded headband and a short dress, turned to the man and winked. A moment later, Jack lost track of the flapper as Peaches embraced him. "Still handsome as ever," she said.

"And you, beautiful as always."

She gave him an extra squeeze and let go. He released her and took a step back. The flapper came around Peaches and smiled. "My turn. Hello, Jack."

Jack tilted his head. There was something familiar . . .

"You remember my sister," Peaches said.

"Cherry?"

"I go by Cherie now," she said, hugging him fiercely and planting a red smear of lipstick on his cheek.

He wiped it off with his palm. "Well, I'll be damned."

"That's not the usual reaction I get when I kiss a man."

"I can't believe it. I thought you were in France."

"I am. Not at the moment, of course, but I mean that's where I live."

"Well, it must suit you. You look twenty."

Cherie dimpled.

He grinned at her. "Cherie, huh?"

"Why not? You and Morgan changed your names, didn't you?"

Jack laughed. "You got me there. Well, good to see you again. And unexpected. Abigail didn't tell me you were coming, too."

"She didn't know," Peaches said. "None of us did, until I got her on the train."

"Too bad. I could have driven Abigail's car instead of my truck. All three of us will have to squeeze into the front seat. It'll be close, but that's the only seat there is. I hope you don't mind."

Cherie clasped his arm with both hands. "We won't."

A porter arrived pushing a hand truck stacked with the sisters' trunks and valises.

Jack eyed it. "Sheesh! I guess it's a good thing I did bring the truck."

Jack's truck was a Ford Model T with the cargo area already half-full of crates. Once their luggage was added and lashed down to the fence-like rails that surrounded three sides of the truck bed, he threw a canvas tarp over everything and tied it with rope. The sisters got in the cab, Cherie in the middle and Peaches next to the window. Jack got the engine started on the first crank. He climbed in the truck and adjusted the idle until the engine chortled like a creek flowing over rapids.

The truck had a small oval rear window, but Jack couldn't see over the stack of cargo anyway. He lowered the driver side window, leaned out, and put the truck into reverse.

Once they were aimed toward the road, he put the truck in low gear. When he reached for the gas lever on the steering column, his elbow bumped Cherie's tit. "Sorry," he said. When he made a right turn onto the highway, it happened again. "Sorry."

"Jeeze, Jack, it's all right," Cherie said. "It's not like you're doing it on purpose. Are you?"

"I . . . no . . . I mean . . ."

He realized she was smiling.

Once they were on the road to Taos, things got a bit more relaxed. That is, until Cherie asked, "How long has he got?"

"Who?"

"Morgan."

"As long as most folks, I hope."

Cherie glanced at her sister. "But I thought he was—"

"Dying? Well, we're all dying someday. I don't see any reason to rush him."

Cherie scowled at Peaches, for some reason. "I don't understand."

"Look, I don't care for this kind of talk," Jack said. "Sure, Morgan had a bad bout with the surgeon. But the one thing he doesn't need is any naysayers."

Cherie opened her mouth to speak.

Jack held up his hand.

He needed to set them both straight before they got to the house. "Don't get me wrong. He'll be excited to see you, but don't come around him with long faces. Keeping him cheered will do more for his health than a bucket of sympathy."

Peaches elbowed Cherie in the ribs, and they rode along with only the rumbles and squeaks of the truck for conversation.

After a few miles, Jack said, "Look, I didn't mean not to talk. I just don't want people saying Morgan's dying."

"I was only asking," Cherie said.

"Well, let's talk about what happened at the depot. I should warn you that won't be the last time you get whistled at around here. The closest most people in New Mexico have come to seeing a flapper was the cover of *Life* magazine."

"Better than New York where schoolgirls are lifting their skirts a few inches, donning a long string of beads, and thinking that makes them flappers."

"Well, what is a real flapper? And why do your eyes look like a raccoon's?"

Cherie punched him in the arm. "Your generation expected women to look gorgeous and act naïve while hunting a husband and then turn matronly and motherly once married."

"I didn't. And don't call Abigail matronly if you value your life."

"You guys were the exception. But think about our mother, for instance, or Emma Deitwiler."

"Actually, I could tell you some stories about Emma."

"Really? Well, anyway, what flappers are doing today is no different from what you and Morgan and Bryce were doing when we met you, only it's women doing it now."

"As I recall, you two were also doing it then."

"Yeah, but we had to hide it from Mother and everyone else in town. To me, a real flapper lives a life free of restrictions and old mores. She cuts her hair, throws away her corsets, and shimmies 'til the break of dawn because she wants to. She drinks, makes love, and says 'damn' when she feels like it, damn it."

Jack laughed. "I think I've got a soapbox in back for you to stand on."

"I'm not preaching to nobody. My life is about fun. The world had enough grief in the Great War."

"Amen to that," Jack said. Cherie's attitude might be just what their situation needed.

"And I have no intention of settling down."

Peaches spoke up, "We're staying at the Columbian. I'd like to check in so we can bathe and change before we go to your house, if that's not a bother."

"Not at all. I have freight to deliver. I'll take you to the hotel first, then pick you up when I'm done."

The Columbian Hotel was located on Taos Plaza. A bell boy helped Jack unload the trunks and carry them to the sisters' room while Cherie started drawing a bath. Jack returned to the lobby and used the hotel phone to let Abigail know they were in town and that Cherie had come, too.

"Oh, Jack," Abigail said. "Don't you dare let them stay in a hotel. Go back upstairs, get their luggage, and bring them here. They can stay with us."

"Where will they sleep? We only have one empty bedroom."

"Well, how many rooms do they have at the hotel?"

"Well . . . one."

"See? No different than here."

One big difference, Morgan. The impressionistic landscape hanging on the opposite side of the wide lobby reminded him. "How's Morgan doing?"

"He's fine, Jack, same as he was when you left."

"I think the house might be too noisy with extra guests. Morgan needs more time to heal."

"Nonsense, Morgan adores the Romero sisters. He just asked about Cherry the other day. Now, go get them before they unpack."

"Too late. They're probably already in the bathtub. I'm going to make my deliveries and then swing back by here. Do you want me to call you again and tell you when we're leaving?"

"No. I want them staying with us."

"I love you, Abigail, but for God's sake let it be. They've had a hell of a long train ride. Don't ask them to repack everything right now. You three can discuss it when you see them. It won't hurt anybody to spend one night at the Columbian."

The phone was silent.

"Abigail?"

"All right, but go tell them not to eat. I'm making a big dinner."

"I told you they're taking a bath."

"Not both at the same time. Just tell whichever one isn't. Love you. Bye."

Jack obediently went to their door and knocked. "It's Jack. Are you decent?"

Peaches opened the door a crack. "Barely."

"I talked to Abigail. She's cooking a big meal, said to tell you not to eat. I'll be back in about an hour. Will that give you enough time?"

"Depends on how long Cherie hogs the tub. I'll hustle her along."

"I'll leave you to it." Jack turned to go.

"Cherie, my turn," Peaches said, closing the door.

# CHAPTER 10

Morgan and Cyrus were sitting in Adirondack chairs under a shade tree when Jack's truck roared down the driveway and skidded to a stop, raising a cloud of dust. Adirondack chairs were unknown in the southwest when they moved here, but Jack remembered seeing them in the Catskills and fashioned a set of four for Abigail shortly after they were married.

Jack jumped out of the truck and raced around to open the passenger door. Peaches made a graceful quarter turn in the seat and put her foot on the running board. Jack offered his hand and helped her down. Cherie slid across the seat and accepted Jack's help. As soon as Cherie was out of the truck, both women began fussing with each other's dresses, smoothing wrinkles, straightening this or that, and fiddling with their hair. Jack placed his hand on the small of Peaches' back and nudged her. "Let's go."

By the time they rounded the front of the truck, Morgan and Cyrus were standing. The sisters hurried to Morgan, surrounded him, and each kissed his cheek.

Jack called toward the house, "Abigail, we're here."

Peaches gave Cyrus a hug, but Cherie just looked at him.

Jack caught up to them. "Cherie, you remember Cyrus, don't you?"

"This handsome man is that little boy Cyrus?"

Cyrus's eyes darted left and right, then fixed themselves on the lawn.

"Cyrus," Jack said, "you and Cherry used to play records together on the Gramophone when Morgan and I owned the Emporium."

Cyrus looked at Jack and gave him a small smile. "I remember."

"That was a long time ago." She offered Cyrus her hand. "Please, call me Cherie."

Cyrus touched her fingertips. Then, the screen door on the porch slammed, and he startled, drawing back into himself. Abigail came down the steps and crossed to them.

Seeing Abigail made Jack's heart jump. Although her figure was, in all honesty, edging toward matronly, she still had a voluptuous body and enjoyed being admired by men. Her dark wavy hair, high cheekbones, almond-shaped eyes, and perfect mouth from her Welsh ancestry were as striking as the day he'd met her. In his eyes, age hadn't diminished Abigail a whit.

When she reached them, there was another round of hugs and kisses. "I'm so glad you've come, and brought Cherry, too."

"I go by Cherie now."

Abigail gave a delighted laugh. "Oh, très *chic, Mademoiselle.* Cherie it is, then. You must stay here with us, both of you."

"We don't want to impose," Peaches said. "You have enough to worry about without us."

"Believe me, it will be my pleasure. As you see, the men outnumber me three to one. It'd be good to have some female company."

"We can talk about that later," Jack said. "Cyrus, would you bring two more chairs from the house?"

Cyrus nodded and left. It looked a little like an escape. Jack could understand that. Cherie might be a little intimidating for him.

"So, Morgan," Cherie said, "how are you, really?"

"Cherie," Jack said, sharply. When her eyes met his, he shook his head.

"Oh, it's simple," Morgan said. "I'm full of cancer."

Jack slapped him on the back. "Full of shit is more like it. Now, who wants a drink? Name your pleasure, beer, wine, or whiskey."

Cherie looked surprised. "They don't have prohibition out here?"

"Hell," Jack said. "New Mexico jumped the gun. We got prohibition three years before the rest of the country."

"Then how . . ." Cherie said.

"Whiskey and wine are legal for medicinal purposes," Abigail said. "Morgan has prescriptions."

Morgan laughed. "Which I keep filled for their benefit. I can't drink anymore. I only have half a liver. The surgeon took the rest."

"Don't worry, someday you'll be able to drink again with the rest of us," Jack said.

"I'm fine with my morphine," Morgan said.

"We buy wine and brandy from a religious order in California who has permission to make it," Abigail said. "Whiskey we get through the local apothecary, and Jack brews his own beer at an old hunting cabin in the forest."

"Aren't you worried he'll be arrested?" Cherie said.

Jack shook his head. "The Volstead Act didn't make possessing alcohol illegal, just manufacturing and selling it. If they don't catch me at the cabin, and I don't try to sell it to anyone, I'm in the clear."

"So, you're not a bootlegger?"

"No reason to, personal consumption only."

Morgan laughed. "Couldn't sell it, if he wanted to. He and Cyrus drink up every keg he makes."

Cyrus returned carrying a dining room chair under each arm. "Free beer—another reason to keep living at home."

"What's everyone having?" Jack said.

"I'm making mint juleps if either of you would like to try one?" Abigail said.

"What's in it?" Cherie said.

"Whiskey with crushed mint and sugar. It takes the edge off the pharmacy whiskey, which is a little harsh."

"If that's what you're having, I'll try it," Cherie said.

"I'll have wine," Peaches said, "if Morgan can spare it."

"No skin off my back. I told you, I quit drinking."

"For now," Jack said.

"Abigail, can I help?" Peaches said.

"No, Jack and I will get the drinks. You two stay here and visit." She tugged on Jack's arm. "Come, husband."

"Yes, dear." Jack started to follow, then stopped and turned. "Morgan, will you be all right?"

"Fine, Jack, I'm surrounded by beautiful women. What more could a man ask?" Morgan pressed on his abdomen with his hand. "Well, maybe a lemonade with a few drops of my morphine."

"You got it, my friend." Jack hurried to catch up with Abigail.

* * *

"Morgan, do you need to sit down?" Peaches said. "Don't feel you have to stand on our account."

"Yes," Cherie said. "This isn't the Victorian Age."

Morgan dropped into the Adirondack chair with an anguished grunt.

Peaches headed toward the house. "I'll tell Abigail to hurry with your medicine."

Morgan patted the arm of the chair Cyrus had been sitting in when they arrived. "Please, Cherie, have a seat and tell me what you've been up to."

She settled into the seat and spent a minute trying to take in the landscape. She'd been working to wrap her mind around being back in Taos since they'd arrived. It was all so familiar—she'd forgotten how the dust tasted—that it was hard to remember who she had been in Paris.

And then . . . seeing Morgan this way . . .

"I wouldn't know where to begin," she said. "It's been seventeen years. Abigail's house looks as lovely as I remember it, and the flower gardens are beautiful."

"As are you. You certainly grew into a gorgeous woman—and a flapper to boot."

"I've been living in France since the war. The feeling there is that life's short and could end at any moment."

"I wouldn't disagree," Morgan said.

"Yes . . . well, we flappers want to spend our time enjoying life and freedom rather than primly staying at home and waiting for a man to marry, like our mothers did."

Cyrus turned away from her. He looked a little pale. She glanced at Morgan.

"It's not you," Morgan said. "Cyrus has bad memories of France."

Something else to wrap her head around. But not now. "I heard that you have a studio out back."

"Yes, Jack built if for me right after Abigail and he married. I mostly paint plein-air when the weather is nice, but it has good light for times I need to paint indoors. I'll show it to you sometime."

Peaches and Abigail returned with a tray of drinks and Jack carried two steins of beer. He handed one to Cyrus.

Abigail handed Morgan his lemonade, and he drank it in one go. "Do you need more?" Peaches said.

"No, this will kick-in in a few minutes."

"I've got some friends in both Europe and America doing morphine for fun," Cherie said. "I've never tried it, but a girlfriend told me it gives her an ecstatic stillness detached from the world's chaos. An utterly self-sufficient pleasure."

"You can drink all my prescription booze, but I'm afraid I can't spare any morphine. I kind of need it for pain."

Cherie blushed. "Oh, Morgan, I'm not trying to take anything from you."

Jack squatted down in front of him. "Are you sure we gave you enough?"

"I'm fine Jack. I can feel it working already. Enjoy your beer."

Jack stood up and Morgan turned back to Cherie. "Your friend is right, though. It not only stops the pain, but it does bring a certain euphoria. I wish I didn't have to be so selfish, but the doctor has to special order it."

"Oh, don't worry about me. If I'd wanted to try it, I could have gotten it easier than booze in a speakeasy."

"They gave us morphine in France," Cyrus said in a flat voice. "Field medics did, trying to cure our headaches and bad memories. But only so they could send us back into battle."

Cherie stared, which she hated doing. But what did you say to something like that?

"Why don't you sit down, dear," Abigail patted Cyrus on the shoulder and guided him to one of the dining room chairs he'd brought out.

Jack held his stein out to Cherie. "You want to try a sip? It's a damn sight better than bathtub gin."

She took a sip, nodded, and handed it back. He was right. "It's very good, Jack. And cold. How do you manage that?"

"I built us a spring house. Cyrus helped."

"A what?"

"I read an article about it. They have them in other states where there are cold mountain streams. It's a stone building, sunk into the ground, with a channel of water running through part of it. The stone walls conduct cold from the water and keep the whole building cool. People build them to keep milk, butter, and cheese cool."

"And beer," Abigail added.

"Of course, beer. That's what I built ours for—we already have an icebox. Anyhow, when I read that article, I thought, our creek is coming from the mountain, and we certainly have plenty of stones. It was just a matter of finding the right size and cementing them together. I'll show it to you later if you like."

"Tomorrow, Jack," Abigail said. "As soon as we finish our drinks, we're going to have dinner."

"Can we help?" Peaches said.

"Most everything is ready. I just have to bake the biscuits and put the food in serving dishes. Enjoy your drinks. We're in no rush."

* * *

They had a couple more drinks as everyone chatted and relaxed, then Abigail left to put the finishing touches on dinner. Peaches and Cherie joined her.

"Is the table set?" Cherie said.

"No, but let Peaches do that. She's been here before and knows where everything is. You can make biscuits."

"Er . . . I don't cook much. Mother never taught us."

"Really? She ran a boardinghouse."

"Yes, but she planned to marry us to men who could afford cooks and housekeepers like Mrs. Hoffsteader had."

"Well, you can do this. Everything's measured in that white bowl, just add buttermilk and mix it."

Cherie opened the icebox and peered in.

"The buttermilk is the bottle furthest back. Just add a little at a time as you stir, until the dough is moist. You don't want it sloppy wet. Here's an apron so you won't get flour on your dress."

Cherie accepted the apron and unfolded it. It had been a while since she'd seen one. There was a strap at the top that looped around the neck and ribbon-like strings that tied behind the waist. She held it out and admired the periwinkle pattern. "Cute." She put on the apron and began to dribble buttermilk into the mixing bowl, pausing to show Abigail the results.

Abigail nodded. "That's enough. Now, put flour on your hands and knead the dough—very little, just three or four times—then dump it on that floured breadboard and dust the dough with a dollop of flour." She handed her a rolling pin. "Roll it evenly until it's about a quarter of an inch thick."

Abigail removed a blue enamel roaster from the kerosene oven, set it on the sideboard, and turned the oven flame hotter.

Cherie made a couple of back-and-forth strokes with the rolling pin, but on the last pass the dough wrapped itself around the rolling pin.

Abigail didn't scold her. "Unwind the dough, put a little more flour on it, and rub some on your rolling pin."

When she tried again, everything worked out. If only their mother had told them it would be this easy.

"Okay, get a water glass from the cupboard over the sink, dip its mouth in the flour, and use it to cut circles in the dough, as close together as you can." Abigail handed Cherie a cookie sheet. "Put your biscuits on this, keeping them about one inch apart. Then gather up the scrap dough, roll it out again, and cut out the rest of the biscuits."

Cherie filled the cookie sheet and slid it into the oven, feeling pleased with herself.

"You mentioned the Hoffsteaders," Abigail said. "Did you know they bought your mother's house?"

"Really? Whatever for?"

"Their daughter, Henrietta, got married. They gave it to her for a wedding present. She must be near your age. Weren't you girls in school with her?"

"Who's that?" said Peaches, coming from the dining room.

"Henrietta."

"She was in my grade," Peaches said. "What can I do next?"

"Get me the large platter from the china cabinet. Cherie, you can toss the salad."

Peaches returned with the platter and held it as Abigail lifted the chicken from the roaster and transferred it to the serving dish. The room filled with the delicious smell of roast chicken and it reminded Cherie of her mother's Sunday dinners.

Abigail drained boiled green beans and poured them into a serving bowl, adding pats of butter. "Peaches, dish up these Harvard beets and take both bowls to the dining room."

Cherie opened the oven door and peeked in. "Um . . . the biscuits are . . . ready?"

"Are the tops brown?" Abigail said.

"A little bit."

Abigail handed her a hot pad. "You're right. Take them out."

Cherie showed her the pan.

"Perfect, we don't want them any browner. Put them in that basket and cover it with a towel. Peaches, tell the men we're ready, and ask Jack and Cyrus to bring in those two dining room chairs."

# CHAPTER 11

Abigail served rhubarb pie for dessert. Cherie couldn't remember the last time she'd had it. "This is delicious," she said. "I forgot how good rhubarb pie tastes."

"Thank you," Abigail said. "We've eaten peach pie every night this week. I thought it was time for something different."

After he ate his pie, Morgan retired, even though it was still daylight. Jack and Cyrus moved onto the porch. Cherie and Peaches helped clear the table and put away leftovers. While the dishwater heated, Abigail scraped the plates. "Oh, dear, Morgan didn't finish his pie."

"No, I saw him," Cherie said. "I think that's Cyrus's pie."

Abigail pressed her lips into a thin line and shook her head. When she looked up, she gave her a forced smile.

"It was delicious," Peaches said. "My, oh my, if I ate pie that good everyday I'd be fat."

Abigail's smile turned genuine. "Morgan likes pie. It's one thing I know he'll eat, so, yes, I always serve pie."

"Have you tried making him shepherd's pie?" Cherie said.

"No, what is it?"

"A piecrust filled with meat, vegetables, and gravy. Then, instead of a top crust or meringue, you cover the pie in mashed potatoes. I ate it in Ireland. It's good. Try it. Maybe Morgan will eat more meat if it's baked in a pie."

"He can't help it. The drugs kill his appetite. I think the sweetness of pie is the appeal, but I'll try anything at this point. Why don't you make shepherd's pie tomorrow and we'll see if it works?"

"Oh, I know how to eat it, not how to cook it. But I'm sure you can figure it out."

Abigail checked to see if the kettle was boiling and handed the girls aprons. "Here, you don't want to splash dishwater on your lovely dresses."

Peaches accepted the apron, but Cherie said, "I'll just use the same one I wore to make biscuits." She slipped the apron over her head and tied the strings behind her back. "So, is Jack secretly a bootlegger? You can tell us, we won't squeal on him."

"Oh, God, no, he really only makes beer for us. Jack runs a trucking service transporting goods from the Albuquerque and Santa Fe train stations to businesses in Taos."

"How did he get into that business? I thought he was a carpenter. After the Emporium went bust, I remember him working on that big house Arthur Manby built."

"I don't know how well you remember Jack. He always had an intense interest in science and is very mechanically minded."

"That's right," Cherie said. "Those hand-cranked generators and electric lights."

Peaches nodded. "Always reading *Popular Science Magazine*."

Abigail smiled. "He still subscribes. Anyway, when we bought our first car, he took the entire engine apart and put it back together just to understand how it worked. It made him a very good mechanic, and he's often called on to help others, but he didn't want to be a mechanic for a profession. When he noticed the local merchants still hauled their goods from the railway by horse-drawn wagon, he decided it was a business opportunity. So, he sold our car and bought that truck. Good for him, but not for me. I wrestled with the Ford twice and ordered a Pierce-Arrow."

The kettle began to hiss. Abigail poured the water into the dishpan and added cold water using the hand pump on her sink. She filled a second pan with rinse water. Peaches washed, Cherie dried, and Abigail put the pans and dishes away.

"I'm so glad you girls are here," Abigail said.

Peaches shrugged. "It's the least we could do."

"I don't mean just for Morgan—though he's the main reason. But for me, too. Trying to hold together three men who are a mess is wearing. It's good to have other women to talk with."

"Three?" Cherie said. "What's wrong with Jack and Cyrus?"

Abigail grimaced. Peaches answered for her. "Cyrus was in the war—never recovered."

"Injured?"

"Mentally," Abigail said. "Nightmares that he won't discuss, bouts of tremors, and disabling headaches. Any sudden loud sound frightens him. He can't decide on a job or keep a girlfriend."

Cherie nodded. And here she just thought he was shy. "I've seen this. A lot of French men are in a similar state. But you said all three men. Was Jack in the war too?"

"Thankfully, no. After the US entered the war, the government enacted three rounds of conscription. Jack and Morgan were too old and Cyrus too young for the first two registrations, but they all had to register for the third round. Fortunately, none of them were drafted. Cyrus, though, got a wild notion and enlisted. In a way, I blamed Bryce Holloway."

Cherie raised her eyebrows. "Bryce? So, he came back?"

"No, I'm thinking of years ago, when Cyrus was a little boy, Bryce filled his head with stories of the Rough Riders. None of which were true."

"Bryce." Peaches sighed. "Have you seen him at all?"

"Not in years. He sent Jack and me picture postcards from California a couple of times, but nothing recently."

Cherie finished drying the plate she was holding and handed it to Abigail. "So, what *is* Jack's problem?"

Abigail touched the edge of her eye with her finger. "His best friend is dying—*our* best friend is dying—but Jack won't accept it. He thinks if we all keep denying it, death can't take Morgan."

"That can't be good," Peaches said.

"Not for any of us. And Jack worries the whole time he's working. He's taken to calling long-distance from Santa Fe to check on Morgan every trip he makes. That's not cheap."

They worked quietly for a few minutes until Abigail broke the silence. "I do hope you'll stay here. Jack can go get your luggage tomorrow."

"I think we should," Peaches said. "What do you think, Cherie?"

"Fine by me." She'd rather not be in downtown Taos anyhow. It wasn't full of happy memories.

Abigail looked pleased. "I've never stayed at the Columbian, but the owner just leased the hotel restaurant to a couple of Greeks, the Karavas brothers.

I don't know if the food is Greek or what, we haven't eaten there since they took over."

"Do you have enough room here?" Cherie said.

"There's an empty bedroom between Morgan's and Cyrus's."

Peaches finished the dishes and dried her hand on Cherie's towel. "We'll need to stay at the hotel tonight, though. We didn't bring any nightgowns with us."

"I'll loan you two of mine and send Jack to collect your bags from the hotel first thing in the morning." She took the last dish from Cherie and put it away. "That's done. Shall we have a brandy in the parlor or join the men on the porch?"

"Parlor," Peaches said. "We're enjoying having you to ourselves."

"And I you. I was hoping you'd say that."

The women removed their aprons, and Cherie followed Peaches and Abigail into the parlor. While Abigail filled three snifters with a dark liquid and handed them out, Cherie admired the room. The walls were painted pale green with gold leaf border at the top. Several of Morgan's paintings hung on the walls. An oriental rug covered a good portion of the hardwood floor. On it, sat a low, polished mahogany table in front of the divan. Lace curtains adorned the windows, and there was an upright piano. It was all a little old-fashioned, but warm and comfortable.

Abigail lit lanterns around the room. It wouldn't be dark outside for hours, but the lamps gave the room a pleasant umber glow. It felt like a real home, nothing like the bare, makeshift apartments she'd lived in since leaving Taos. She sniffed the brandy. "Is this from before prohibition?"

"No, the Christian Brothers operate a vineyard in Northern California that's permitted to make it for medicinal purposes."

Cherie took a sip. "Not too shabby." She lifted her glass. "God bless the Christian Brothers."

"I'll drink to that," Peaches said, taking a swallow.

"Please be seated." Abigail offered them the divan and sat in an arm chair next to it.

Cherie sat next to Peaches on the sofa and looked at Abigail. "You have no idea how much I always admired and envied you."

"Oh, it's me who envies you, living so free, without a care as to what other women think. When I divorced Cyrus's father, that was massively scandalous in Taos. I always had to guard my reputation. Twenty years later, it still hasn't changed."

"But you're a powerhouse in Taos," Peaches said. "An astute business woman who owns parcels of real estate, and even the bank."

Cherie's eyes widened. "You own the bank?"

"I bought it from Mr. Hoffsteader last year, but I have to let a man run it. Businessmen won't bank there otherwise."

Cherie cocked her head. "Why not Jack or Morgan?"

"Oh, the last thing Jack would want is to be cooped up in a bank. To him it'd be worse than jail. And Morgan's paintings sell so well he doesn't need another job—thanks in good measure to your sister's gallery, by the way."

Peaches blushed. "Only because you and Morgan helped me set it up."

"I had very little to do with that."

"You helped us get mother's affairs settled and kept the crooks from robbing us of her estate. The only reason I had the money to start a gallery was because you convinced us to save the proceeds."

"Women had to fight for their rights back then," Abigail said. "We couldn't even vote. New Mexico got statehood in 1912, but women didn't get to vote until two years ago."

"At least you can now," Cherie said. "Women still don't have the vote in France." She finished her brandy and held up her glass for more. Abigail got the decanter and refilled all their glasses.

Cherie glanced out the door to see if the men were listening. No one was on the porch. They'd probably gone to the spring house for more beer. "Abigail, I don't know why you say you envy our freedom. You're the one who taught Peaches and me to be free-thinking, sexually independent women."

"I don't know what you mean."

"You don't remember teaching us that trick of using sulfate of iron for birth control? No other woman in this town would have, even if they'd known about it themselves. You told me if I took command of my own woman-hood I could have all the sex I wanted. I was only sixteen, but I've never forgotten."

Abigail shrugged. "Just common sense advice."

"I was clueless about your sex life back then," Cherie said. "But looking back, I realize you could've been having affairs with anyone you wanted."

Abigail swirled her snifter and studied the color of her brandy.

"Not that I'm prying."

"Of course not."

Except that she was. "You did build Morgan a studio in your backyard, and he's lived with you and Jack ever since. Don't the wags in Taos question your living arrangements?"

"No one's ever dared ask, and I wouldn't answer if they did."

"Nor should you," Peaches said. "But birth control has improved beyond what you taught us. I have a Dutch Cap now."

"Me, too," Cherie said. "You can't buy them in America, but I was fitted for mine by a doctor in the Netherlands."

Peaches glanced at Cherie. "I was lucky enough to get mine from Margaret Sanger before the police in New York shut down her clinic."

Abigail looked interested. "What is it? How does it work?"

"It fits over your cervix," Cherie said. "The best part is you don't have to trust a man not to get you pregnant."

"I don't know how much longer I need to worry. I'll be forty-three soon."

Cherie couldn't let that go. "Wasn't Abraham's wife ninety?"

"Oh, God, I'd hate that. Wouldn't you?"

They heard Jack and Cyrus come up the porch steps and open the screen door. "Abigail, are you still up?"

"We're in the parlor, Jack."

"I'm ready for bed."

"Go ahead. I'm just going to get the girls a couple of my nightgowns and then I'll join you."

"Have you checked on Morgan?"

"No, why would we?"

"To make sure he's all right."

"He's fine, Jack. Don't go in there and wake him."

After Jack disappeared upstairs, she hugged Peaches and then Cherie. "I'm glad you're staying. I am so comfortable around you. I don't have to watch every word I say, like I do with the ladies in Taos. Besides, compared to your wild lives, my past seems mild. Of course, holding together Jack, Morgan, and Cyrus has been pretty challenging as of late."

# CHAPTER 12

Two days later, Morgan heard a soft knock on his door. "It's Cherie. Are you decent?"

Yesterday, Jack had moved Peaches and Cherie from the hotel into the room down the hall. Morgan lacked the strength to help Jack carry their trunks, but after some urging, Cyrus lent Jack a hand.

Morgan wasn't feeling exactly sociable last night, but this morning was better. "Yes, come in." The door opened slowly and Cherie slipped in. She was wearing yet another outfit he had not seen before, and he wondered that youth took such pleasure in clothes. Today she wore a cream-colored skirt whose hemline ended in uneven points, like a large handkerchief held up by one corner. A plum-colored sleeveless blouse fell well below her hips, around which she had tied a wide emerald green sash.

Morgan was dressed, sitting on the edge of the bed. He put one hand on the footboard and pushed himself up, standing carefully like every old man he'd ever seen.

She rushed over to help him.

"I can do it," he said. "Let's go outside."

She hovered around him as they made their way downstairs and onto the porch where he collapsed into a rocker, exhausted from the effort.

"Can I get you coffee or something?"

"A coffee would be great, and ask Abigail if she has a biscuit or anything left from breakfast."

"Abigail's not here. She and Peaches went to town. Peaches is paying Art Society members for their paintings she's sold."

"I'm glad. They can probably use the money. I don't see Jack's truck."

"No, he's in Santa Fe. Left me in charge. Said he'd be back as soon as he could."

"He worries over nothing, you know."

"Uh-huh. Let me get that coffee." Cherie left. When she returned with the coffee, she also brought a small plate of toast with a lump of jam on the side. "I didn't know if you liked jelly on your toast, so I left it for you to decide."

Morgan smiled at her, accepted the plate, and took a sip from the cup. "Mmm-mn, that's good! Thanks." He balanced the plate on his knee, took a triangle of toast, and dipped a corner in the jam.

"Oh, I forgot to bring you a knife." She dashed away.

"Cherie, don't worry about it. I'm not an invalid . . ." But she was already out of earshot.

She was back in seconds holding a butter knife.

"Thanks. Now, have a seat." He spread the jam on his toast and took another swallow of coffee. "Tell me what you've been doing. I haven't seen you since I put you and Rebecca aboard the R.M.S. *Umbria* for Ireland."

"What a memory! I don't think I could have recalled the name of our ship."

"Oh, my mind's not gone. Just the morphine makes it a little fuzzy sometimes."

"Well, the crossing took a week. We docked the following Friday in Queenstown—that's in County Cork. It was summer, so Ireland wasn't too cold when we got there. But we were there for a year, and experienced our share of damp, bitter weather, and snow. Often we stayed with Irish relatives Rebecca had never met, but who welcomed us none-the-less. Other times we lived in damp hotels and drank Irish whiskey in cozy pubs to warm ourselves after a day tramping around outdoors."

Morgan remembered Rebecca. She was nearly as tall as Bryce, but plumper. She seemed timid on first meeting, but when she preached her voice could take over the room, and she had a strong singing voice, leading hymns a cappella. He recalled her dark hair and green eyes. She'd graduated Tufts College and was ordained a Universalist minister in 1904, so she must have been about the same age as he, Jack, and Bryce. Taos had been her first church, and she hadn't kept the position long. When Cherie and Peaches became orphaned, it was his idea that Rebecca take Cherie with her as a lady's travel companion. Apparently it all worked out—at least for a year.

"Yes," Morgan said. "I recall she was on a quest to find what her people called 'thin places.' She gave a sermon about it just before she was fired."

"Oh, quest we did. Rebecca took us from one end of the isle to the other. Every sacred nook and holy promontory, we were there."

"I always told her I thought thin places must be the same as places you find on Taos Mountain that possess a sense of the sacred."

Cherie gave a quick shake of her head. "I wouldn't know. Mother never let us go up into the Taos mountains."

Morgan finished his toast and set his plate down. "That's a pity. What I want to know, though, is if you perceived any specialness in the Celtic places you visited?"

Cherie rolled her eyes. "They were dripping with it."

He laid his hand on Cherie's arm. "Seriously?"

Cherie sobered. "Okay. Yes, there were . . . times. We'd hike up to some windy crag and meditate until she was satisfied. She carried a small note book with her and would make notes about the experience afterwards."

"I'd love to know what was in her notes."

"I never read them. I thought it might be too personal, like reading some-one's diary."

"But what about you?"

"I don't keep a diary."

"No? You started to say there were times when you . . . Tell me about those."

"Hints, of something, I suppose."

"Did the distance between our plane and heaven seem narrower?"

"That's what the Irish say. I've never seen heaven, so how would I know? I will say that when we'd meditate in those places, I'd feel . . . I don't know, lighter. I stopped noticing the rocks pressing on my butt. I had no weight as if my head were a zeppelin and my consciousness was pulling me up."

"Wow. No wonder Rebecca sought out those places."

"They weren't the only places we visited. After tramping around Ireland for a year, Rebecca decided we should travel to France to visit Lourdes. Although she was a Universalist minister, her relatives were Catholic, espe-cially those we stayed with in Ireland. They were all on about Saint this and Saint that and Holy Mary. By this point, we were going anywhere locals said was a spiritual place."

He scooted his chair a quarter turn so he could stop looking sideways and see her straight on.

"I'd have moved, if you'd asked."

"I can do things. Please continue your story."

"We took a boat to some port in southwest France near the Spanish border. From there it was only a short train ride to Lourdes. We stayed there two weeks. I haven't been back to Ireland since."

"What was Lourdes like?"

She shrugged. "There's a huge church and hundreds of pilgrims everywhere. The main thing is a grotto with a spring where people bathe in the flowing water, drink it, and fill little bottles to take home. Reverend Sullivan was in the throes of the miracle-ness of it, but it was all too Catholic for me. Too much like all the Holy Days when Mother dragged us to church. But France . . . oh, France, I wanted to stay forever. I convinced Rebecca we shouldn't leave France without visiting the Basilica of Sacré-Cœur. That got us to Paris with its street cafés and Montmartre—cobblestone alleys full of painters imitating Monet and Renoir."

"My heroes," Morgan said.

"I begged her to leave me there, but of course she wouldn't. We sailed to Boston and stayed with her brother and his wife. She showed me her college and tried to get me to finish school, but I was almost eighteen by then, and the only thing I wanted was to find a way back to France. So, she bought us tickets to New York City, and delivered me to Peaches, who was living in Greenwich Village with a painter she modeled for. I forget his name— there were many."

Morgan smiled. "I know."

"A younger sister put a cramp in her plans, but Peaches did the honorable thing and rented us a crappy room with a shared bathroom two floors down. As soon as my eighteenth birthday came, I started looking for a ship back to France. I met a spoiled young cakie with a private cabin who didn't mind buying an extra ticket."

"Trading favors for passage?"

"It's not like I was a virgin, and he was nice enough, though a little dull. I dumped him as soon as I got situated in Paris."

"Sounds a bit callous."

"Don't judge me, Morgan. I was eighteen, unmarried, and sexually liberated in the City of Light. There were artists and interesting people everywhere. Peaches opened her gallery with our inheritance and regularly sent me a small stipend. I rented a room even smaller than the one Peaches and I shared in the Village, if that's possible. But it didn't matter. I never spent any time there. It was just a place to bathe and change clothes. I ate in cafés unless a man took me to dinner at a good restaurant. Paris was cheap, and I quickly learned that if you didn't spend money, you didn't need much to live on."

"Reminds me of when Jack and I were young."

"Peaches and I were talking about that just last week at a speakeasy in New York." She stood up and stretched.

Morgan noticed her full breasts strain the sides of her blouse. All the Romero women had been buxom. She caught him staring and winked. He looked away.

She picked up his plate, cup, and saucer. "I'm going to use the privy. Can I bring you more coffee on my way back?"

He shook his head and opened the screen door for her.

The telephone rang. She set the dishes on the hall table and scooped up the phone, putting the earpiece to her ear. "Oh, hello, Jack, are you still in Santa Fe? He's fine. We've been having coffee together on the porch . . . No, she and Peaches are in town . . . Stop worrying, I've got this, no need to rush back. We're enjoying each other's company . . . All right, I'll tell him. Take your time. Bye."

She spoke through the screen door. "That was Jack."

"I overheard."

"He's still in Santa Fe. The train's delayed. He said to tell you not to overdo it."

Morgan laughed. "He's worse than a mother hen."

# CHAPTER 13

When Cherie returned from the privy, Morgan said, "Have you seen my studio?"

She hadn't. It seemed intrusive to poke around on her own, so she'd waited for an invitation. They walked behind the house and entered a building brightly lit by windows on all sides. A barely started painting—nothing more than a few long brush strokes—was propped on the easel with a stack of blank canvases on the floor beside it.

The place smelled of turpentine and linseed oil. Finished paintings leaned against the walls below the windows on three sides of the room. There was a small writing desk in the corner, a chaise lounge by the opposite wall, and a small table strewn with dead petals from a vase of wilted flowers.

Morgan opened a window, and Cherie opened several others. A pleasant breeze blew through, carrying the paint smells away. Not that she minded them. She'd hung around his previous studio in Taos, and art studios in New York and in Paris, seemingly most of her life.

He eased down on the chaise lounge and stretched out. "I need to lie down for a minute." He scooched over, making room for her. "Sit here."

She bit her lip. He couldn't possibly be inviting her to—

"Oh, nothing like that," he said. "I'm too old for you."

She kneeled on the bed, folded her feet under her butt, and sat, angled so she faced him. She tucked her skirt around her knees and patted his chest. "No you're not. I've been with men your age."

He lifted her hand from his chest and kissed it. "Thank you for saying that, but I didn't bring you out here to seduce you."

"With me it's usually the other way around."

He let go of her hand. "If you remember, I always supported a woman's sexual freedom. You don't have to keep trying to shock me with how wild you are. Now, why don't you tell me more about your life in France?"

"Well . . . the wonderful thing about living where everyone around you is an artist, even if you're not, is that although you can't afford them, you see all your friend's wonderful pictures, and you can spend as much time looking at them as you want. No one minds. The artists are glad for the attention."

Morgan gave her a knowing smile. "Taos is like that now, with the Taos Society of Artists and all the other painters who have come."

"Do you mind if I look at your work?"

"Not as long as you keep talking."

Cherie untangled her feet and stood. She began at the nearest wall, looking at each one, then moving it and looking at the ones behind it. "Oh, Morgan, these are wonderful." Cherie picked up a small metal Eiffel Tower. "Did I send you this?"

"No, I bought that at the St. Louis World's Fair for a friend in New York who was holding my paintings. Then plans changed. Jack and I came straight here from the Fair and I never got to give it to her."

"But you've returned to New York many times since then."

He smiled ruefully. "I kept forgetting to take it with me. Soon the Fair was long forgotten, and no one would care for such a trifle."

*I would.* She set it down, and moved to the next painting. "You should come back to Paris with me. I'll introduce you to everyone."

"I don't think I'd make it to the train station, let alone the ride east."

She frowned. "I'm sorry. That was insensitive of me."

He waved it away. "Don't worry about it. Go on with your story."

"I hung out in Paris and started spelling my name Cherie. For seven years I was in heaven, but then the old European rivalries had to go and blow everything up. I didn't want any part of war, so I fled. I stayed with Peaches for a while."

He propped himself up on his elbows. "I made several trips east during those war years. It's funny we didn't see each other then."

"Oh. I took up with a graduate student writing a book on Gaugin and he took me with him to Tahiti."

"That sounds wonderful. What's Tahiti like?"

"Gorgeous! Even prettier than Gaugin painted it. The water actually *is* turquoise and aquamarine." She was looking at one of his Taos landscapes, studies in reddish-brown and sage. "I wonder what you would have made of the place. Gaugin was long dead, of course, but his work compels you to look for the brown-skinned lovelies he painted there. Or at least that's what my fellow told me."

Morgan chuckled.

"When the war ended, I returned to France, but everyplace north of Paris was in ruin. I was tempted to come back to stay with Peaches in New York, but then a poet I knew took me along when he visited Gertrude Stein."

"Stein? How did you and she get along?"

"My having been to Gaugin's Tahiti roused her interest, as her brother owned two of his paintings. But there's only so much you can say about Tahiti, so on subsequent visits, I was relegated to her companion, Alice, who served tea to wives and girlfriends while Miss Stein talked to the men. That grew old quickly, but I did meet other American writers there."

"Was it she who turned you into a flapper?"

She picked up another painting that somehow captured the height and space of a canyon deep in the mountains. For a second, she felt that sense of lightness that Rebecca's thin places had given her.

"Miss Stein? Goodness, she's no flapper. Alice and Gertrude are old. She is a lesbian, though—she, and Alice, and dozens of women I know in Paris. It's a common thing there. A funny memory that sticks in my mind is the first time I went to their apartment. Miss Stein was wearing thin sole shoes, without a heel, almost like a sandal, except the toe of her shoes curled up like the sultan's shoes in *Arabian Nights*."

Cherie set down the painting and turned toward Morgan. "Women became flappers in reaction to all the death. Millions of men lost on the battlefield, and then the Spanish flu took millions more. I caught it myself. Obviously, I survived, but I admit it frightened me. If you recall, La Grippe killed our mother. I thought for sure fate was going to take my entire generation."

She'd done it again. Why was she talking to Morgan about death? She avoided looking at him by moving to the opposite wall and examining the paintings stacked along the floor. Smaller studies. Glimpses into the Taos light and space.

"So you became a flapper because . . ." he said.

"We just want to extend our youth and enjoy life and freedom with the days we've been given." Damn, she had to quit reminding him. Change the subject.

"We frequented the cafés on the Boulevard Montparnasse and Boulevard Raspail, just to be seen. Maybe our lover's name might appear in one of the gossip columns where up-and-coming writers and artists were desperate to be mentioned. So we went there regularly and made a show of ourselves for the sake of the attention. When someone sold a painting or a story, we'd dine at Michaud's, a very fine restaurant on the corner of rue des Saints-Pères and rue Jacob. There, perhaps we'd see other writers I'd met at Miss Stein's. Famous artists too—once I saw Picasso dining there with two of his models."

Cherie turned to see his reaction to her mention of Picasso.

Morgan was asleep.

She smiled and crossed over to the chaise. The pleasant breeze made her feel sleepy too. She stretched out next to him and rested her head on his chest. The gentle rise and fall of his breathing soon lulled her into a peaceful dream.

# CHAPTER 14

Peaches rode in state in the back of Abigail's Pierce-Arrow. Abigail sat in front, next to Cyrus who was acting as their chauffeur for the day. Abigail and Jack lived on the outskirts of town, so Peaches could easily have walked. But she had a lot of artists to visit, and since Abigail had business, too, they decided to make a day of it.

The car was extraordinarily comfortable with a smooth ride. Jack liked to brag about its ruggedness and said its four-speed transmission allowed it to go places you would not expect for a fancy automobile. He carried on about horsepower and its inline-six engine with dual valves, but all that was lost on Peaches. She liked the nice upholstery and the way the body looked with its headlights housings molded into the flared front fenders. Cyrus said he liked the way it drove.

First stop was the bank. Abigail went in to meet with the manager, leaving Peaches with Cyrus. They were silent for a while, but it wasn't a comfortable silence, with her lounging in the back seat and him still gripping the wheel, staring straight ahead. After a time, she said, "It's nice of you to drive us."

Cyrus nodded and continued to stare at the windshield.

"I'm sure you had better things to do today than chauffeur us around."

Cyrus gave a brief shake of his head.

"Cyrus," she said. "I've known you since you were a child, and we've seen each other on many of my previous trips back to Taos. You don't have to be shy with me."

He turned in his seat and faced her. "I'm sorry. Was I being rude? Sometimes I forget how to act, even with people I know."

"Are you worried about Morgan?"

"Not the way Jack is. I worry more what life will be like after he's gone. I barely remember the time before he and Jack became my fathers."

"You're so lucky to have them. Cherie and I lost our father when we were little children."

"So did I. Mine wasn't dead, no, but he may as well have been. Morgan and Jack have always felt like my real dads."

Peaches winked. "Two men and one mom must have been an interesting house to grow up in."

Cyrus ran his finger over the nap of the upholstered seat. "I can't imagine what you're inferring."

But he didn't seem upset by the idea. "Cherie and I never saw them as fathers. We had something else in mind. Of course, when they came to Taos, we were grown-up girls, or thought we were anyway."

Abigail came out of the bank and got in the car.

"Where to next?" Cyrus said.

"Let's start at the Phillips's house."

Minutes later, Cyrus parked in front of the adobe hacienda and Abigail and Peaches exited. "Are you sure you won't come in with us?" Peaches said. "We could be awhile. I don't want you to be bored."

"No, I'll wait in the car. I'll be fine."

As they walked to the house, Abigail said, "Thanks for trying. He's not very sociable. It's only by making him drive me that I even get him to go anywhere."

Rose Phillips answered the door and smiled when she saw who it was. "Please come in. I was just making tea. Oscar's here as well. He and Bert are in the parlor. Go on through and I'll join you in a minute."

They entered the parlor and everyone greeted each other. Oscar Berninghaus was another member of the Taos Society of Artists whose paintings Peaches exhibited.

"Oscar, I sold that painting of the two Indian women walking from the Pueblo," Peaches said. "But I didn't know you were here for the summer already, so I sent the money to your house in St. Louis."

He brightened. "A sale, Bert."

"Good for you, Oscar."

"I've got money for you too, Bert," Peaches said.

Bert smiled. "And it's much appreciated."

While Bert showed Peaches his latest paintings, Rose brought in a tray with cups and a teapot. She poured and passed around cups. "Abigail, how is Morgan faring?"

"He has his good days," Abigail said, but Peaches noted a quiver in her lips.

Abigail turned away from them and studied a batik wall hanging.

"Rose's mother made that," Bert said.

Peaches wondered if New Yorkers might buy batiks. "Taos has become a real art colony, hasn't it?"

Oscar nodded. "Someone counted a hundred artists in the area now."

"How many are members of the Art Society?" Abigail said.

"Ten."

"All men, I bet," Peaches said.

Bert nodded. "But some of us are arguing to let in Catherine Critcher."

"I hope you do," Abigail said. "You've heard that women can vote now?"

"You going to see Walter Ufer?" Oscar said.

Peaches nodded. "Later today."

"Take my advice and don't bring up the election with him. He'll go on a tear about why we should have elected Eugene Debs."

Peaches laughed. "Okay. We didn't come to discuss politics, anyway. Abigail and I had better go now. We have a lot of stops to make." She handed Bert his check and thanked Rose for the tea.

Cyrus was out of the car and leaning against the side when they came out. He straightened and opened the door for Peaches, leaving Abigail to fend for herself.

"Thank you, Cyrus."

"You're welcome. Where to next?"

"Ernie and Mary Blumenschein's, on Ledoux Street."

"I know where they live—in Buck Dunton's old place." Cyrus turned the corner and only drove a few blocks before they were there.

A courtyard in front of the house was planted with colorful flowers, and several of Ernie's paintings were set out for passersby to peruse. The front door was propped open. Peaches called, "Hello, anyone home?"

Mary came to the door, brushing flour from her apron. "Oh, hello Abigail, Peaches. Ernie's not here. He's gone over to Doc Martin's."

"He's not sick, I hope," Abigail said.

"No, Doc bought one of his paintings and he took it to him. I'm not sure if he's coming straight back or going elsewhere from there. I'd invite you in, but I'm in the middle of baking."

"That's all right," Peaches handed her an envelope containing a check. "Just give him this. It's for a painting my gallery sold."

Mary took the envelope. "I'll give it to him as soon as he gets back. Will you be in Taos long?"

"That depends on Morgan. We're staying at Abigail and Jack's."

"Oh, Abigail, how is Morgan doing?"

"His spirits are good. He seems happy that Peaches and her sister are here."

"You have a sister? I don't think I know her."

"You wouldn't," Peaches said. "She moved away right after school and hasn't been back since."

"Is that Cyrus in your car?"

Abigail nodded. "He's our chauffeur today."

"Is he any . . . better?" Mary said.

"Pretty much the same."

The bell of a timer rang inside the house. "Oh! I better check the oven."

"You go ahead," Peaches said. "We'll visit another time. Goodbye."

Mary made her goodbyes and left for the kitchen. Peaches and Abigail returned to the car and Cyrus drove them to Walter Ufer's house. Walter answered the door holding a wet paint brush and bid them to follow him into his studio.

Peaches smiled at the sight. Walter was dressed in khaki pants and jacket. His pant legs were tucked into knee high riding boots and he wore a flat-brim hat that reminded her of old photos of the Rough Riders. With his round wire-rimmed glasses, he looked like a young Teddy Roosevelt.

His wife, also named Mary, sat in one corner of his studio, reading. She put down the book and greeted them. Walter picked up his palette and returned to his easel, where he was adding the faint image of an Indian ghost to an unfinished landscape of Taos. He had surrounded himself with Indian artifacts, barely leaving a corner of the room free for Mary's chair.

"The Indian has lost his race pride," Walter said to no one in particular. "He wants only to be an American. Our civilization exerts a terrific power. We don't feel it, but that man out there in the mountains feels it, and he cannot cope with such pressure."

"I see you're working," Peaches said. "We don't want to disturb you. I have a check for that small painting we sold."

Walter held up his full hands. "Mary, can you take that?"

"We'll go now," Peaches said. "Good luck with the new piece, Walter. Let me know when it's finished. I'd like to see it. You can reach me at Abigail's." They made a hurried exit and spotted Jack's truck idling next to the Pierce-Arrow, blocking the road.

Cyrus sat in the car talking to Jack through the window. Abigail and Peaches walked over to Jack's truck. Abigail stepped up on the running board and kissed him. "Did you just get back from Santa Fe?"

"Yes. I haven't started my deliveries yet, but I saw your car parked here."

"We're visiting artists I owe commissions," Peaches said.

"Who's with Morgan?"

"Cherie," Abigail said.

"Yeah, I spoke with her when I telephoned from Santa Fe, but I didn't know Cyrus was with you."

"Jack, Cherie's there."

"Sure, I know, but does she know where all his medicines are and when to give them?"

Abigail patted Jack's shoulder. "Morgan knows what to take and when."

"How soon are you going home?"

"Not for a while," Peaches said. "We're going to Buck Dunton's next, then several others. Taos artists have had a good year."

"Maybe I should swing by the house before I start my deliveries," Jack said.

"It'd be a waste of gas, and you know it." Abigail kissed him goodbye and stepped off the running board. "Don't be so anxious, Cherie's with him."

# CHAPTER 15

Cherie was awakened by a firm hand shaking her shoulder. She lifted her head from Morgan's chest and turned to see Jack leaning over her. He put his finger across his lips and motioned for her to follow. Morgan made a soft opiated sigh as she unwound herself from him, stood, and followed Jack out of the studio into the glaring afternoon sun.

"Abigail and Peaches still aren't back?" Jack said.

Cherie shrugged. Why was he asking her? She'd been napping with Morgan. She shaded her eyes with her hand and looked toward the open doors of the empty garage that had once been a carriage house. "I guess not."

"I thought they might get here before me."

"I don't know. It's just been me and Morgan."

"I finished my deliveries as quick as I could. Now, it's time for a cold beer. You want one?"

"Maybe. Should we eat something first?"

"Did Morgan have lunch?"

"No. He had toast for breakfast, and then he took his medicine and fell asleep."

"He's never going to get his strength up unless he gets more food in him. A bird couldn't survive on what he eats some days." Jack left for the spring house and returned with two glasses of golden liquid. Beads of sweat formed on the outside of the glasses, while thin streams of bubbles effervesced upward. Jack had already taken several sips and had bits of foam on his mustache. He handed Cherie her glass and motioned toward the Adirondack chairs. "Let's wait for the others in the shade."

Cherie sat on the edge of the seat and rested her glass on the wide wooden arm of the chair. Jack sank all the way back in his chair. The backs and seats of Adirondack chairs were angled so that when you slid against the back, your body pointed slightly toward the sky. It was a new experience for her, and she rather liked it. But unless she perched on the edge, she found it difficult to see the person sitting beside her.

Cherie handed Jack her beer, picked up the heavy chair and turned it to face him.

"I'd have done that if you asked."

"Women are perfectly capable." She retrieved her beer and sat down. "That's better. I can see you, now."

She studied Jack. He had aged handsomely—still recognizably the tall, attractive man who had walked up to her mother's porch with Morgan when she was fifteen. They were New York dandies then. Covered in soot from the train ride and dust from the stage coach, but once they'd bathed and changed clothes, they were the most exciting men she and her sister had ever met. They'd actually lived in New York City, when New York was a magical land of culture and sophistication.

Jack smiled at her. "You grew up nice. Beautiful, in fact."

"Do you really think so?"

"There must be something in the French waters. You look young as the day I met you."

"I did take the waters at Lourdes." She batted her brown eyes and took a small sip of beer. Jack wore his hair longer than men did on the Right Bank, but not as long as some bohemians. She spotted a few gray hairs along his temples, but it helped more than hurt his looks.

"Except your hair's shorter," he said. "I remember you with long, wavy, brown hair, always tied with a velvet ribbon that matched your dress."

"I was a schoolgirl." *And you gave all your attention to Peaches.*

"You like your hair short?"

"And sassy. Hats fit better too."

Jack laughed. "Still cheeky." He finished his beer and stood. "Ready for another?"

She shook her head. Her glass was still full.

"Okay, I'll be right back."

Minutes later, Jack returned from the spring house with a fresh beer. He held it up. "Today got me a little keyed up. Normally, I pace myself."

"You do?"

"Oh yeah. You have to understand yourself. Now, take me, I'm a thirsty drinker. I drink liquids in volume. That's why I prefer beer. Over the years I found that a pint of beer every half hour will let me drink all night without leaving that happy, inebriated state and becoming falling down drunk. You can't do that with whiskey and wine. A pint of either will push you over the cliff and shorten your night."

"But that's your second beer, and it hasn't been a half hour."

"I know. I'll take it slower with this one. But you're young yet. Let me teach you how to drink. It's a scientific principle I discovered—one drink every half hour."

"Does that work with champagne and cocktails?"

"Well, I have been known on occasion to have a bump of whiskey with my beer, and it seems fine. You just have to be aware where the edge of sloppy drunk is for you."

"I love to dance. The black bottom and the shimmy seem to help burn the booze off."

"I like to dance, too, but don't let it fool you. My half hour rule still holds true."

"I bow to the master."

The Pierce-Arrow rolled down the long driveway and stopped. Peaches and Abigail got out, and Cyrus backed the car into the garage. The women came over, and Jack stood and kissed Abigail, who said she and Peaches were going to start dinner.

Cherie stood up. "Do you need help?"

"No, Abigail and I are enough," Peaches said. "Besides, you said you can't cook."

"Well, I don't cook. But I could do something. Abigail shouldn't have to do it all."

"I don't mind, you're my guests," Abigail said. "Stay out here with Jack and enjoy your beers."

"Speaking of which," Jack said. "Is there enough time before dinner for me to run out to the cabin? I need to start a fresh batch of beer. We don't want to run out now we have extra company."

"I can drink something different," Cherie offered.

"No, no, don't worry. I can keep us all in beer. It's just that it takes ten days to ferment, so I want to start another batch before we need it."

Abigail gave him a squeeze. "Wait until morning, dear. I'm reheating leftovers and I don't want to have everything ready and you not back yet."

Cyrus carried two baskets of groceries to the kitchen. Abigail and Peaches followed.

"Abigail, are you sure you don't need help?" Cherie called after her.

Abigail waved her hand. "Keep Jack out of my hair."

"I hope Abigail's not just being polite. I don't want her to feel like she's running a boarding house while we sit here on our butts."

"She doesn't. Abigail runs things around here better than ten women could. It keeps her mind from worrying about the rest of us."

"You mean Morgan and Cyrus?"

"Me, too, though God knows why. I'm fine—hale and hearty as a dollar."

"She says you're too anxious about Morgan."

"We all are. It's nerve wracking waiting for the doctoring to do its magic."

Cherie saw Morgan come out the studio door. He shuffled over to them. "Sorry, Cherie, I guess I dozed off while you were talking."

"You didn't miss anything."

"How are you feeling?" Jack said.

"You say that as if I should be feeling poorly."

"I didn't mean that."

"It's all right. Fact is, I'm not going to get any better."

"Nonsense. As Bryce used to say, 'Time wounds all heels.'"

Cherie laughed. "He was a card, wasn't he?"

Jack nodded. "What he was, was a bullshitter. But he was our bullshitter. I wish we knew where he was. We could use a little more humor around here."

"You're funny enough," Morgan said.

"Just trying to keep things light."

Peaches called from the porch, "Abigail says to wash up. Dinner's almost ready."

That was quick. They started walking toward the house, Cherie at Morgan's side and Jack hovering near.

"Morgan, if you're up to it, we can go for a drive after dinner. The weather's nice and it would get you off this place for a change."

"I appreciate the thought, Jack, but that old truck bounces my insides too hard."

"We can take the Pierce-Arrow if Cyrus left any gas in it. Hell, we can all go."

Morgan managed a wan smile. "Let's see what I feel like after supper."

* * *

Serving dishes were passed around the table and everyone filled their plates. When Morgan didn't take as large a portion as Jack thought he should, he spooned an extra helping onto Morgan's plate.

"How was your day in town?" Morgan said.

"It was good," Peaches said. "Everyone asked about you and sends their good wishes."

"There are a lot of respectable artists here now, more than just those ten in the Society. Must be a hundred, all told."

"That's what Oscar Berninghaus said. I'll have to see some of their work—perhaps take some on consignment when I go back to New York."

"Morgan can introduce you around one day," Jack said. "Be good for him to get out."

"That's not necessary, Jack," Abigail said. "Cyrus can do it. Anytime you want to go, Peaches."

Cyrus, who had eaten quickly, excused himself, and started to leave the table.

"There's dessert," Abigail said.

"No thanks, I've had enough."

Peaches took a sip of wine and patted her lips with her napkin. "When we were in town today, I couldn't help thinking how we chose opposite paths. You guys ran away from New York City to come here, and Cherie and I ran away from Taos to live in New York City."

"Well, *you* did," Cherie said. "I moved on to Paris."

Peaches pinched her sister in the ribs. "You're so continental."

Abigail reached over and brushed Morgan's shirt front with her napkin. "You've got ketchup on you. It's not coming off. Wait, we didn't have ketchup. Are you bleeding?"

Peaches leaned close to Morgan and touched the spot with her finger. "No . . . it's lipstick."

Morgan shook his head and shrugged.

Peaches looked at Cherie.

Jack raised his glass. "Ain't fate shit. I drank to excess, but Morgan lost his liver."

"I drank my share too, Jack."

Jack drained his glass. "Morgan, tell the girls that funny story about when you were in the hospital recovering from surgery and the guy in the next bed shit himself."

"Jack!" Abigail said. "Please, not at the dinner table."

Jack rolled his eyes. "I only wanted everyone to laugh."

"Who wants dessert?" Abigail said.

# CHAPTER 16

Jack pulled off the side of a winding dirt road and set the handbrake, putting the Ford in neutral. "Wait in the truck."

Cherie watched as he got out, picked up the end of a fallen tree, and hauled it to one side, his biceps straining the sleeves of his shirt. He returned to the truck, drove forty paces into the woods, stopped, and went to drag the tree back over the entrance.

She'd been bored this morning. Morgan was sleeping, Cyrus morose, and she'd had more than enough girl talk. Jack was outside, happily whistling as he loaded a soup pot, two canning kettles, a bucket, a washtub, and a third kettle on his truck. She asked if she could come with him. It took him a moment to answer. Finally, he nodded. "It's a secret place. You can't tell anyone."

"Who would I tell?"

"I guess you've got a point."

"Let me freshen up my lipstick and put on my hat. A woman never leaves home without a hat."

"Don't make a fashion decision out of it. We're only going out in the woods."

She hadn't realized he was serious. They were in deep forest. Even though she'd grown up in this part of New Mexico, she had no idea where they were.

As Jack wound the Ford over ruts and tree roots on a trail only he could see, Cherie's body slammed against the door and her head bounced on the roof. Then he edged down a sloping bank and began driving through the shallow water of a stony creek. They followed the stream for a mile until he came to another place where the land sloped gradually up from the water. He downshifted, gunned the engine, and turned out of the creek.

Finally, Jack parked in front of a decrepit old cabin, maybe built by some hunter or trapper last century and apparently not used since then. "We're here."

He got out of the truck and began tossing aside tumbleweeds strewn in front of the cabin door.

Cherie opened the passenger door and stood on the running board. She looked at her feet, wishing she'd worn something more practical than her patent-leather Mary Janes.

Jack put his shoulder to the cabin door, and it creaked open. "Come on in."

The inside wasn't much better than the outside. A small woodstove on the far side of the room and a crude sideboard was all there was to it. Not even a chair. A couple of nets containing dried weeds hung from the rafters.

Jack opened the stove door, put in a bit of kindling and two pieces of split wood, struck a match, and got a fire going. "I prefer to do this on a foggy morning. One thing the Indians got right is that a column of smoke can be seen from a long way on a clear day. But it's early. Anyone sees our smoke will hopefully just think some hunter or fisherman is cooking his breakfast."

He motioned for her to follow him outside and around to the back of the cabin. There, spanning two tree stumps, lay a pair of large window screens stacked together and clamped. Jack began removing the clamps on one side and indicated she should do the same on her side. Once the top screen was free, he raised it three or four inches, shook it vigorously, and then stood it upright against a tree.

While Jack gathered up clamps, Cherie examined the split kernels of brown grain spread in an even layer over the bottom window screen. "What is it?"

"Malted barley." He took the clamps back to the truck, and she followed. Jack climbed on the truck bed and handed her a pail. "Fill that with water."

She looked around. "Where's the pump?"

He dragged the washtub and the canning kettle to the edge and jumped down. "No pump. Get it from the creek."

Cherie removed her shoes and stockings and put them in the truck. Barefoot, she waded into the creek and turned the bucket on its side, but when righted, it was only a quarter full. "Jack, I can't get it filled, the creek's too shallow."

Jack carried over the kettle. "Sorry, that's what this is for. Empty your pail in here, and repeat until you figure you have two gallons."

"You mean you've been serving us beer made from river water?"

"Why not? You can't get purer water than a mountain stream. Scoop out a handful and taste it."

"I don't think so. What about all the rocks and sand in this creek?"

"When you get water from a pump, what do you think is at the bottom of the well?"

"I never thought about it."

Jack spread a square of muslin over the kettle and held it from slipping as she poured water from her pail through it. "I was only teasing you about the dirt. You'll see there won't be any on the cloth. I only strain it to make sure there aren't any leaves or twigs."

After Cherie emptied her pail, Jack lifted the muslin and saw how full it was. "A couple more buckets should do it."

When he decided they had enough water, she held her hand out, and he steadied her as she climbed out of the creek. "You may as well leave you shoes off. We're going to need more water later."

Jack asked Cherie to take the empty washtub around back where the screens were, while he carried the kettle of water inside and set it on the stove.

Cherie picked up one of the kernels from the screen to examine it, and its little white root fell off. She hoped Jack wouldn't be upset. It was only one kernel; there were thousands. When Jack arrived, he took the kernel from her and pried it open with his pocketknife. "See this small leaflet inside the grain? It's called an acrospire. I soaked the barley and then let it germinate about two-and-a-half days until the acrospires were nearly as long as the grain. Then I stopped the germination and dried them in these screens. You can dry them in a low temperature oven if you can control the heat, but I can't do that out here, so I dry mine in the sun. I came up with the idea of clamping two screens together to keep the birds and critters from stealing my malt. Works pretty well."

Cherie was constantly amazed at Jack's ingenuity.

"Now, what we're going to do is shake the screen until the little white roots fall off. If the malted barley is sufficiently dried, they usually come right off."

Once Jack had his malted barley separated from the rootlets and into the washtub, he carried the tub into the cabin, took a piece of firewood, and ground the barley a bit. He tested the kettle water with his finger. "Good, not too hot yet." Cherie watched him scoop handfuls of the crushed grain into the water kettle. "This part is like making tea. We want the water hot, but not boiling. We'll let it steep about a half hour."

While the barley tea steeped, they went back to the creek and filled the second kettle with filtered water. When they returned, Jack felt the side of the pot and decided it shouldn't get any warmer, so he set it on the sideboard and put the new kettle on to boil.

"I'm beginning to see beer is a lot of work," Cherie said.

"Nah, the yeast does all the work. It takes us a few hours to get the ferment ready, but that typically makes enough beer to last weeks."

"Not with us around."

"Oh, I'm glad to have you here. Abigail's happy, Morgan's happy, maybe even Cyrus. I can't really tell about that kid." Jack opened the door to the stove and added more wood. "I'm glad you came with me today. I wasn't sure how to bring this up, but since this is going to take a couple of hours, I may as well . . ."

"What is it?"

"Yesterday, when I found you with Morgan—"

"Oh, you don't think—No, nothing happened. We just took a nap."

"Don't get me wrong. Having sex with a beautiful young woman may be the very thing Morgan's morale needs, but I'm not sure his body is up to the challenge."

"Jack, we weren't even petting. Really."

Jack pulled out his pocket watch and checked the time, then looked to see if the second kettle was boiling.

"You don't have to defend your honor to me. I've always advocated a woman's right to love who she pleases when she pleases."

"I heard that about you. But I wasn't trying to have Morgan."

"I don't mind if you do. Just, give him a few more days to get stronger."

Cherie picked up a third kettle and started out the door. Clearly, Jack could have this conversation without her. "You're going to need more water, right? I'm going to the creek."

* * *

When Cherie returned with the water, Jack had the door to the woodshed open and was pouring boiling water into two tall pickling crocks. He yelled over his shoulder, "Put your kettle on the stove, and then refill this one, please." Jack sloshed the water around in the crocks and then dumped it on the ground. He divided the remaining water from the kettle between the two crocks and handed her the empty pot.

The creek water was cold, but she hadn't run barefoot since she was a child. It was a delight she'd forgotten in city living.

The second pot came to a boil. Jack set it aside, put the third pot in its place, and checked his fire. "See, Cherie, no reason to worry about creek water. We boil it. Not because you can't drink it as it is, but because we don't want anything growing in the ferment but what we put there."

Cherie nodded and watched as he set Abigail's good soup pot on the floor beneath the pot of malted barley "tea." He took the lid from the soup pot and set it in the barley kettle, but the lid was too small and it sunk. "Doesn't fit," she said.

"Not supposed to, it holds the mash on the bottom while we siphon off the good stuff." Jack took a length of rubber hose and started the liquid from the barley draining into the soup pot. When the flow stopped, he added boiled water to the barley pot and siphoned again.

Jack poured the remaining boiled water into the ferment crocks, and added the third pot which was now boiling. Next, he chose the largest kettle, one like her mother had used to heat jars during canning, and emptied the soup pot into it. Cherie peeked in. It was barely half full. He set it on the stove and added more wood to the fire. "When this boils it's going to foam up pretty high. I learned early on to use a pot big enough not to boil over."

He handed her the kettle of barley mash. "We don't need this anymore. Dump it somewhere far from the cabin, then rinse out the pot in the creek."

When Cherie returned, Jack was preparing the dried weeds that hung from the rafters. "What's that?"

He held up a three inch long cone. "*Humulus lupulus neomexicanus*, wild hops. They grow all over this part of New Mexico. I harvest mine from a little canyon—my secret place."

Leave it to Jack to know the Latin. Cherie looked into the kettle which had reached a roiling boil. The surface was covered with thick, smooth foam that reminded her of the head on a beer. Jack checked his watch and then went out to split more wood.

Suddenly she noticed a change, and things started floating in the foam. She ran to the door. "Jack, something's wrong. It looks like Chinese egg-drop soup."

Jack put down the ax and came in. "That's good. Now we add the hops." He put in half the hops and stirred the brew with a long wooden spoon. "In about thirty minutes, we'll put in more hops, and the rest about fifteen minutes before it's done."

"How long does it cook?"

"An hour. Nothing to do until then but feed the fire. You can stir it once in a while to make sure it doesn't scorch."

Jack went outside and returned with an armload of wood he dropped on the floor. He took the spoon from her, gave the wort a stir, and handed the spoon back.

"Listen, Cherie, I understand women have certain needs, same as men."

Not this, again.

"If you want to be of some help while waiting for Morgan to get healthy again, why don't you turn your wiles on Cyrus? The boy doesn't do anything but mope."

So now it was Cyrus? "Jack, I don't need you to set me up."

"I'm not saying you do. I'm only saying—"

"Men! They always think sex is the solution to everything."

"As a member of that gender, I can state scientifically, after years of experimentation, that sex takes a man's mind off his problems. Inversely, unfulfilled urges impair his ability to concentrate. I don't know if it's the same for women."

Cherie laughed in his face. "Just because I practice free love doesn't make me a whore, Jack. You can't decide who I sleep with."

Jack turned red and looked away. "I never meant to imply . . ." He went to the stove and stirred the wort. "You know I respect you, don't you?"

Cherie chewed the inside of her cheek. Maybe she was a little harsh.

"Why don't you get Cyrus to take you to a movie? You can take Abigail's car. It's a nice car to drive."

"I can't drive."

"That's okay, Cyrus does." Jack checked his watch and added the rest of the hops. "And the Pierce-Arrow is a comfortable ride."

Cherie decided to change the subject. "When we drove to the hotel the first day, I noticed Deitwiler's has gone out of business."

"Yeah, sad. Fred closed up after Emma died."

"Died? Emma?"

"Yes, breast cancer. You didn't know?"

Cherie clutched her breasts. "That's horrible. She hardly had any tits in the first place."

"You can let go of yours. Size doesn't seem to have anything to do with who gets it."

"It must have been hard for her to go through."

"Cancer's a bitch."

Cherie saw his mind had jumped to Morgan. "Well, having a German last name during the war couldn't have been easy for Fred, either."

"No, people forget pretty quickly that all of our ancestors came from somewhere else."

"How much longer does this cook?"

Jack looked at his watch and handed her a hot pad. "You can help carry. In about five minutes, we'll set the kettle in the creek so it cools quickly."

When time was up, Jack covered the pot so water wouldn't splash in, and they carried it to the creek. While it cooled, Jack dug a hole, put the burning embers from the stove in it, and covered them with dirt. He loaded the two screens, the washtub, bucket, and all the pots and pans onto the truck. "We're almost done. I always take everything home to keep the place looking abandoned."

Jack closed up the cabin and threw tumbleweeds in front of the door. Cherie walked with him down to the creek.

"Penelope, too," Jack said.

It took a moment for her to connect to their earlier conversation. "Abigail's sister? Dead?"

Jack nodded. "Four years ago; Spanish Influenza took her."

Cherie grimaced. "I caught that. I lived, but it was damn scary. Must have been hard on Abigail, losing a sister."

"Harder on Walter. He pretty much stopped coming over after she passed."

"They had children, right?"

"His boys are grown and help him farm. They got drafted, but it was at the end of the war so they didn't have to suffer what Cyrus is going through. Shame is, they only visited Cyrus a couple of times after they got back."

They carried the wort to the woodshed. Jack felt the water temperature in the crocks with his hand, added yeast, and divided the wort evenly between the two crocks, filtering it through cloth as he poured. He covered the crocks and closed the woodshed door, stacking logs in front of it. "That's it. You can get in the truck. The yeast will do the rest of the work."

She climbed in, looked at her dirty feet and decided not to put her shoes and stockings on. Jack set the canning kettle in the back, cranked the motor, and got in. He backed the truck in a half circle, put it in low gear, and headed up the creek.

Cherie turned in her seat toward him. "Didn't Penelope and Walter have a daughter as well?"

"Dead, too. She married and moved to Albuquerque, but died having a baby. Everybody young is dying now. It's just not right. Didn't it used to be you had to get old before you died?"

"Jack, you guys have been through deep shit."

"Yeah, I know." He let the truck chug along a moment. "That's why it's so important we keep Morgan alive."

# CHAPTER 17

Cherie left Jack to unload his beer making equipment and walked to the house carrying her shoes and stockings in her hand. She scuffed her bare feet on a mat by the door and tiptoed down the polished hallway, trying to reach the bathroom without leaving any tracks.

The door was ajar, but as she pushed it open, it banged against a metal pail. Cherie gave an involuntary shriek. Abigail's head snapped toward the door. "Oh, Cherie! You gave me a start. I didn't hear Jack's truck."

Morgan perched on the edge of the bathtub, shirtless. Abigail was washing his face and chest with a wet cloth. Cherie's jaw dropped. Not because the once handsome Morgan was half naked, but because his pale skin clung to his chest like a wet camisole, outlining every rib. His abdomen, concave as a serving bowl, was marred by a brutal six inch scar that ran diagonally from just below his sternum toward his right side. Crosscut with stitches, it resembled barbwire.

She looked away, a crimson flush creeping up her neck and inflaming her cheeks. He surely didn't need to be gawked at.

His shirt lay crumpled on the floor, and there was vomit in the bucket. Abigail pointed toward the pail. "Would you take that outside and fetch Morgan a clean shirt from his room, please?"

Cherie glanced at her feet. "Um, I need to wash the mud off first or I'll track up your floors."

Abigail tossed her a towel. "For now, just rinse off at the pump out back. And wash out the pail while you're at it."

Cherie tucked the towel in the crook of her elbow and pinched her nose closed. With her other hand she grasped the handle and carried the bucket at arm's length. Abigail laughed, and this even brought a chuckle from Morgan.

After washing her feet, emptying and cleaning the pail, and bringing Morgan his shirt, she helped Abigail steady him as he walked upstairs to his room. Abigail softly closed his door, and the two women stood in the hallway outside his bedroom.

Impulsively, Cherie wrapped Abigail in her arms and began to sway. "Oh, you poor dear woman, what you have been through. I only learned today about the death of your sister and niece. I am so sorry for you."

Abigail tried to squirm out of her embrace, but Cherie held on, rocking her back and forth.

"You keep this up and I'm going to bawl."

Cherie patted Abigail's back. "Go ahead. You deserve a good cry. I can't imagine how it would feel to lose Peaches."

Abigail's shoulders began to quake; she buried her face in Cherie's neck and the dam broke. Cherie began to weep, too. The women leaned into each other and hugged for . . . Cherie didn't know how long. It was as if time suspended.

Abigail's nose ran. She lifted her head and looked at Cherie's collar. "I'm sorry. I've soiled your good blouse."

Cherie stopped crying and sniffed. "Making beer with Jack already did that."

"And I've kept you from your bath."

"This is more important."

Abigail wiggled out of Cherie's arms, pulled a hankie from her pocket, wiped her eyes, and blew her nose. "Yes, thank you. But Penelope died a long time ago. I need to start supper. Why don't you have your bath and then come help me? I'll teach you how to bake a pie."

Cherie dried her eyes with her palms and nodded. She started away, stopped, and turned back. "Never tell Peaches I said I'd miss her."

Cherie retrieved her bathrobe from her room and proceeded to the kitchen, where she filled two copper water kettles from the hand pump in the sink and put them on the stove to heat. While the stove did its work, she cleaned the bathroom. It was a simple chore, but one less thing for Abigail to contend with.

Fortunately, ever-clever Jack had constructed a platform outside with a galvanized tank that acted as an elevated cistern. A pipe from it ran through the wall to a faucet on the bathtub. She turned the handle, and lukewarm water gushed from the tap. The kettles on the stove boiled, and she poured their contents in, creating a steamy cloud. She tested the water with her hand, turned off the faucet, slipped out of her clothes, and settled into the tub.

Cherie soaped a washcloth and replayed the conversation she'd had earlier with Jack. She wasn't about to allow Jack to decide who she slept with, but his suggestion that she might bring Cyrus out of his shell had merit. Not only would it help him but it would also lessen one of Abigail's principal concerns.

She gently moved the washcloth down her arms, up her legs, across her shoulders and over her breasts. She imagined the rough texture of the terrycloth to be Cyrus's hands. He was a beautiful man with full lips, his mother's Welsh cheekbones, and dark wavy hair. She continued washing, massaging her breasts, then sliding the soapy cloth down her abdomen, she scrubbed the thick nest of her pubic hair. Letting go of the cloth, she sought out the familiar nub that was her pleasure point. It'd been a while since she'd had a man—the writer she'd sailed to New York with, but he talked better than he performed. She closed her eyes and imagined kissing Cyrus. She tangled her fingers in his hair and pulled his face to her. Her toes curled and her body stiffened.

She'd almost gone over the edge when a series of sharp raps on the door intruded.

"Cherie? Are you still in there?"

The excitement evaporated in an instant. "Yes, Jack."

"Don't drain the tub. I need a bath, too. No reason to waste the water."

"Well, I'm not finished, yet."

"Take your time. I'm in no hurry."

"Okay. Go away, now. I'll let you know when I'm done."

Cherie managed to find her way back into matters at hand, and when satisfied, rinsed herself, stood, and toweled off. She wrapped her head in the towel, put on her robe, tied the sash, and threw open the bathroom door. "Tub's all yours, Jack."

In her room, she removed the towel, rubbed her hair vigorously, and ran a wide-tooth comb through it. She loved having bobbed hair, so easy to deal with. Opening her trunk, she began sifting through various outfits, finally settling on a white sailor top with blue stripes, and a navy blue skirt that was a little short, almost up to her knee. For shoes, she decided on an older scuffed pair of Mary Janes.

After carefully applying her makeup, she stepped back and checked her appearance in the tall mirror that stood in the corner, turning to one side and then the other. Not bad. She went downstairs to find Cyrus. Looking out the screen door, she spotted him sitting in the grass under the cottonwood tree where he often was. He appeared to be carving trenches in the dirt with a large hunting knife.

She strolled over to him, waiting to catch his eye, but he seemed focused on his task. "What'cha doing?"

Cyrus's eyes snapped up to her face briefly, then back to the ground. "Nothing."

"Good. Do you know where I can find a basket?"

"What for?"

"Berries."

"Mom probably has one on the back porch."

Cherie bent down and reached for his hand.

Cyrus jerked his hand away. "What are you doing?"

"No need to worry. I thought I'd be helpful and pick berries for your mother's pie."

Cyrus gave her a sheepish look. "Sorry. Just . . . a reflex, don't take it personally. It doesn't mean I don't like you."

Oh? She held his gaze and smiled gently. "I understand. You're not alone, you know. I've seen many men in France with similar struggles."

He looked away.

She held her index finger in front of his face and slowly swept it toward where she was standing. His eyes followed until she had him looking at her again. "I need your help."

"You do?"

"Surely you know where berries grow in the woods. You've lived on this property all your life."

"Yes."

"Well, I don't. So I need you to show me."

He shook his head.

Cherie offered her hand. "Come. We're only going to places you played in as a child."

Cyrus tentatively accepted her hand and stood.

She gave him a smile that could melt butter.

# Chapter 18

Later that week, Abigail was going into town to conduct some business. Peaches suggested to Cherie that they ride along with her and visit their mother's grave.

"Thanks, no," Cherie said. "Do you really think I want to relive unhappy scenes of our childhood?"

"Cyrus is driving," Peaches said. "Abigail and I'll ride in back. You can sit up front."

Did Peaches think Cyrus was enough inducement to get her into a grave-yard? He was a handsome man, but she wasn't in love with him. Not even in lust with him, much. And she'd buried Mama seventeen years ago.

Of course, when their mother expired of La Grippe, Peaches was bedridden with the same disease. Cherie hadn't caught it yet, and the doctor said she couldn't stay in the house or she would. When no one from her church would let her stay with them, it was Jack who convinced Rebecca to take her in until Peaches recovered. Father Ignacio told his parish that he was displeased they'd abandoned her to a Protestant woman minister, but members of his congregation had a greater fear of La Grippe than of their padre's disapproval.

When Mother died, she and Peaches had no nearby relatives, and none of her mother's fellow parishioners would help wash and prepare the body.

So, Jack had paid the undertaker out of his own pocket. Her sister eventually recovered, but not in time for Mother's funeral. Jack and Abigail had accompanied Cherie to the funeral. They weren't even Catholic, but Jack said he didn't want her to have to sit in the front pew alone.

Peaches might feel they were indebted to Morgan for helping them get started, but Cherie suddenly realized it was Jack who stepped up while the rest of Taos turned their backs. She wasn't going to whore for him, but she owed him something. And mending Cyrus wouldn't be unpleasant. It wouldn't be easy, though. While she found Cyrus amenable to her charms —he was clearly attracted during their berry picking—she hadn't succeeded in getting him to ask her out. He said it wasn't her, and she could believe him. He was reluctant to leave home even to drive Abigail on her errands. Whatever good Cherie could do him probably wouldn't involve going on a real date.

"Come with me," Peaches said. "You've never been to her grave."

"I have. I buried her. You're the one who missed the funeral."

"I was barely alive. What did you expect?"

"That wasn't a complaint. You were as sick as Mother. I feared I was losing you, too. It was right that you didn't attend."

"Then why are you angry at me?"

"I'm not. I just don't want to visit her grave. The once was enough."

"It's what daughters do for their mothers. We can take some of Abigail's lovely flowers. She won't mind."

"You go."

"Not without you. It's well time we honored her and put the past behind us."

Cherie turned away. It was hard to tell the difference between honoring the woman and honoring the past. And there wasn't much to honor in a mother whose main intent had been to raise them to marry rich dullards. Cherie sometimes wondered if their mother hadn't ruined marriage for both of them.

Peaches clasped her sister's hand and slowly drew her into Abigail's large flower garden. "I brought shears. Cut whichever colors you like."

And, yet, Cherie let herself be led along. She'd do it. But she'd do it for Peaches.

* * *

They dropped Abigail off in town. She told them not to hurry. She had plenty to do until they came for her. The cemetery was situated behind the Catholic Church. Cyrus said he would wait in the car. If the sun got too hot he'd move it into the shade, some place where he could see when they came out.

Peaches handed Cherie the flowers and retrieved a rag and a brush from the car trunk. They skirted the church, taking a path down the side of the adobe building.

"I know where the grave is," Peaches said. "I've been here before."

Cherie nodded. She also knew. Burned in her memory was the exact place where Father Ignacio stood praying over the hole containing Mother's casket. She surveyed the cemetery. "Do you think this is where Abigail will bury Morgan?"

"A Jew on consecrated ground?"

"Oh, right."

At the grave, Peaches brushed dirt out of the lettering on the simple stone marker, and then wiped the surface with the rag.

An old man carried a cane-back chair to a nearby grave, sat down, and began to talk to his dead wife. "God has ordered up a bright, beautiful, sun-shiny day for us."

"Excuse me," Cherie said. "Do you come here every day?"

Peaches threw her an annoyed look.

"I used to. Now, only once a week, when the paper comes out. I read to her what's happened to the people she knew and tell her about those who moved here since she passed."

"You don't really think she hears you in the ground?"

"Of course not. She's not here. She's in heaven. I do it to comfort me. I'm the one who's still here."

"I apologize for my sister's interruption," Peaches said. "You go on with your conversation, please."

"I don't mind. We're in no rush. My wife and I got all the time in the world to talk. Your sister seems a little jumpy, though."

He looked at Cherie and his grizzled face bent into a sympathetic smile. "If it helps, I'll tell you, so was I. After her funeral, I put off coming here for the longest time. I expected it would hurt too much and all I'd think about was the day I buried her. But that wasn't what happened. A lot of tears were shed that first time, I'm not ashamed to admit it. A great sense of peace came upon me and my tears were actually because of the fond memories I had of her."

That was the problem, though. Cherie tried to dredge up any fond memories of Mama, but couldn't find any.

Peaches took the flowers from her and arranged them on the grave. "There you go, Mother."

Was Peaches talking to the dead now, like the old man?

Peaches moved to the next grave, their father's, and set to work. Father's headstone was fancier, with a large bronze crucifix riveted to the granite, a particularly gruesome rendition of Christ in deep anguish. Why had Mother chosen such a thing? Peaches brushed vigorously, tickling the suffering savior's underarms with her bristles. When she finished, she stood between the two graves, closed her eyes, and bent her head in silent prayer. She made the sign of the cross and hooked Cherie's arm. "Are you ready to go?"

"Past ready."

As they started away, a single cloud opened and released a summer shower. The old man folded up his newspaper, picked up his chair, and hurried toward a church alcove. Raindrops struck Cherie's face, mingling with tears that appeared as suddenly as the cloudburst. She had no idea what she was crying for, but she couldn't stop.

She raced for the car and practically dove into the backseat. Without a word, Peaches got in the front with Cyrus. He put the car in gear and pulled away.

Cherie watched out the car window as the rainfall dissipated as quickly as it had begun. A double rainbow took its place, wrenching a sob from somewhere deep inside her.

# CHAPTER 19

Jack sipped his beer and looked at the blue afternoon sky. A single dark cloud over Taos had threatened to come their way, but it had disappeared and the sky was clear. Cyrus and the women were all in town. He and Morgan were sitting under the cottonwood tree. Morgan had been nursing morphine-laced lemonade all afternoon and acted pretty happy.

Jack thought it might be the right time to bring up the matter of Cherie.

"I don't think you're strong enough for sex, yet."

Morgan shook his head. "Why, has Abigail said something?"

"No."

"Jack, I think that part of my life is over. A naked woman could sit right where you are and it wouldn't even get a rise out of me."

"Oh, don't be so hard on yourself—pun intended. Once you kick this cancer, your sex drive will bounce back."

"Jack, I'm terminal."

"Oh, hell, Morgan, we're all terminal, from the minute we're born."

"Well, me more than most." Morgan turned toward him, a quiet grin on his face. "You need to understand, Jack, I am dying. Maybe not today, or even tomorrow, but I *am* dying."

"Maybe not even next week."

Morgan raised his eyebrows. "No, maybe not next week."

"If not then, why not next year, or twenty years?"

Morgan shrugged. "All right, so why did you bring up sex?"

"I found you and Cherie sleeping together."

"I never—"

Jack held up his hands. "Hey, it's not that I blame you. Cherie is a beautiful, grown-up woman, old enough to do what she wants. It's just that you should have waited until you recovered a little more. You don't want to pop a stitch."

"I honestly have no idea what you're talking about."

"The other afternoon in your studio."

Morgan looked puzzled.

"How else did her lipstick get on your shirt?"

"I have no memory of it, and I'd think I would."

"Well, I hope you don't mind. I said something to her about it."

"You what?"

"Just the same thing I said to you. I asked her to hold off until you were a little stronger."

"Jack, I'm sure you thought you were helping, but really it's not necessary. I can barely get around."

"That's what I told her."

A man about Morgan's height appeared at the end of the driveway walking toward them. Jack stood up and shielded his eyes. The man wasn't dressed like a farmer, but not like a salesman, either. On his head he sported a white straw boater, a hat typically reserved for summer boating events and picnics back east. "Is that one of your artist friends?"

Morgan rose slowly and looked where Jack pointed. "Not that I can tell."

The man called in a loud voice, "I'm looking for a couple of eastern dandies who live with the prettiest woman in Taos."

"Bryce?" Morgan said.

Jack recognized the voice at once. "Bryce Holloway!" Jack ran to him and picked him up in a bear hug, swinging his feet off the ground.

Jack set him down, threw his arm across Bryce's shoulder, and started walking with him toward Morgan, who was steadying himself with one hand on the chair back. Bryce paused to retrieve his hat which Jack's enthusiasm had knocked to the ground.

"Fancy hat," Jack said, "don't see those anymore."

Bryce put the boater back on. "Standards must be maintained, my good man."

Jack slapped him on the back. "Where have you been?"

"California, mostly. Pasadena for years, more recently San Francisco." They were closer to Morgan now. "Hi, Morgan, you okay?"

"Hello, Bryce. Yeah, I'm fine. Just got a little dizzy when I stood up."

Bryce embraced him. "Good to see you, old friend."

"You, too. A complete surprise, though. The last person I imagined seeing."

"I hoped you wouldn't mind my coming."

"Mind?" Jack said. "Hell, we're delighted. How'd you get here?"

"I took the Atchison, Topeka and Santa Fe from San Francisco to Tres Piedras and hitched a ride from there."

"You should have continued on to Santa Fe and called me. I'd have picked you up."

"Didn't know you had a telephone."

"You could have called Taos information. Well, no matter, you're here now. Sit next to Morgan and I'll get you a drink. What's your poison, whiskey, wine, or beer?"

"Have you got anything else?"

"Shit, Bryce, it's prohibition. What do you expect, champagne?"

Bryce glanced at the glass in Morgan's hand. "What are you drinking?"

Morgan sat down and took a sip. "Lemonade with morphine."

"I'll have a lemonade without the morphine."

"You're kidding," Jack said.

"Jack, I haven't had a drink in years."

"You? I think I'm going to faint. You're the last person I'd take to be a teetotaler."

"I decided I must be allergic. Every time I went on a bender, I came down with handcuffs."

Morgan laughed. "Bryce, you're witty as ever."

Just then the Pierce-Arrow rolled down the drive and turned into the garage.

"Abigail's back," Jack said.

Bryce gave a low whistle. "Beautiful motorcar. Is that yours?"

"Abigail's. I drive that truck." Jack jerked his thumb toward the Ford.

Abigail was the first one out of the garage. Peaches and Cherie trailed her. Cyrus came last, carrying a box of groceries.

Jack waved. "Honey, you'll never guess who is here."

Abigail smiled. "Can that be Bryce Holloway?"

Bryce took her extended hand and kissed it lightly. "You haven't aged a day."

Abigail blushed. "Liar. I see that hasn't changed." She withdrew her hand and reached for Peaches. "You may not recognize these young women."

"Oh, I'd never forget Peaches." He opened his arms to her, and she rushed into his embrace. Peaches kissed him on the mouth long and hard, until Cherie tapped her on the shoulder. "Move over, sister."

Cherie took his face in her hands and kissed him on the lips.

Bryce looked into her eyes. "Cherry? The last time I saw you, your mother was dragging you from our store for dancing to ragtime."

"I go by Cherie now. And the last time I saw you, you were shirtless and barefoot, dancing in a circle of Indians."

"Hey, Morgan, how come you and I didn't get a welcome like that?" Jack said.

"I kissed you at the train station, and you wiped it off," Cherie said.

"A kiss on the cheek. Piffle."

Before Jack could stop her, Cherie whirled around and gave him a prolonged kiss on the mouth.

Jack moved to Abigail's side and gave her a squeeze. "That was . . . unexpected. Cherie, I was only teasing."

Abigail laughed. "You *were* kind of asking for it."

Cherie looked into his eyes. "Today, I realized that when my sister was sick and my mother dying, it was you who took care of us. Found me a place to stay and even paid for Mother's funeral. I never thanked you, just left Taos without a word of gratitude."

Jack ran his fingers through his hair. "That was ages ago. Besides, it was Abigail who saved your estate from the vultures."

Cyrus stood outside the circle of old friends, still holding the box of groceries. Bryce gave him a friendly smile. "I don't see wedding rings on either of you girls, so I assume this handsome young man is someone's boyfriend."

Abigail stepped forward. "Bryce, this is my son. Cyrus, you remember Jack and Morgan's friend, Bryce, don't you? He used to be their partner in the emporium when you were five or six."

"This is little Cyrus?" Bryce said. "My, didn't you grow into a fine man? And why haven't one of you girls claimed him?"

"We just got here," Cherie said. "Give us time."

"They're much older than Cyrus," Abigail said

Cyrus set the box of groceries down and shook Bryce's hand. "Of course, I remember you. You used to visit my mom and played trains with me when I was a kid."

Bryce met Abigail's eyes and smiled. She glanced at Jack. All of them remembered what those "visits" used to be about.

Jack winked at her. "I was just about to get drinks. What's everyone having?"

Jack took drink orders and asked Cyrus to bring out extra chairs. Cyrus picked up the box of groceries and followed him into the house.

"Please, everyone, have a seat," Abigail walked over to Morgan, tilted his chin up, and looked into his eyes. "Have you had a good day?"

Morgan lifted his glass and grinned. "Feeling no pain."

"That's good." She kissed him on the forehead. "Are you hungry? Should we start supper?"

"Oh, Abigail," Cherie said. "Have Jack build a fire and roast something out here. Bryce just arrived. It's not fair for the women to be relegated to the kitchen."

Abigail bit her lip and seemed on the verge of tears.

"We don't have cook outs anymore," Morgan said quietly. "The smell of flesh on an open fire upsets Cyrus too much."

"No, I'll make dinner," Abigail said. "I do it all the time. Meanwhile, you ladies can entertain the men."

"At least wait for your drink," Cherie said.

"Oh, I'm not going inside yet."

Cyrus brought two chairs and left to get a third. Abigail sat down. "Bryce, tell us everything. And make sure at least half of it is true."

# CHAPTER 20

Abigail really didn't want to miss a moment of Bryce's colorful stories, but the orange and fuchsia sky to the west warned her the day was drawing to a close and she hadn't started dinner. She decided she'd serve a smorgasbord. She had leftover roast beef and some cold lamb in the icebox. She could slice it thin, and it would go far enough. There were several types of cheeses in the springhouse.

At the next pause in the conversation, Abigail stood. "Let's move this party indoors. Cyrus, will you put the leaf in the dining room table? Jack, get the cheeses from the springhouse. Peaches and Cherie bring lettuce, radishes, and scallions from the garden. Bryce, please carry these chairs back into the house."

"What can I do?" Morgan said.

Abigail patted his cheek. "Make your way to the dining room."

Abigail sliced meat and bread and opened jars of home-canned pickles and beets while Cherie washed vegetables and Peaches made a salad. In no time, Abigail had serving platters spread along the table. Jack refilled everyone's drinks. The sisters jockeyed positions to put Bryce between them, but Cyrus won out, taking the chair on Bryce's right, and leaving them to fight over the other seat.

Throughout the afternoon, Cyrus had hung on Bryce's every word. That worried Abigail. Bryce looked good—better that when he'd left them all those years ago, in fact. He was clean, well-dressed, but not lavishly. Ordinary cut of clothes, not Fifth Avenue. He seemed a changed man, but Bryce could fool anybody for a while.

"What brings you back to Taos after all these years?"

"I ran into Louis Sharp in Pasadena. He has a studio there in addition to the one he keeps in Taos. He told me Morgan didn't have long."

"Louis doesn't know his ass from a hole in the ground," Jack said. "Morgan's going to be with us a long time."

Bryce glanced at Morgan, who even fully clothed, looked skeletal.

"Well, it's good to see you," Morgan said. "Though we all thought you'd become an Indian shaman after you disappeared."

Bryce smiled. "No, Abigail was right. The Indians were never going to share their deepest secrets with a white man, no matter how many times we took peyote together. But my quest took me on a different path to the real kind of Indian."

"What tribe was that?" Cyrus said.

"Not a tribe, a whole continent of people with sacred knowledge more ancient than Moses. You know, America's Indians aren't from India. Columbus just called the natives that because he was lost."

"Have you been to India?" Cherie said.

"No, I only made it as far west as California. But there I met a woman—"

Jack laughed. "I'll bet you did."

Bryce ignored him. "She introduced me to Theosophy and Raja Yoga."

"To what?" Morgan said.

"The Theosophical Society. They used to have their headquarters in New York City when we lived there, though we knew nothing about it. Mrs. Tingley moved the international headquarters to Lomaland about 1900."

Jack slapped the table. "Tingling, raja, lotus-land, I swear you're making up these names."

"Not lotus-land, Lomaland, it's a real place near San Diego, a large community of spiritually minded people. There's the Raja Yoga College and a School for the Revival of the Lost Mysteries of Antiquity. We even built the first open air Greek theater in America."

"What did you do there?" Peaches said.

"Studied secret doctrines, yoga, and meditation."

"What did you do for work?" Abigail said.

"Mrs. Tingley established a symphony orchestra, and every student in her school was required to learn at least one instrument, so I taught piano. The educational goals of the school involved not only the intellect but also moral and spiritual development."

Jack laughed. "I hope they didn't put you in charge of moral development."

Cyrus made a face at Jack and turned to Bryce. "What's yoga?"

"It's a Sanskrit word that means union. Its aim is to connect us with the divine. Mrs. Tingley used to say we are like a piano. Every string has to be tuned before it can produce harmony."

"I can't imagine you in a monastery," Peaches said.

"It's not. In fact, around sixty percent of Lomaland was female."

Jack laughed. "I knew it."

"Abigail, you'll be pleased to learn that the executive positions were also about sixty percent women. Something you won't find anywhere else in America."

Abigail smiled. "Is this philosophy the reason you quit drinking?"

"No. I'm sure there are Theosophists who have a glass of wine on occasion, but not to excess. I've always had trouble with the 'not to excess' part, so I found it was better to just not start. You might remember I had a trust fund. Still, I was always broke. Then I made, what to me was an amazing discovery—when you stop spending every penny on booze and women you suddenly have money left. Now, because I live modestly, I'm able to work at what interests me."

"And that is?"

"Deep secrets of yogis, hidden in India for three thousand years."

"Sounds like balderdash," Jack said.

"Jack, let's talk about this again when you've had less to drink. You're interested in science, and India's ancient scientists understood far more about the structure and underlying principles of the Universe than writers in *Popular Science Magazine*. It will fascinate you, I promise."

"Science, huh?"

"Yes, so far western scientists have only looked at one side of the equation. About a year and a half ago, I attended a conference in Boston and heard a swami who had come from India lecture on the scientific basis of yoga meditation. Fascinating speaker."

Abigail stood up and started to clear the table. "Where are you staying?"

"I was hoping to stay here."

She frowned. "I'm sorry. We don't have an empty room."

"Mom," Cyrus said. "We can make him a pallet in my room."

"I don't think that's a good idea. You lose control if anyone even enters your room while you're sleeping."

"Bryce can stay in my studio," Morgan said.

Abigail considered a moment, then nodded. "That works."

"Even better," said Bryce, "I can meditate in private there. Of course, it's your studio, Morgan. If you need to paint, come on in. I'll understand."

"Oh, you'll be up hours before Morgan," Jack said. "He sleeps half the day."

Abigail patted Bryce on the shoulder. "Come along, I'll get you blankets and a pillow."

"Give them to me," Peaches said. "I'll make up his bed."

"He'll need a lantern," Cyrus said.

"Don't everyone fuss over me," Bryce said.

Abigail almost smiled. People always had.

# CHAPTER 21

Cyrus doesn't know what day it is, sometime around the beginning of November, maybe the last of October. It's certainly early dawn, but the moon is still out. He's lying on the ground next to a field ambulance. It's bitter cold, and he is shivering.

Someone touches his forehead. His eyes flutter open briefly.

A nurse brushes the hair from his forehead and places her hand there to see if he has a fever. Her dress is white, translucent in the full moon, almost sheer enough to see through. How has she kept it so clean in the muddy battlefield? She has brown hair. He feels like he knows her from somewhere. Perhaps she's cared for him in the past. "Mademoiselle?"

"Oui," she says.

"Water, please."

*"Oui, mon Captaine."*

He's a private not a captain, but he doesn't argue.

She leaves him—he panics a bit—but in a moment she's back, carrying a pitcher. He'd expected a canteen. She places the spout to his lips and tips gently.

The effort of swallowing wears him out. His head falls back into the mud. The nurse soothes his face with her cool touch. But then a dark shadow falls between him and the nurse.

Abigail appeared in Cyrus's doorway. "Cherie?"

Cherie was standing near Cyrus's bed holding the water pitcher from his washstand. "I heard him thrashing, so I came in to check. He can't seem to wake up."

Abigail pressed her lips together and nodded grimly. "It happens a lot. Far too often. I've got to give Morgan his medicine. I'll check on Cyrus when I return. You should go back to bed. I'm sorry he woke you."


The shadowy figure bellows, "Private Wythe!"

"Yes, Sargent."

"Stop this malingering and get back into the field."

He rolls to his feet and stumbles back to the trenches. He hopes the kind nurse will be all right.

The battle is the Meuse-Argonne Offensive, and he is barely trained. After he landed in France six weeks ago as part of the American Expeditionary Force, his unit was turned over to British officers for training just outside the theater of war. Hah, theater. What a joke. He and a million other men have been fighting and dying since September twenty-sixth, in trenches that are little more than muddy swamps. Mortar and artillery shells launch with distant thumps. There is nothing to do but hunker down and hope they miss. If one lands in the trench, blood and body parts will splatter all over the dirt walls.

This particular volley fails to reach them, instead blasting craters in the no-man's-land between him and the Hun line.

Lice also live in the trenches, and live a lot better than he does. They certainly eat better, mostly on him—biting unmercifully and making him itch. He can take it no longer. He lays his M1917 rifle on the ground above him and climbs out of the horrid trench.

A few dozen yards across no-man's-land, a Hun does the same.

Cyrus charges him, firing until his magazine is spent. The German continues to fire, but Cyrus turns sideways to him and somehow all the rounds miss him.

Finally the German too, runs out of ammunition. He pulls his knife and charges. Cyrus yanks at his own knife, but it's jammed in its scabbard and he can't get it out before they are locked in hand-to-hand combat.

The keen edge of the Hun's blade glints in the morning rays as it nears his throat.

He grabs at the Hun's wrist and flips him onto his back. Somehow, the ground is soft and yielding. And the Hun screams like a woman. He goes for the enemy's throat.

Then the Hun snaps his knee up and catches Cyrus in the crotch. He rolls to one side, clutching his groin, and falls to the floor.

He's wrapped in sweat-stained sheets. Above him the nurse—no, Cherie—looks over the edge of the bed. And the enormity of what just happened hits him.


Cherie touched the damp hair on the back of Cyrus's neck with her fingers, and he jerked away. He pulled himself up and sat on the edge of the bed with his back to her. Cherie got off the bed and smoothed her nightgown. She shrugged her shoulders and arched her back, trying to break the adhesion of sweat-soaked material on her skin. Finally, she reached behind her and tugged the fabric.

Cyrus avoided looking at her.

She thought about getting a robe—the damp gown was pretty revealing. Not that she minded being naked in a man's bedroom, but she didn't really know this version of Cyrus, the grown man. The one she'd just kneed in the groin. "I'm sorry I hurt you."

"I deserved it."

"No, no, never say that." She walked around the bed where she could see him. "Your mother told me not to be in here, and maybe she was right. But I heard you and came in to see if I could help."

He turned his face to the wall and wouldn't look at her.

"We don't have to talk about it," she said.

"We don't?"

"No. Not if you don't want to."

He buried his face in his hands. "Ever since I came back, everyone wants me to talk about the war. But how can I?" His voice was oddly calm and even. "How do you tell your neighbors about the man in the trenches whose socks grew into the flesh of his feet, or that time you were spattered by bits of one of your buddies during a mortar strike?"

Cherie took a step toward him and reached out one hand without touching him. "You were having a bad dream."

He nodded. "Happens often."

She brushed his face and turned it toward her. "What can I do to help?"

"Nothing I know of. The Army calls it shell shock. But it doesn't have any-thing to do with shells. I just . . . can't be with anyone. Someone surprises me in my sleep like you did, I might try to kill them."

"I'll be more careful." Cherie laughed. "I might have killed you."

He actually managed a wry grin, or something like it. "Oh, a knee to the groin hurts like hell, but I don't think anyone ever died from it."

Unsure what to do next, she walked to the other side of the bed and started stripping the sheets.

"You don't have to do that. Mother has a cleaning woman who comes today."

Cherie didn't know what to do. She crossed her arms and rested her hands over her nipples. She had felt them harden and thought they might be visible through the fabric. "Well, I hope you're not mad at me."

Then Cyrus turned somber again. "I hope you're not afraid of me after the things I've told you."

Cherie rushed to him and kissed him lightly on the cheek. "You can talk to me about anything, any time."

He truly smiled for the first time that morning.

She turned and left.

In the hall, she looked to see if anyone was around, then dashed into her room, grabbed her robe and ran downstairs to the bathroom. She smelled like Cyrus's sweat. If she ran into Abigail, she'd think they'd been rutting. Cherie turned the faucet on the pipe connected to the cistern and filled the tub. The water was cold, but she couldn't waste time waiting for kettles to boil on the kitchen stove. The whole house would be up soon. She slipped off her gown, climbed into the tub, and broke out in goose bumps.

That was okay. A good cold bath would help tamp down the excitement.

# CHAPTER 22

Chilled from her cold bath, Cherie hurried to her room, crawled back into bed, and snuggled up against her sister to warm herself.

Peaches yelped and pushed her away.

Daylight was beginning to pry its way around the edges of the drapes. Cherie tossed and turned for a while, but then smelled coffee and decided to hell with it, she might as well get up. She dressed and headed for the kitchen to see if she could help Abigail with breakfast. Along the way, she discovered Cyrus sitting at the dining room table with his head buried in his arms. A half-finished cup of coffee sat cooling. As she passed behind him, she ran a soothing hand across his shoulders.

He jerked up, then looked embarrassed, and left the room without explanation. What was going on here?

When he didn't come back for breakfast, Abigail went to check on him, but returned alone. Morgan wasn't at breakfast either, but that wasn't unusual. Jack made up for their absence by eating twice as much.

After breakfast, Peaches and Cherie washed and dried the dishes while Abigail made pie dough and rolled it out into two pie shells. They had just finished when Bryce strolled into the kitchen. "Peaches, care to go for a walk?"

Her heartbeat sped up. Ever since he'd arrived yesterday, she had been interested in getting him alone. Maybe it was just the magnetic pull of nostalgia, but she wanted to find out. She took off her apron and whispered to Cherie, "How's my hair?"

Cherie wet her finger and stuck a stray curl back in place. "All set."

Peaches turned and smiled at Bryce.

She gave Bryce a tour of the springhouse Jack had built.

"He's always had a knack for the ingenious," Bryce said.

Peaches nodded. "Abigail says he reads a lot of science magazines."

"Always has—ever since we were kids."

The stream that fed the springhouse made a pleasant murmur, and they decided to follow it, strolling arm in arm.

"So, how did you guys meet?" Peaches said. "I mean you were from the upper set, and they . . . weren't."

"I was a perpetual wiseass. After I got kicked out of my third private school, my parents had to put me in public school. That's where I met them, and we stayed friends for life."

"Until you left Taos."

"Well, I'm back now." Bryce stopped walking and looked her in the eye. "No, seriously, we parted as friends and I've kept in touch, sending them postcards whenever I moved on."

"I wish you'd done the same with me." Peaches batted her eyelashes. "You know I've been in New York this whole while. You could have stopped by anytime you were in the city and received a warm welcome."

"Honestly, I never knew where you were."

"And would you have come if you did?"

"Perhaps. But I took my life west, not east. I've only gone back there for funerals and whatnot."

"You know you weren't the first boy I ever had, but you were the first who made certain a woman got as much pleasure out of the encounter as he did." Her voice edged toward dreamy. "I'll never forget my eighteenth birthday."

"Nor will I."

She shook her head. "Shame it's been so long."

Bryce tickled her under the chin. "Don't kid a kidder. Where'd you say you lived, Greenwich Village? That's not exactly a convent."

"Never said there aren't men in my life. I only feel sorry you aren't one of them." She realized it was true as she said it.

They continued along the brook. The path narrowed, and they had to walk single file. Peaches took the lead and Bryce followed. A few minutes later she stopped, and he bumped into her. She reached behind her and clasped his hands, wrapping them around her waist. They proceeded onward like two showmen in a vaudeville routine.

As they approached the babbling sound of a small rapid, the path sloped upward and broadened into a clearing. Bryce gripped her waist and turned her to face him. "As you said, 'shame it's been so long.'"

He leaned toward her, and she into him. Their lips met and their bodies pressed together, squeezing out a decade and a half of lost time.

When they paused to breathe, he ran his finger lightly around her lips, down her throat and into her cleavage. He attempted to ease her back into a soft landing on the grassy overlook. But Peaches stepped back and steadied them upright.

A confused look passed over his eyes.

She took his chin in her hand, and kissed him firmly, but briefly. "I'm too old to roll in a hayfield."

Bryce grinned. "It's grass, not hay."

"We've waited this long, it'll keep."

Bryce kissed her on the nose. "You know where I'm staying."

"I do." She took him by the hand and started back the way they'd come.

* * *

Abigail checked the kitchen clock. It had been nearly fifteen minutes since she'd stopped stirring the pie custard and put a lid on it. Steam streamed from the bottom pan of the double-boiler. She cracked an egg and separated the white by pouring the yolk back and forth between the shell halves. She dropped the yolk into a separate bowl and separated three more eggs.

Today she was making an extra pie because with Bryce here, they would need more than before. Since pie was the one thing she knew Morgan would eat, she wanted to have plenty.

When the fifteen minutes were up, she beat the yolks, stirred them gradually into the cooking mixture, and let it cook five more minutes. Just before removing it from the heat, she added lemon juice and butter, which she mixed in well. She turned off the flame and removed the top pan of the double-boiler, setting it aside to cool.

A shadow in the doorway caught her eye. She turned. "Hello, son."

"Hi, Mom."

"Feeling better?"

"I'm all right."

"Are you hungry?"

"Nah, I'll wait 'til supper."

Great. Now she had two men who weren't eating like they should.

"What are you making?"

"Lemon meringue pie." Abigail opened the oven door and checked the temperature on the thermometer hanging from the middle rack. Perfect.

She wondered if Bryce's arrival had been behind Cyrus's bad dream last night. His mere presence was a reminder of his old stories about the Rough Riders and the glory of war—

She stopped that train of thought. She knew better. He'd been having nightmares for four years. It'd be unfair to blame Bryce. Despite her misgivings, it was good of him to come all the way from California to see Morgan before he passed.

Abigail turned her attention to the egg whites for the meringue, beating them with a whisk until they were frothy. She added sugar and a teaspoon of vanilla extract and beat them some more. Morgan was going to enjoy this. She hadn't made lemon pie for a while.

"Cyrus?"

"Yes, Mom."

"About last night . . ."

He gave an involuntary shiver. "Bad dream, that one."

At least he was talking. Abigail continued whisking the egg whites. "Better, now?"

Cyrus nodded. He got a water glass from the cupboard and filled it from the hand pump. He took a long drink, then another, set the empty glass in the sink, and turned to go.

"You woke Cherie," Abigail said.

"I know."

"Did that embarrass you? Is that why you didn't come to breakfast?"

"Nah, it wasn't her. I was just wrung out, needed to keep my head down."

"Because, you know, they don't have to stay here. Yes, it's nice they came for Morgan. But you're my son. If having too many people around makes you uncomfortable, we can put them up elsewhere."

Cyrus spun on his heel. "No! Don't send them away. She . . . she—"

"What?"

"Understands me."

*And your mother doesn't?* Abigail lifted her whisk, and the mixture formed stiff peaks. She divided the lemon custard evenly between two pastry shells she'd baked earlier, and then spread the meringue over the filling, making sure it touched the edges of the crust all the way around. She slid the pies into the hot oven.

"So finding her in your room didn't unsettle you?"

Cyrus blushed. "I'm the one who upset her."

"In what way?"

"In my dream I . . . thought she was a German soldier."

Oh! That couldn't be good. Abigail set the dirty mixing bowls in the sink. "I saw her in there and told her to go back to her room. She should have listened."

"I'm kind of glad she didn't. Cherie's nice. With her, I don't feel any pressure."

Abigail sighed. Some days, the burden of three broken men weighed on her to the point of breaking. If her shell-shocked son had finally found someone he'd talk to, it could be a blessing. "Well, Cyrus, Cherie is a very open-minded person."

She glanced at the time and opened the oven door. The peaks of the meringue had turned a lovely shade of tan. Just right. She took the pies out and set them on a rack to cool.

Cyrus kissed her on the cheek and left. She put her hand to her face and smiled. That hadn't happened in a while. Through the screen door she heard Cyrus, "Hi, Bryce. Where you been?"

# CHAPTER 23

It was a lazy Sunday. Bryce and Peaches had gone for another of their now frequent walks—about which Peaches would say nothing, which said something. Cherie was sitting in the shade with Morgan, but he'd dozed off. Cyrus came out of the house. Cherie noticed he was freshly shaved, shirt pressed, pants creased, and shoes shined. He crossed the lawn and stopped in front of her, twisting his driving cap in his hands. "There's a movie called *The Flapper* playing at the picture show. I was wondering if you would like to go with me. We can take Mother's car."

Well, well. This was undoubtedly Jack's doing. Cherie had heard of the movie, but she'd been in France when it was released last year, and so never saw it. Apparently movies took as long to reach small western towns as they did to reach France. "Keen. Sure, I'll go. Let me change my dress and freshen up."

In the darkened theater, Cherie waited through the newsreel and the cartoon for Cyrus to make the first move. When he hadn't by the time the main feature started, she'd decided he was either too inexperienced or shy. She reached over the armrest between their seats and felt for his hand. Cyrus jumped up, ready to fight. Cherie's heart leapt to her throat.

People in the row behind them shouted for him to sit down. He shriveled back into his seat, stammering apologies, and adding, "I know it's no excuse, but I startle easily."

"Shut up," a man behind them said. "You're drowning out the piano."

Cherie thought Cyrus's apology couldn't ruin the accompaniment more than the two-bit pianist hired to keep up with the film was doing already. Cyrus was hard to figure out. He hadn't been afraid to touch her when he'd helped her from the car. Again, after buying tickets he had no problem linking arms as they walked down the carpeted aisle to their seats. Maybe it was the darkness?

The two of them sat in stony silence, as separate as heads on Easter Island. The movie was about Genevieve, a schoolgirl from Orange Springs, Florida. A few minutes into the film she sneaks off in a boat with a boy.

About that time Cyrus's hand snaked over to touch Cherie's arm. She clasped his hand in her lap and smiled at him in the flickering black and white projector light.

Genevieve's strict father finds out about the boy and sends her to a private boarding school in the north. There, she lies about her age to get invited to a country club dance by an older man. The headmistress catches her at the dance, and as she is being scolded, a moose head mounted on the wall starts winking at her. The theater audience roared. Cherie stole a glance at Cyrus and saw he was laughing, too. Good.

Unfortunately, *The Flapper* wasn't. Winking moose aside, the scrapes Genevieve got into were ridiculous and contrived, and the staunch moralists won out in the end. Genevieve bore as much relationship to the real flapper lifestyle as Chaplin's Little Tramp did to genuine hoboes.

Later, as they left the theater, Cherie failed to conceal her disappointment in the movie.

"You didn't enjoy the picture?" Cyrus said.

She wrapped her arm in his and walked closer to him. "I enjoyed being with you."

"Even though I made a fool out of myself?"

"Only a little. Besides, I shouldn't have startled you."

"I don't understand what's wrong with me," he said. "I shouldn't have re-acted like that."

"Hang on, hang on. Saying something is wrong with you is like saying it's your fault. I don't buy that for a minute. You saw some terrible things that stayed with you. You're not alone. France is full of former French soldiers languishing like you are. They returned home, put on civilian clothes again, and to their mothers and girlfriends look very much like the young men they'd known before the war. But they aren't. They're subject to sudden moods, queer tempers, and fits of confusion. Many speak bitterly and lose control of themselves."

"Like I've done with you, twice now."

"Yes. But it's no more your fault than it was theirs. I want you to know that you can talk with me about what happened. I've heard it all before. But don't feel you have to unless you're ready."

Cyrus looked at his feet and left it to Cherie to steer where they walked. She guided him into an ice cream parlor. "Let's have a sundae."

He brightened. They sat at a table near the window, and a boy about four-teen, wearing a white hat and white apron, came over. He took their order and left.

"All I want to do is just forget the war. I try every day. But the war won't forget me."

"Tell me how I can help. And don't be afraid to let me know if anything I say or do isn't helpful."

"I'm sorry. I'm not very good at talking with girls. I mean, I used to be—before the war and when we first got to France. The odds of meeting girls there were slim, though. Ten thousand Americans arrived every day, so the French girls had their pick. Still, I met a few. I wish I'd have met you then." He shook his head. "No, I don't. I'm glad you weren't there. It was a bloody mess."

But she had been—at least when it started. And afterwards. She knew firsthand how awful it was for the men. And while she was ready to listen, she wasn't going to force him to talk about it. The war was over. He'd made it home, and he was doing better than some Frenchmen.

Cherie reached across the table and patted his hand. He didn't jump. Good. That was progress.

He gave her a small smile. "Thanks. Let's just talk about the movie."

Cherie nodded. "That girl was certainly no flapper."

"No? But it had some funny bits. I liked the moose on the wall."

"Yes, but why call her a flapper? She was just a silly high school girl. She didn't have her hair bobbed, wear flapper dresses, have sex, or even kiss a man. For God's sake, she drank soda pop, and that was supposed to be shameful! And there wasn't a single person at the country club dancing the shimmy or black bottom."

"Is that what it takes to be a flapper?"

"Well, those are things flappers do, but it's more an attitude toward life. Flappers aren't like our grandmothers' generation. We aren't clinging vines. Our fashions mock their bustles, corsets, and petticoats and let us move free. We are no longer as susceptible to the tyranny of society. We're standing on our own."

"Are you a suffragette?"

"We're the next chapter. Women already won the vote. Flappers aren't waiting for someone to give us our rights, we're exerting our right to do what we like. We're called brash for wearing makeup, drinking, smoking, casual sex, but after the ruination of war it seems life should be lived with panache."

The boy arrived with two sundae parfait dishes on a tray. He placed napkins and spoons on the table and then served their ice cream. Cherie scraped a bit of syrup from her sundae with the spoon and licked it. "Damn, that's the cat's pajamas." She winked at Cyrus. "Oh, we swear, too."

"Hell, I don't mind."

Cyrus dug into his ice cream, exhibiting an appetite she'd not seen so far.

# CHAPTER 24

By the time Morgan got up on Monday, it was nearly lunchtime. He was spending more and more time asleep. Maybe it was the morphine. Maybe it was practice for what was to come. He slowly made his way downstairs by holding onto the banister. The house was empty. He heard Abigail and Bryce laughing on the front porch. And God bless Bryce for that. Laughter wasn't a sound she made often enough lately. Until the last few years, they'd lived a merry life. Then everything went to hell at once. She'd stood strong, but he could see it weighed on her, and she'd sacrificed her mirth to pay the freight. He blamed himself. Sure, Cyrus was part of it, too. But his cancer was her real burden.

Abigail opened the screen door and held it while he shuffled to a chair. "I was just going in to make a fresh pot of coffee."

"Sounds wonderful. Where is everybody?"

"Jack left for Santa Fe early. He's already called to ask about you. He'll be home after lunch. Cyrus drove the girls into Taos. I'll be right back." She let the screen door close and disappeared into the house.

Abigail returned ten minutes later, handing them each a cup on a saucer. Morgan's hand trembled a bit, spilling coffee over the rim of the cup. He lifted up the cup and sipped from the saucer.

The coffee had a pleasant aroma, but he didn't have the taste for it he once had. That wasn't Abigail's fault. She used the same brand of coffee she always had and made it in the same coffee pot. No, the only thing that had changed was him.

Bryce finished his coffee, and Morgan handed Abigail his still half-full cup. She left to make their lunch. Bryce helped Morgan walk to his studio.

Morgan sank down on the chaise and looked at Bryce. "Are you comfortable enough out here? This daybed wasn't exactly designed for a good night's sleep."

"I've slept in worse places, believe me." Bryce sat in the chair next to the bed. "Besides, it's quiet. I can meditate."

"You mentioned that before. This isn't the Bryce I grew up with."

"No, I've changed. And some part of you must be glad, because I sure used to cause you and Jack a lot of trouble."

"Well, you never meant to."

"No, but that was part of the problem. I had no idea what my intentions were or should be."

"Oh, don't be hard on yourself. All three of us were wild eastern dandies, trying to lighten up people's lives with a little fun."

"Like a balloon ride, with us supplying the hot air."

Morgan grinned. "God, I've missed your wit. It's been too long. So, you live near San Diego? What's the Pacific Ocean like?"

"Beautiful sunsets, but I'm in San Francisco now—went there in 1915 to see the Panama-Pacific International Exposition and never left."

Morgan's eyes took on a dreamy look. "I've never forgotten the World's Fair in St. Louis with its dozen neo-classical palaces."

"Me either. Those memories were what drew me to the San Francisco Fair, and I wasn't disappointed. Even though it was only about half the size of the one in St. Louis, it had a beautiful Palace of Fine Arts, and a four hundred foot tall Tower of Jewels covered with cut glass gems that sparkled in the sunlight. At night they illuminated the tower with powerful searchlights. It was a spectacular light show."

"I wish I'd seen it."

"I'm surprised you and Jack didn't go."

"I can't remember now why we didn't. Somehow life got in our way. I was traveling back and forth to New York a lot. Peaches had started her gallery and my paintings were selling well. I think that's when the Taos Art Society formed, too."

"But you never became a member?"

"I'm not much of a joiner. But its members are all close friends."

"Good," Bryce said, "and good that you and Abigail and Jack have stayed together all these years. I'm sure that's raised more than a few eyebrows."

"You remember what Hamlet said to Ophelia? 'Be thou chaste as ice, as pure as snow, thou shalt not escape calumny.'"

Bryce laughed. "I believe the rest of that quote is: 'Get thee to a nunnery.'"

Morgan smiled. "You know I've never been one to tell tales out of school. I'll just say, in all the time we've lived together, Abigail never acted jealous about any of my past lovers."

"Including Peaches?"

"Oh, Peaches was never on the list. I slept with some of my models, yes, but Peaches wasn't one of them. You on the other hand—"

"What?"

"She told me she had you when she was eighteen."

"*She* had *me* is the truth. It was more her doing than mine."

"I'm not buying it. Remember Bryce, I knew you back then."

Bryce flapped his arms like a bird. "All right, all right, enough with the past. I want to talk about you and now."

Morgan shrugged. "What do you want to know?"

"You're really dying?"

"I am."

"But Jack says—"

"Jack doesn't want to believe it. He figures if everyone denies it hard enough, it can't happen. It's like playing hide-and-seek with a toddler who thinks when they cover their eyes no one can see them."

"But your eyes are open."

"Yes, I'm not hiding from it. I see clearly. It's an occupational hazard. Artists learn to see things as they really are."

"And is your eye single?"

"Meaning what?"

Bryce touched his middle finger to the center of his forehead. "If thine eye be single, thy whole body shall be full of light."

"I'm Jewish, remember? That's in your Bible, not mine."

"Which text doesn't matter—it's a principle of the universe. Learn to concentrate on the single, inner eye, and your conscious life force will rise up within you to reveal a brilliant light."

"Have you come to convert me to . . . whatever this is?"

"I am here because we've known each other since we were school boys, and you are about to go someplace none of us have ever been. Conversion in the ordinary sense means nothing. But there is a change that can come from a man's own higher nature." Bryce scooted his chair closer to Morgan. "I have stood face to face with myself and found that to be true, first, at Lomaland, and later, from the words of two great Indian swamis. The only authentic conversion is when we transcend our self-created limitations. For no one gains the supernal palace while peering out the windows of our smaller self."

Morgan laughed. "You sound like a preacher in search of a pulpit."

"Yeah, sorry. But, Morgan, really, all the trouble I put myself—and you guys—through was because I didn't understand the divine laws governing human life and spiritual evolution." Bryce took a breath. "Find your interior self, ride it up to the single eye, and dive into the light."

Morgan slapped the chaise cushion. "You've lost me."

"Okay . . ." He thought a minute. "Imagine walking through Abigail's flower garden. You sense fragrances, but you can't see them."

"True."

"Well, while we here in the west have been uncovering the principles of steam locomotives and light bulbs, ancient sages, high in the Himalayas, have been paying attention to subtler things. They've perfected techniques of meditation that bring states of ecstasy and the peace that pass all understanding."

"So . . . meditation gets you ecstasy? You used to say that about drinking alcohol and taking peyote."

"No, it's . . . you know what my life was like then. I was a mess. And it left me bound. I needed my next drink in order to get happy again. What I'm doing now has freed me from all of that."

Morgan smiled. "Remember when we all took peyote together?"

Bryce smiled as well. "Maybe not the best way to get to enlightenment, but something in those pleasurable hallucinations had a very transformative effect."

"I remember you being amazed at the falling snow. You said the snowflakes were dancing a ballet. Are you still taking peyote with that shaman?"

"No, I gave that up when I started practicing meditation. But that doesn't mean you have to. Swami Vivekananda said that once a man has understanding, then wealth, pleasure, and duty aren't stumbling blocks. Hell, I could drink wine, if it didn't make me do stupid things. Jesus did."

"I can't. The doctors cut out my liver."

"Oh, right. My point is, I'd be happy to teach you Raja Yoga. It doesn't require any physical exertion, and you may find it helpful. I did."

Abigail appeared in the doorway. "Morgan, lunch is ready. Will you come in the house, or shall I bring yours here."

Morgan stood. "We'll come there." He turned to Bryce. "Oh, why not? At this point, what have I got to lose?"

# CHAPTER 25

Jack lowered the hood of the Model T and fastened the latches. He'd tightened the leather fan belt and refilled the oil reservoir behind the fan bearing —he thought he'd heard a slight squeal. He'd also tweaked the carburetor a bit. An overly lean air-fuel mixture could cause the Ford to backfire, and that wouldn't do around Cyrus. Opening the driver's door, he lifted the seat, unscrewed the cap off the fuel tank and inserted a clean stick of wood. When he pulled it out, he estimated the tank was half full. Today's trip to Santa Fe hadn't used as much as he thought.

He returned his tools to the garage and wiped his hands on an old towel he kept for that purpose. The Ford was simplicity itself to work on, and its regular maintenance was a comforting part of his weekly routine. He checked his pocket watch and considered whether it was too early for a beer.

A loud moaning came from Morgan's studio.

Jack raced across the yard. How could Morgan be in that kind of pain? Abigail never forgot to give him his medication. What if this was something new?

He twisted the knob and threw open the door. Morgan was sitting up on the daybed, eyes closed, mouth open, repeatedly going, "A-a-a-a-w U-o-o-o-u M-m-m-m."

Jack rushed to him. "Where does it hurt? Did you take your morphine? Has the pain worsened? Should I call the doctor?"

Morgan's eyes snapped open as if he'd been asleep.

"Simmer down, Jack," said a voice from the other side of the room.

Jack whirled around. "Bryce? I didn't know you were here, too. Why didn't you help him?"

"Because I'm not in any pain," Morgan said.

"Then, what the hell?"

"We're chanting," Bryce said. "I'm teaching Morgan to meditate. Join us. I'll explain."

Bryce was sitting on the floor cross-legged like an Indian. Jack gave him a dubious look and turned back to Morgan, who nodded. "Try it. What harm can there be?"

"Do I have to sit on the floor?"

"Floor, chair, anywhere you like," Bryce said. "It's what's going on inside of you that matters—where your consciousness is seated."

Morgan patted the daybed. "Here, there's room for two."

Jack bit his lip, glanced at Bryce, smoothed his mustache with his fingers, and sat next to Morgan. Whatever it was, Morgan seemed to be for it. May as well give it a try. "So, what are we doing here?"

"AUM is the ancient symbol of the Absolute Self, the cosmic universe. Its powerful, profound sacred meaning has been passed down from sages of antiquity, the Rishis."

Jack crossed and uncrossed his legs. "Ree-shes?"

"They said AUM is the root of all that existed before and since. What our Bible means when it says, 'In the beginning was the Word.' By meditating on AUM, we realize our true nature is the Absolute Self."

Meet your Self by chanting a nonsense word? Jack shook his head as if bothered by a blue bottle fly.

Bryce held up his hand. "Jack, I know how it sounds. But you have a scientific mind. Let me break it down for you. At the highest level, the self and the Absolute Self are identical—pure consciousness, pure bliss."

"That sounds more grandiose than scientific." Then again, Bryce had always tended toward flamboyancy.

"Sorry, let me start again," Bryce said. "We can't conceive of Absolute Self because it's not tied to the sensory perceptions we use to understand the world. But we can access it through the three mystic sound vibrations of AUM." Bryce folded his palms together and looked toward the ceiling as if he were about to pray, then he shivered.

"Is that what you were doing when I came in," Jack said, "vibrating your way to this . . . Absolute Self?"

Bryce nodded. "Believe me, it's a lot easier to experience than explain. The first letter, A, pronounced drawn out as A-a-a-a-w, refers to the first state of self, the experiencing self. Say it with me."

Oh, why not? Jack joined Morgan chanting, "A-a-a-a-w."

"The second letter, sounds like U pronounced with a long O sound. That symbolizes our mental self. Let's try it together."

"U-o-o-o-u."

"The third sound is M-m-m-m, representing the oneness. As the three states merge, they form one cosmic vibration in which the consciousness transcends self-identification, gaining liberation, and ultimately attaining a true state of pure consciousness."

Bryce had kind of wandered off a little at the end, but Jack wasn't about to challenge him. "Okay. Let's give it a try."

Bryce led the chant. "A-a-a-a-w U-o-o-o-u M-m-m-m. A-a-a-a-w U-o-o-o-u M-m-m-m." Jack joined in, trying to listen to the sounds.

"Just let one AUM blend into the next," Bryce said.

"This sounds like the chants you did with the Pueblo Indians," Jack said.

"No, this is different. Start again, then after a while stop making the sound with your voice, and continue it only in your mind. But don't get distracted with other thoughts. Let it be a locomotive engine that pulls you deeper into it and carries you upward."

Jack imagined riding a train up a steep incline.

The three friends chanted together without further interruption from Bryce. It made Jack feel like they were one, together again on some great adventure.

Their mystic intonations gradually grew softer until there was stillness. A great peace came over the room, and even Jack's breathing quieted.

Presently, Jack got bored. He opened his eyes. Bryce, sitting across from him, had a blissful smile on his face. He turned to look at Morgan. Something was wrong. He didn't seem to be breathing. Jack watched him a while longer, but couldn't detect the slightest movement of his chest. He held his finger beneath Morgan's nostril to feel for air. Nothing. He moved it closer.

Morgan's eyes popped open, and he slapped Jack's hand away. "What the hell are you doing?"

"I'm making sure Bryce hadn't meditated you to death."

Morgan stared at him for a moment and then burst out laughing. "I swear, Jack, when I die, you won't be the first to know."

# CHAPTER 26

That night, after a fine dinner, Abigail suggested they have brandy in the parlor.

"Or whatever your preferred drink is," Jack said.

Murmurs of agreement mingled with the noisy scooting of chairs away from the dining table. Bryce smiled at Abigail. "If it wouldn't be too much trouble, I'd appreciate a cup of coffee."

"No trouble at all," she said. While Abigail brewed coffee, Peaches and Cherie started clearing the table. When they brought the dirty dishes into the kitchen, she said, "Just leave those on the sideboard. We'll wash them later. Let's join the men in the parlor."

When the coffee was ready, Abigail set a cup on a saucer, filled it, and Peaches carried it into Bryce. Abigail and Cherie followed.

"Thank you," Bryce took a sip. "Damn, that's hot! I burned my tongue."

Abigail laughed. "What did you expect? It just came off the stove."

Peaches leaned into his ear and whispered, "Do you want me to kiss it to make it better?"

Bryce winked at her. "Maybe later."

Abigail turned to Morgan. "Would you care for a coffee, dear?"

Morgan stood, stretched his arms over his head, and yawned. "Thanks, but no. I'm going to turn in."

"Awww," Jack said. "It's early."

Abigail kissed Morgan on the cheek. "Don't listen to him. You go to bed if you need to."

"I will. Good night, all."

Everyone wished him well as he departed. Abigail poured snifters of brandy and handed them around.

Bryce set his cup and saucer on the credenza and wandered over to Abigail's piano, a 1900 Baldwin upright made of beautiful mahogany, decorated with three panes of Art Nouveau filigree molded on the upper panel. Bryce lifted the fallboard and studied the keys. "Isn't this the same piano we had at the emporium?"

"Yes," Jack said. "And it's a beast to move."

"I thought I gave it to Rebecca's church."

"You didn't notice it at the time, but it wasn't yours to give. Abigail and I took it back so Cyrus could take music lessons."

Bryce struck the A key and nodded. Then he hit C and G. "Still in tune after all these years."

"Not 'still,' Bryce. Abigail has it tuned every year."

Bryce turned to Cyrus. "How long did you take lessons?"

"Nine or ten years."

"Play us something."

Cyrus shrunk back into the couch cushions and shook his head. Cherie took a seat on the couch and slid next to him. "No, Bryce, why don't you play? I haven't heard you since I was a girl."

Bryce pulled out the piano bench, sat down, and fingered the keys. He ran up and down a scale a few times. "Okay, this one's for Cherie."

Peaches recognized the lively foxtrot, pointed to her sister, and laughed. No one else knew the song, so they waited until Bryce finished, and then clapped politely. Bryce turned to acknowledge their applause and noticed their puzzled expressions. "Is my playing so poor no one recognized 'Hot Lips?'"

"I did," Peaches said.

"Never heard it before," Jack said.

"It's a big hit in New York this summer," she said.

Bryce nodded. "California, too. Cherie, I thought you liked jazz. Don't you know Paul Whiteman's Orchestra?"

"I do. I guess his latest record hadn't reached Paris before I left."

Jack stood up and began pushing furniture around, clearing a space in the center of the room. "Play something we know. Cyrus, help me roll up the rug."

Abigail stepped out of the way. "What are you doing, Jack?"

"Creating a dance floor. Come on, Cyrus. Get off your butt and help me."

Cyrus reluctantly stood up and assisted Jack with the carpet.

Jack wrapped Abigail in his arms and said, "Okay, something lively, Bryce —a song we know."

Bryce nodded and began "Sheik of Araby." Everyone joined in singing:

> I'm the Sheik of Araby,
> Your love belongs to me.
> At night when you're asleep
> Into your tent I'll creep . . .

Cherie took Cyrus's hand and tried to drag him on to the dance floor, but he pulled free and walked over to watch Bryce. Cherie shrugged and started dancing with Peaches. By the time the song ended everyone was laughing and clapping.

"San Francisco may not be the size of New York," Bryce said, "but it doesn't mean I've been living in a hole."

Jack laughed. "Or a monastery. Play some of your old ragtime tunes."

Bryce slid over and patted the piano bench. "Have a seat, Cyrus. We'll play four-hand."

Cyrus wrung his hands. "I haven't played since before the war."

"That's okay. I'll do the hard stuff. Ragtime is really just your basic chords in repeating patterns played with the right hand. We'll start with 'The Chrysanthemum,' one of Joplin's easiest pieces. Sit down. I'll show you your part."

Cyrus glanced at Abigail, who nodded. He sat next to Bryce and watched as Bryce showed him a combination on the upper register. "Now, you try it." Cyrus repeated what Bryce had shown him and did a pretty good job of it.

"Okay, now drop down an octave, play the same notes four times, then go back up scale and repeat. I'll work around you."

Bryce began a stride rhythm with his left hand and nodded to Cyrus.

Cherie beamed proudly at Bryce. Peaches grabbed her hand. "You still remember the ragtime two-step?"

The sisters joined Jack, jumping wildly around the floor, with Abigail trying hard to keep up. Bryce increased the tempo, and Cyrus kept right up with him. By the time the song ended, everyone was out of breath.

Cherie's eyes filled with merriment. "Now, these are the times with Jack and Bryce that I remember. Cyrus, you play beautifully."

Cyrus met her eyes and gave a shy smile.

Abigail rested her head on Jack's shoulder and whispered, "I think Cyrus is actually enjoying himself."

Jack nodded and tilted his head in Cherie's direction.

Abigail smiled, but then she gave a worried glance toward Morgan's room, and said, "I wonder if we aren't disturbing Morgan's rest."

Peaches lay her hand on Bryce's shoulder. "Maybe she's right. We better stop."

"One more," Jack said. "Morgan won't care. He's probably glad to hear a little joy instead of doom and gloom."

Abigail squeezed his arm. "Just one, all right, Jack?"

Bryce scratched his head. "Hmmm, a song to end on . . . I know. 'Toot Toot Tootsie Goo'bye.' Cyrus, just follow what I do, and jump in when you're ready."

> Toot, toot, Tootsie, Goo' Bye!
> Toot, toot, Tootsie, don't cry,
> The choo choo train that takes me,
> Away from you no words can tell how sad it makes me,
> Kiss me, Tootsie, and then,
> Do it over again . . .

# CHAPTER 27

Saturday, Abigail and Peaches prepared a nice supper—roasted chicken with stuffing, mashed potatoes and gravy, and a salad of fresh greens.

Cherie hadn't been around to help. She and Cyrus had gone for a walk along the creek that ran behind the property, the same path Bryce and Peaches frequently explored. No need to ask her sister what that was about. She and Cyrus never got up to anything much there besides hand holding and the odd affectionate caress. He no longer acted afraid to touch her and didn't jump when she touched him, but she was still proceeding slowly. Sure, there was a decade difference in their ages, but in Paris Cherie had always felt and acted younger than she was, and the war had aged Cyrus beyond his years. To Cherie it seemed as if they were contemporaries. She thought Cyrus felt the same.

At dinner, Cherie said that since she hadn't helped cook, she should at least clear the table. She stood up and began gathering dirty dishes. As she reached for Cyrus's plate, he stopped her hand.

"I'm sorry. Weren't you finished?"

"I am. I want to ask you a question."

She felt everyone at the table watching. "Go ahead."

"What do you like to do best? If you could do anything while you're here, what would it be?"

"Go dancing."

"Really?"

"Yes. There has to be somewhere around here where people do the two-step or the shimmy or the black bottom, it doesn't matter. There used to be saloons here, after all."

"Things have calmed down since then," Abigail said. "We're all so respectable now."

Cherie made a noise, then turned to Cyrus. "Do you know how to dance?"

"Not all those, but I can dance."

No one else said anything. Cherie waited. Cyrus required patience.

Finally, he spoke. "We should go. If that is what you like best, then we should go."

"That'd be the bee's knees. You mean tonight?"

"Uh . . . okay. I don't know where they have bands though. I haven't been out since before the war."

Cherie turned to Jack and raised her eyebrows.

Jack grinned at her with approval. "The Grange hall holds dances every Saturday. Abigail pays dues. Shouldn't be a problem getting in. And I'd guess we could persuade the band to stretch their abilities some."

"You belong to the Grange?" Cherie said.

"It's one of the few fraternal organizations that allow women to join. Not only that, but four of its leadership positions can only be held by women." Abigail clapped her hands with joy. "We should all go."

Jack shook his head. "Morgan's not ready to jig."

"I'll stay here and hold the fort," Morgan said. "The rest of you can dance in my place."

"You kids go. Abigail and I'll stay," Jack said.

"That's hardly fair to Abigail," Peaches said. "How long has it been since the two of you went out dancing?"

"Not counting the other night in the parlor?" Abigail said. "More than a few years."

"Well, someone has to be here with Morgan," Jack said.

"No, someone doesn't," Morgan said. "I'll be fine on my own for a few hours. Go ahead. It'll do you both good to get a night out."

Jack crossed his arms. "Sorry, no."

"I'll watch over Morgan," Bryce said.

"Me, too," Peaches said rather quickly.

Morgan made a dismissive gesture with his hand. "I don't need a nanny."

Peaches stood and helped Cherie gather the dishes. "Bryce and I will stay with Morgan. The four of you go out."

* * *

Jack parked and turned off the engine. Cherie could hear music. It wasn't jazz, but it had a steady beat. It would have to do. Cherie stepped out onto the dirt parking lot and worried about her gold glacé shoes. She'd chosen them because they complimented her dress, a pale green fabric embossed with gold figures. It was backless, with thin shoulder straps, and draped loosely over her torso and hips. Not the sort of thing you could wear with cowboy boots she expected to find in the Grange.

Jack took Abigail's hand and strode boldly toward the door. Cyrus offered Cherie his arm, not shy at all.

As soon as they entered the hall, Cyrus found seats in a corner where he could keep his back to the wall. Something about that nagged at Cherie's memory, but she couldn't put words to it. She shook it off. The band was already in full swing, and it was time to get on the dance floor. Cyrus resisted. "I need to loosen up first."

"Okay, let's go to the bar," she said. "I suspect they have lubricants available."

"You mean Coca-Cola?" Cyrus said. "You can't buy alcohol in America."

"Not even in a private lodge?"

He shook his head.

"See, that's why all the great writers have flocked to France. You can't write without fuel."

"Get us four colas," Abigail said. "Jack has a flask."

Cyrus left to buy sodas, and Cherie said, "Come dance with me, Abigail. In Paris girls dance together all the time."

"Not so fast," Jack said, "I want the first dance." He wrapped his arm around Abigail's waist and began to sweep her around the room, dodging other couples.

After sitting out the next few songs, Cyrus eventually got his feet moving. He wasn't a great dancer, but she loved the sensation of his warm hand on her bare skin. A backless dress had been a good choice.

In the gap between songs, she showed him a few steps and how a change in hand position could signal that he was about to spin her. He had less experience than her, but she was careful to let him lead. And giving her-self to him allowed him to give himself to her. It was turning out to be a wonderful night.

On the drive home, she could tell the evening had been good for Jack and Abigail, too. After Jack parked the car in the garage and everyone got out, he and Abigail lingered outside gazing at the moon.

Cyrus walked Cherie to her room. At her door, he hesitated, then grabbed her arms and kissed her.

At first, his kiss seemed unschooled, tense. Then his lips softened. Cherie parted her lips and began to flow her body against him. They wrapped their arms around each other and he pulled her closer. Cherie slid her hand up his back and wove her fingers in his hair.

She heard the front door open, and Jack and Abigail enter the foyer laugh-ing. Abigail hadn't laughed much lately. This was good. It was all good.

Cyrus startled, breaking their embrace and turning toward his room. Cherie spun him back, gave him another small kiss, and said, "Goodnight. Thank you for taking me dancing. And for this."

Cyrus beamed at her, his eyes twinkling.

Cherie slipped into her room and closed the door, leaning against it with a sigh. She maneuvered around the crowd of trunks and furniture and lit a lantern on the dresser. In the cast of yellow light she saw that Peaches hadn't come to bed yet. She hoped Morgan was all right.

Pulling off her dress, she caught a whiff of her sweat. Well, it had been hot, and she'd danced a lot. She finished undressing, poured water into the basin and washed her underarms with a cloth. She'd take a bath tomorrow. For now, she put on her nightgown and fell into the soft embrace of the feather mattress.

* * *

Cherie gradually slipped from that pleasant state just before wakefulness when the day seems like a smile and her featherbed cloudlike. She giggled for no reason and stretched. She reached for her sister.

Peaches' side of the bed was empty.

Cherie didn't know the hour, but it was late enough that birds were singing. She glided out of bed and put on her robe. No reason to dress yet. She planned to take a bath first.

Abigail and Jack were in the kitchen, swaying to a melody only they could hear. Abigail had coffee ready and broke her embrace with Jack to pour Cherie a cup.

"I'll get it," Cherie said. "Go back to what you were doing."

Jack grinned.

"No, I better start breakfast," Abigail said.

"I'd like a bath first," Cherie said. "Is Peaches in the bathtub?"

Abigail cocked her head. "No. Isn't she still in bed?"

Cherie bit her lip. "Okay. If no one wants the tub, I'm going first." She filled two large copper water kettles and set them on the stove.

* * *

Back in her room, freshly scrubbed, Cherie stood before the mirror holding an assortment of dresses in front of her. She contemplated how each dress made her feel, before tossing it on the bed and trying another one.

Peaches entered and looked at the pile on the bed. "One of those kinds of days?"

Cherie glanced at Peaches' reflection the mirror. "Would that be the same dress you were wearing last night?"

"Would that be any of your business?"

Cherie laughed. "I assume you spent the night with Bryce."

Peaches smiled as well. "In Morgan's studio . . . After we helped him to his room, of course."

"Aren't you worried what Abigail will say?"

"Why should she say anything?"

Cherie shrugged. "I don't know, a couple of her remarks made me think Bryce wasn't in her favor."

"That's about Cyrus enlisting. Has nothing to do with Bryce and me." Peaches scooped the pile of Cherie's dresses from the bed, deposited them on a chair, and fell onto the bed. She tucked two pillows behind her head and watched Cherie continue to pull garments from her trunk. "Don't bother repacking any of those. Hang everything in the wardrobe. It's time we got these trunks out of here. We can barely walk around."

Their room had a double bed, a wardrobe, a dresser, a table with a pitcher and basin, a nightstand, a chair and a tall mirror on a stand. The addition of their two trunks made it an obstacle course.

"I could have left my steamer trunk in New York and just brought a suitcase," Cherie said. "You're the one who said I should bring everything."

"Well, we had no idea how long we'd be here."

"I assure you I never thought I'd stay long enough to need all this."

"Yet here you are, trying on dress after dress. Aren't you glad you listened to your sister?"

"If I had brought less, I'd have fewer decisions to make."

"And probably wouldn't like any of them," Peaches said. "When you've run through your choices, you can try on some of mine."

Cherie laughed. "Is that a trick to get me to unpack your trunk, too? Besides, we don't know how much longer we'll be here."

"As long as it takes."

"Maybe Jack's right. Morgan's going to live forever."

Peaches got up. "You know that's not true." She selected a dress from her trunk. "After I bathe, I'll speak to Jack about storing our trunks in his garage."

# CHAPTER 28

A swallowtail butterfly landed on a painting Morgan had done of red hollyhocks growing near an adobe wall. Bryce studied it with fascination.

They'd left the studio door propped open, and the yellow and black butterfly had fluttered in while Morgan and Bryce were meditating. After their meditation, which Morgan had to admit did make him feel better, the men opened their eyes and had been watching it investigate the studio ever since.

The vase of desiccated flowers on the table next to the daybed held no interest for the swallowtail. Instead, it perused the canvases stacked against the walls, pausing at any picturing bright flowers. It eventually figured out that the blossoms didn't have any nectar and moved on to the next. Bryce crawled on his hands and knees, following the butterfly's progress. Morgan stretched out on the chaise, turned on his side, and watched Bryce and the butterfly from there.

"Bryce, do you remember Rebecca Sullivan, the woman Universalist minister?"

Bryce paused in his observation of the swallowtail and looked up. "Of course."

"Were you still in Taos the day she gave that sermon on Celtic Thin Places?"

"No, I was living with the Indians by then, but I recall you and Jack talking about it later. It must have made an impression."

"Well, the gist of it was that people in Ireland and Wales believe that in certain wild, beautiful places the distance between heaven and earth is thinner, narrower than elsewhere. I've always believed there were places in the Taos Mountains like that. When I'd paint there, it felt like a sacred space."

Bryce stood up and brushed dust off his knees. "The Apache have a proverb. 'Wisdom sits in places.'"

"I've thought so, ever since we moved here. In certain locations the holy and earthly seem to touch. There, God's presence seems more . . . present." Morgan sat up. "But as I get closer to death, I'm becoming aware that Thin Place is within us."

"Meditation will do that to you."

"Perhaps, but this isn't the first time we've seen the veil between heaven and earth become so thin that we could peer into other realms."

"You're talking about peyote."

"I am. I'm remembering it more clearly. That time you, Jack, and I drank peyote tea, there was something more happening. We had a transcendental experience together."

Bryce smiled and nodded.

"I would like for the three of us to revisit those ineffable realms once again before I have to go there alone."

Bryce shook his head. "I don't think—"

"I realize you've been away a long time, but surely one of the tribe remembers you and would get you enough peyote for three of us."

Bryce rubbed his neck. "You don't need it. The meditation technique of raising your Shakti—spiritual energy—will take you beyond where peyote can."

"Yes, but the three of us, one last time together . . ."

"Morgan, I understand the attraction of nostalgia, believe me. But I don't take drugs anymore."

Morgan sighed. "I don't have that luxury. For me, it's all day, every day, but the morphine just makes me sleepy. It doesn't give me a transformative experience I can share with my oldest friends."

"It wouldn't be the same as you remember. I participated in a lot of peyote ceremonies, and I learned the state of mind you bring to the ceremony flavors where the journey is going to take you. Jack is carrying a truckload of anxiety about your disease. If we take peyote together, he is likely to find himself fighting the lord of death for your soul."

"You don't really believe in the River of Styx and those Greek gods and goddesses."

"I believe every culture has a mythic god of death. But whether they're real or not isn't my point. Jack isn't in any fit state to take hallucinogens. Also, we can't predict how peyote will interact with your medications. As for myself, I quit using drugs when meditation left me in a state of consciousness higher than the peyote took me. I found my new normal was here . . ." Bryce held his hand above his head. "And when I take drugs, I'm here." He lowered his hand even with his forehead.

The butterfly found the doorway and flew out.

# CHAPTER 29

Cherie's naked, soft breasts pressed against Cyrus's ribs as they lay panting. He had rolled off her and she was nestled against his side, breathing hard. He was catching his breath, too. He hadn't been with a woman since France. A young country girl named Chantelle. He was handsome then. His mother said he was still handsome now, but he *felt* handsome then and apparently the French maiden thought so, too.

The war changed that. He'd been numb at first, but later he got moody and depressed and irritable. Worst was his guilt for having survived while everyone in his battalion died.

"*Everyone?*" a voice in his head asked.

"*Well, the American Expeditionary Force lost 25,000 lives in the six-and-a-half week Meuse-Argonne Offensive. I was only there for the end of it, but the dead men outnumbered the living.*"

He'd hesitated to make love with Cherie, though his balls were metaphorically turning blue from wanting her. She had made plain her willingness from the moment he first kissed her. His fear was that he would spend himself in an instant and be of no use to her. But Cherie knew better than he. She quickly granted his release and then revived him so they could continue until she pleasured, as well.

He kissed the top of her head. "Thank you for making me try. I admit I've worried about this for days."

"Me, too."

He raised up and looked at her. "Did I misread you? I thought you wanted to—"

"Oh, I wasn't worried about having sex. I was afraid it would somehow upset you."

"Not unless you set off artillery. Sudden loud noises, sure, but not sex with a beautiful woman. No, I was afraid I would be too quick and leave you frustrated."

Her fingertip stroked the river of fine hair that ran down his sternum past his navel. "You didn't fail me in the slightest."

He squeezed her affectionately and let go. "You know, you're the first person I can talk to about difficult things."

"You can, and I'll listen whenever you like. But never feel you have to explain. I left France during the war, but afterwards I saw the ruined lands where you fought. Although I can't imagine the horror of the battles, I have some sense of place."

"I don't know how you can live there. I could never go back."

"And I don't understand why anyone wants to come back to Taos. This place is . . . provincial."

"Well, I hope you're not leaving anytime soon. There's not a soul here our age that will spend time with me."

"What about Walter's boys, aren't you near the same age?"

"Walter, Jr. and Jimmy?" Cyrus made a face.

"Weren't they in the war, too?"

"Sort of. I joined up and was already in France before they got drafted. They reported to some base in Alabama or Texas for training on November first, but the war was over ten days later, so they never made it as far as the Atlantic. They were soon mustered out. The army didn't need extra men hanging around at that point."

"Your mother thinks you enlisted because of Bryce's Rough Riders stories."

"Really? He had nothing to do with it. I hadn't seen him since I was six or seven. No, it was patriotic fervor. Every one of my classmates talked about putting on a uniform and killing Huns. I was the only one foolish enough to do it."

"You and a million others."

"Yeah, but most of them didn't come back with shell shock."

"Most of them didn't come back. And as to shell shock, there are more of you than you'd guess. The streets of London and Paris are filled with men who aren't right in their mind."

"Is that what you think I am?"

"No, my love, I think you had a perfectly sane reaction to an insane experience, and you'll be right as rain in due time." She kissed him and let it linger.

He enjoyed it as long as it lasted. "Well, Jimmy and Walter, Jr. say I'm too crazy to be around. They won't come over anymore."

"And do you ever go over there?"

"Nah, they and Uncle Walt work that farm like three bachelor farmers."

"So it goes both ways?"

"Hey, whose side are you on?"

"Yours, my sweet, always yours." Cherie rolled on top of him and parted her legs.

His eyes widened. "What, again?"

"You know you want to."

Yes. He did.

# CHAPTER 30

Jack checked the oil in the Pierce-Arrow and was closing the hood when Abigail came out. "Is the car all right?"

"Purring like a satisfied woman."

She raised her eyebrows. "You're in a state. Do you have freight deliveries today?"

"None that I know of."

"Good. Then, will you stay with Morgan while Cyrus drives the girls and me on some errands?"

"No problem." They could AUM together.

Abigail adjusted her hat, tucking a loose strand of hair in place. "Bryce is going with us, so you'll be on your own with Morgan. I'm not sure how long we'll be gone."

"Doesn't matter." But without Bryce they probably wouldn't AUM.

Creases formed on Abigail's brow. "It's just that Morgan's pain has reached the point where the morphine isn't helping."

Jack's face froze. How had he not known? "What's Doc say?"

"I spoke to Morgan's surgeon on the telephone yesterday. Bayer makes a stronger form of morphine called Heroin. The doctor gave the pharmacist a prescription, but he didn't have any in stock and had to special order it. I called him this morning, and he said it will be in today. He's going to send his boy out with it as soon as it arrives. Someone needs to be here when he comes."

"I'll stay right here."

* * *

Hours went by, but the boy never arrived. Abigail hadn't returned either. Jack came over to Morgan. "I'm sorry your medicine's late. I telephoned the apothecary, and they said the boy left an hour ago."

Morgan was sitting in one of the Adirondack chairs, holding his arm across his eyes. "Jack, it's only pain. I've had worse."

"I don't understand where that boy could be."

"There's probably a good reason for his delay."

"If he's having a petting party with some chiquita while you're suffering, I'll throttle him."

"Oh, don't go overboard, Jack. What if he is? We had our fun when we were his age."

"Why are we waiting? We'll send Cyrus in to get some."

"He's not here," Morgan said. "He drove Abigail and the girls to town."

"Oh, yeah." How did he forget that?

"Maybe you can call Cyrus and have them bring it home with them."

"What?" Jack said. "You think there's a magic telephone that somehow allows you to call people in their cars while they're driving?"

Morgan laughed. "I guess not. Wouldn't that be great, though?"

"We can take my truck. I don't know why Abigail asked the pharmacist to deliver it in the first place. Let's just go get it ourselves."

"Thanks, Jack, but I don't think I can ride in the truck anymore. It jars my insides. What's left of them."

"I'd go by myself, but I don't want to leave you alone."

"Then just calm down and forget it."

"No. I'll telephone Doc Martin and find out if he has anything he can bring you."

Jack ran into the house to make the call. He returned shaking his head. "No one answered."

A gangly teen appeared at the end of the driveway, walking his bicycle. Jack ran to meet him. "About time."

"I'm sorry, Mr. Diamond. My bicycle got a flat tire."

"I can see."

"Then there was this bull—"

"Bull?"

"Yes. I saw a farmhouse across the field and I went to see if the farmer could patch my tire. But when I was halfway to his house his bull saw me, and . . . Well, I barely made it back to the road."

"Okay, but where's the medicine?"

"I lost it."

Jack turned an unhealthy shade of scarlet. "Lost it!"

"Dropped it somewhere in the field."

"Well, why didn't you look for it?"

"He's a very large bull, sir."

Jack pointed at Morgan. "That man is in terrible pain. Don't you realize how important this is?"

"I do. I'm sorry, sir."

"Why didn't you call your dad to have him bring more?"

"I'm going to, but you're the only house on this road with a telephone. That's why I walked the rest of the way here."

Jack stalked off to the house. He returned looking glum. "Your dad said he only got the one package he sent with you."

The boy began to quake, and his eyes welled up with water.

"For God's sake, Jack," Morgan said. "Don't be so hard on the kid. You're going to make him cry."

The boy looked at Jack and sniffed. "You know anything about bulls?"

"No, but I'm about to."

"If you can fix my bike, I'll go back."

"We haven't got time for patching tires. Get in my truck and show me where this field is." He turned to Morgan. "Sorry to leave you, amigo, but it seems unavoidable. I'll be right back."

Morgan waved him away. "I'm not going anywhere."

Jack drove out the driveway, and as he turned onto the road, he saw the Pierce-Arrow coming toward them. He braked and waved his arm out the window. Cyrus pulled up beside Jack's truck and rolled down his window.

"Perfect timing," Jack shouted over the engine noise. "You guys stay with Morgan while this boy and I search for the medicine."

"Search for—?"

"Long story. Ask Morgan." Jack waved goodbye and took off. As soon as he got the Ford into high gear, he increased the throttle as far as it would go. The Model T's twenty-horsepower gave it a top rated speed of forty miles per hour, and Jack pushed it for all it was worth. "What's your name, son?"

"B-B-Billy."

Hitting bumps at that speed with no load in the back nearly lifted the Ford off the ground. Jack had the steering wheel to hold on to, but Billy was getting tossed around and clung to the edge of the seat for dear life.

"Slow down, Mr. Diamond. You're going to miss it."

"Call me Jack, Billy."

"Okay, but you just passed it."

"What? That field back there?" Jack throttled down and slammed on the brakes, raising a cloud of dust behind them. He made a three-point turn and headed back the way they came.

"Excuse me, sir, but you drove by it, again."

"On purpose. That's the Lopez ranch. I'm going to get us some help with that bull." Jack turned off the road and raced down a long lane, skidding to a halt in a patch of grass between the house and barn. A woman, taking laundry off the clothesline, turned and squinted at them. "Jack?"

Jack waved, turned off the truck, set the brake, and got out. "Afternoon, Mrs. Lopez. Is Carlos around?"

"Hi, Jack. He's in the barn."

Just then, Carlos came out. "Jack? Is everything all right?"

"Will be. I need your help though. The pharmacist's boy was bringing Morgan a new medicine when your bull chased him. He dropped the package somewhere in your field—doesn't know exactly where. If you could pen up that bull and help us search I'd appreciate it. Morgan needs it pretty bad."

"Of course." Carlos put two fingers to his mouth and made a loud whistle. A half-dozen children of various ages appeared. "Kids, help Jack find something he lost in the field. Jack, I'll take care of the bull."

Jack motioned for Billy to get out of the truck. When he came over, Jack said, "They're going to help. Tell them what we're looking for."

Billy held out his hand. "It's about the size of my palm. A small brown bag, folded in half, and taped shut."

Jack looked out at the brown dirt field covered with brown grass. Great! Had to put it in a brown bag, did he? "Okay, kids, form a line arm-length apart and we'll walk the field in a grid."

* * *

Once the medicine was found and Morgan had taken some, Jack pushed Billy's bicycle into the garage and patched his tire.

Billy looked at Jack as if he'd hung the moon. He put his foot on the pedal, ready to throw his other leg over the crossbar. "I don't know how I can thank you, Mr. Diamond."

"Jack."

"Yes, Jack . . . And I'm real sorry for all the trouble I caused you today."

Jack patted his shoulder. "Well, now I've seen that beast, anyone with half a brain would have run from him."

Billy smiled.

Jack smiled back. The boy hadn't been slacking off as he'd suspected at first. No, Billy proved himself dependable and bright. Tried to find a phone, walked his bike here. Hell, the kid reminded him a little of Cyrus before the war. "Put your bike in the back of the truck, and I'll give you a lift back to town."

"You will?"

"I just said I would. Let's go."

Jack turned the ignition switch to battery and retarded the spark. He walked to the front of the truck and gave the crank a sharp jerk with his left hand. The engine started on the first try—he loved it when it did that. He went back to the driver's side, reached in the open door, set the switch to magneto, and moved the spark lever down until the engine idled smoothly. Jack noticed Billy's eyes follow his every move.

"How old are you, Billy?"

"Sixteen."

"You know how to drive?"

The boy shook his head.

"You want to learn?"

A grin exploded on Billy's face. "Yes, sir!"

"Well, slide over here."

Jack got in the passenger side. "Now, a Ford doesn't operate like other cars."

"I've never driven any car."

"Well, I'm just warning you."

Billy put both hands on the steering wheel and nodded.

"That lever on your left sticking up from the floorboard is the handbrake. All the way back, like it is now, puts the car in neutral and sets the brakes.

Halfway forward releases the brakes, but the transmission is still in neutral —the motor isn't connected to the back wheels yet. All the way forward lets you put the vehicle in gear."

Jack reached for the lever on the right of the steering column. "This is the throttle, controls how fast the engine turns. Up is slow, down is faster." Jack moved the lever down and the engine raced. He pushed it back up, and the engine returned to an idle. "Now, look at your feet. You see those three pedals? The left one makes the car go forward. The center pedal is reverse, and the one on the right is the brake. Got it?"

Billy shook his head excitedly.

"Okay, push the right pedal as far down as it will go. Then, put your other foot on left pedal and hold it halfway down." Jack watched Billy's feet. "Good. Now, the release the handbrake, pull the throttle lever down a little, and press the left pedal all the way to the floor."

The Ford made a shrill whining sound and got under way. Billy looked both frightened and elated.

Nearing the end of the driveway, Jack said, "Up here you're going to have to stop and check for traffic. Let your left pedal come halfway up while you step on the right pedal."

Billy did as he was told, and the car stopped about twenty feet from the road.

"Well, you did it. But maybe a little too soon. Let up on the right and push the left back down." The truck started moving, again. "Now, let the left pedal halfway up, and just coast to the road, then step on the brake."

Billy stopped at the end of the drive and looked both ways. He let off the brake and pushed the left pedal down as he turned the steering wheel to the right. Once he was going straight on the road, he turned to Jack and grinned.

"You're doing fine." Jack pointed to the throttle lever. "Give her a little more gas."

Billy did.

When the Ford reached about ten miles per hour, Jack said, "Let up on the left pedal."

"What?"

"That's how you change gears. Down is low, halfway is neutral, up is high gear."

Billy took his foot off the pedal and truck jerked, kicking like a mule. Billy panicked and stomped on the right pedal. The engine stalled.

Billy put his head on the steering wheel and peeked at Jack from the corner of his eye.

"Put her in neutral." Jack reached over, snapped the ignition off, then turned it to battery. The engine backfired and started. He flipped the switch back to magneto.

"How'd you do that?" Billy said.

"Sometimes when the motor's hot, and the coil is buzzing, you can get the engine to catch without cranking. Now let's try that again. When you get up to speed, just ease into high gear gently, like you're moving your hand up your girlfriend's leg."

Billy's mouth fell open. He glanced at Jack then straight ahead. But he did what Jack said and soon had the Model T rolling along at a good clip.

* * *

Jack dropped Billy off and returned home about the time Morgan and Bryce usually did meditation. Jack went out to the studio with a mind to join them. Like Morgan said, it couldn't hurt, and it definitely wasn't too strenuous for Morgan. In fact, there wasn't anything to it. Chant some nonsense sounds. Then, sit still and imagine that drawing in a breath pulled energy up your spine. If it helped Morgan, he was for it. Kind of reduced his anxiety too, for a few minutes at least.

Bryce and Morgan were there when he arrived, but Morgan was passed out on the chaise with his mouth hanging open. Jack walked over and checked his pulse. The new medicine had really knocked him under.

Bryce, sitting on the floor cross-legged, looked up at Jack, waiting expectantly.

"What's the point?" Jack said. "He's out."

"Sit down, Jack. Fill the room with calmness. Raise your conscious energy and let it lift Morgan up."

"You think it has that kind of effect at a distance, like magnetism?"

"I know it does."

The door opened. Peaches entered and smiled at Jack. "I'm going to join you."

"Really?"

"Yes. Bryce has been teaching me to meditate."

Jack rubbed his cheek. Well, he couldn't get out of it now. "Here, you take the chair. I'll sit on the floor like Bryce."

Peaches sat down, put her hands on her lap, palms facing up, and straightened her spine. Jack sat on the floor next to Morgan's bed and leaned back against it.

Bryce began to AUM. Peaches joined in, and finally, Jack, too. Eventually, the chant became silent and internalized. Later, Bryce spoke in a soft, resonant tone, as if from a distance, "As you practice the breath technique, visualize the energy pouring from your forehead and surrounding Morgan."

He tried, but damn, the floor was hard. If Peaches was going to join them regularly, she'd need the chair. He should bring himself a couple throw pillows from the parlor. Abigail might not appreciate her good pillows on the floor, but she'd go along with it.

"If the mind drifts, bring the attention back to the movement of the breath," Bryce said.

Jack scratched his head. How the hell had Bryce known he was woolgathering?

# CHAPTER 31

Cherie in his bed had become a regular thing—this was the third night in a row. The others didn't know, or if they did, no one mentioned it. Although someone must have noticed the rhythmic squeak of bedsprings that resounded off the walls of his room, Cyrus figured it wasn't any of their business, anyway.

He was deep in post-coital slumber with Cherie spooned against his back when a flash of lightning on a distant mountain lit up the room, waking him. Many seconds passed before the inevitable pounding of thunder filled his ears. It had felt like waiting for the other shoe to drop.

The next flash struck closer, sounding like a two-hundred-and-fifty-pound howitzer shell. Cyrus couldn't help it. He started to tremble. Cherie threw her arm over him in her sleep. He shrugged her off and brought his knees to his chest, trying to hold the fear in, trying to cling to the present moment. The rain clouds broke open and torrents of water struck the roof and cascaded off, falling past his window.

And he is in a trench in the Argonne Forest. The sounds of German guns are coming more frequently, shells landing closer as the gunners adjust their range. Rain begins to pour, and the trench quickly becomes muddy. Every flash illuminates the corpse-strewn killing field in front of him.

Stretcher bearers dash through the gunfire, tossing any breathing soul onto their litter and scrambling into the trenches to offload the wounded man and rush out again. As the field grows impassible, the stretcher bearers step on dead soldiers to keep from sinking into water and mud so deep it would knock the wounded off their litter. Men as stepping stones.

His trench quickly turns swamp-like. An artillery shell explodes in front of his position, blowing corpses into pieces and carving a crater into which parts of random men finally receive burial.

Cyrus collapses against the trench wall and screams.

Cherie awoke at the first sounds but knew enough not to touch Cyrus, curled in on himself at her side. Outside, rain pounded down, with an occasional flash of lightning. That must be what had done it.

She slid from the bed and began lighting lanterns around the room. When the room was awash in yellow lamplight, she stood near the bed, just out of reach, and said, "Cyrus."

Cyrus rolled over and opened his eyes to the warmly lit room. He sat up and shook off his disorientation. This was his room, his bed. The shoes by the door were his.

He noted how far away she stood and started to weep. "Have I done it again? Have I hurt you?"

Cherie rushed to him and began covering his face with kisses. "*Non, mon amour.* It was only a bad dream. I was perfectly safe."

Cyrus fought for control. When he could speak, he said, "The thing is, it wasn't. A dream, I mean. The storm woke me when it started, and I was here, and I was me. Then, somehow, I was back on the front. It all seemed so real, but I wasn't asleep. That's the really scary part."

Cherie got in on his side of the bed, clambered over him, and sat, leaning against the headboard. She pulled his head down onto her chest, and swayed them in a rocking motion. "You didn't do anything wrong."

"But I might have hurt you."

"You couldn't. I know now not to startle you. As soon as I heard you, I got up and lit all the lamps so you could see where you were."

He straightened up and looked into her eyes. "I thought I was getting over the war, starting to forget." He exhaled. "A measly little thunderstorm and I'm back where I started."

She petted him. "This is no little storm. It's really pouring. On the bright side, the cistern's going to be full."

There was a knock on his door, and his mother opened it a crack. "What's going on?"

"The storm," Cherie said.

"Ah. Are you all right, Cyrus?"

He smiled weakly.

"It was me," Cherie said. "I'm the one who lit all the lanterns. This sure is one heck of a storm. I forgot what they can be like here."

His mother nodded and looked at him again.

"I'm fine," he said. "Really. Go back to bed."

"In a moment. As long as I'm up, I'm going to check on Morgan."

"Goodnight, Mother."

She closed the door, and he looked at Cherie. "You were about to say something."

"That we're going to have more than a few nights like this. But don't blame yourself. The only fault here is the horror you had to endure."

"But if they can come back even when I'm not sleeping, I have no control."

"Perhaps. But you're not back where you started." She hugged him close. "Now, you've got me."

# CHAPTER 32

The downpour ceased before dawn, but disquiet lingered at breakfast. When Cherie reached for Cyrus's hand beneath the table, he folded his hands over his plate as if about to say grace. She patted his thigh and returned her hands to her lap. How many mornings would she have to remind him not to rebuke himself? Not now, in front of the others, obviously.

Later, when they were alone.

Abigail selected a piece of toast and buttered it. "Morgan hasn't eaten or drunk anything in two days."

"I blame the new medicine," Jack said.

"The doctor agrees," Abigail said. "I telephoned him this morning, and he's switching Morgan back onto morphine. Cyrus, when you finish eating, I need you to walk into town and pick up his prescription."

"Walk?" Cyrus said.

"Sorry," she said. "Jack's disassembled the Ford, and he's leaving for Santa Fe as soon it's back together. I need to keep the car here in case we have to rush Morgan to the doctor."

Jack drank the last of his coffee and stood up. "Burned an exhaust valve on my way back yesterday. I'll have them lapped and the engine buttoned back up in a few hours. I can get Morgan's prescription before I go to Santa Fe."

Abigail furrowed her brow. "We don't want Morgan to suffer. Last night's dose is starting to wear off. It won't kill Cyrus to walk."

"We don't mind." Cherie patted Cyrus's leg again. This time he didn't object.

Abigail shook her head. "Cherie, I need you to wash the breakfast dishes and then start lunch."

"I'll do that," Peaches said.

"No, I want you and Bryce to give Morgan a bath this morning. Hopefully, that will perk him up. At least he'll smell better. Also put fresh sheets on his bed. This is my day to bake bread, and that takes all morning. I can't do everything."

No. And they shouldn't let her. Cyrus was going to have to walk into town on his own.

There was a scuffing of chairs as everyone stood and headed to their assigned tasks. Cherie walked with Cyrus out onto the porch and kissed him good-bye. When she returned, Abigail was stacking dirty plates. Cherie carried a stack into the kitchen and saw that Abigail already had a kettle of water on the kerosene stove. She scraped the plates into a garbage pail and set them in the dishpan. The water wasn't hot yet, so she returned to the dining room and picked up the remaining dishes.

Abigail folded the corners of the long tablecloth toward the center, capturing the breakfast crumbs, and followed Cherie into the kitchen. "Set those dishes on the sideboard for a minute and help me shake this out." She proceeded out the backdoor and Cherie followed.

Cherie took one end and stepped away from Abigail until the cloth was fully extended. They gave it a vigorous shake. Abigail looked it over and said, "I think we can eat another meal on this." Cherie walked forward, handed her corners to Abigail, bent down, slipped her hands into the fold, and backed away until it was taut. It was something she'd done with her mother, and it felt suddenly familiar.

Abigail came to her and took her end from her. "You're quite a bit older than Cyrus, as you know."

There it was. She'd been expecting some sort of comment. Cherie watched Abigail finish folding the tablecloth. It dawned on her that Abigail had a purpose in mind when she'd sent Cyrus on a long walk.

Even though Cherie owed her independence to Abigail's mentoring, the old hen wasn't getting rid of the young hen quite so easily. "Cyrus is almost twenty-four. In New York and Paris, I'm considered twenty-five."

"But you're not, are you?"

"Aren't you older than Jack?"

"Yes, but only by a year. You're nine years older than Cyrus."

"Age doesn't make a difference to us."

"But it will soon."

"No it won't."

"Trust me, it will. Someday, not far off, you'll want children, and realize you don't have many years left to start a family."

"Cyrus isn't ready to be a father."

"Which is my point. And you've said a hundred times you're leaving for Paris as soon as Morgan passes. I admit you've had a steadying effect on Cyrus, and thank you. But he's not a flapper's plaything. What's going to happen if the two of you get deeper involved and then you leave?"

So, that was what this was about. Abigail wanted her out now, before Cyrus's feelings intensified. Maybe it was already too late to prevent that. But then again, after last night's storm, Cyrus hadn't acted the same toward her at breakfast. Either Cyrus was unsure about them or afraid of his mother's disapproval. Either way, Abigail had a point. Now was the best time to leave, for everyone involved.

Cherie felt the urge to run away, and she did just that. Racing in through the back door, she turned off the boiling kettle and kept going, leaving by the front door.

From the porch, she spied Jack hunched over the Model T engine compartment, tightening something with a wrench. If she packed now, she could get a ride to the station before Cyrus came back. She trotted over to him. "Jack, can you help me take my trunk up to my room? It's too heavy for me carry by myself."

Jack showed her his greasy hands. "Now wouldn't be a good time."

"How long until you finish?"

"I don't know, soon. What's the hurry? Peaches just had me store them the other day."

"Oh, you can leave hers there, just help me fetch mine."

"If you forgot to unpack something, wouldn't it be easier to just open your trunk in the garage, and carry stuff in than cart the whole damn case into the house and back out again?"

"No, I need to pack."

He stood up from under the hood and gave her the side-eye. "What the hell for?"

"I want to catch today's train. At breakfast you said you were going to Santa Fe."

"I am, but why are you leaving?"

"Obviously, it's time."

"It's not obvious to me. What the hell are you talking about?"

Cherie's throat tightened. She felt her eyes begin to well up. "You guys are making me crazy. You tell me to go to bed with Cyrus, and now Abigail doesn't want me around him. I have feelings, too, you know."

"Hang on, hang on. Don't be rash."

"I'm not. She wants me gone, and she's right. I can't stay here and become a Taos housewife, I just can't. And it's unfair to Cyrus to lead him along. I'm just going to pack my trunk, catch the train east, and find a boat to France."

Jack wiped his hands on a rag and opened the driver's door. "Just sit here while I find out what's going on."

Cherie stepped on the running board and slid onto the seat. She hated to leave Cyrus without saying goodbye. Oh, hell, she may as well admit it, she'd fallen for him. God knows, she hadn't intended for that to happen, but a sweet man hid under the moodiness. Still, he'd seen enough battle. If she truly loved him, she couldn't put him in the middle of a war of feelings between her and his mother.

Bryce came out of the studio and emptied a washbasin. She watched him exchange words with Jack, who continued into the house.

Bryce walked over. "You're not really leaving? Morgan's up."

"That's good news."

"Yes, Peaches is bringing him out on the porch now."

"You're strong. Well, strong enough. Help me carry my trunk from the garage to my room."

"Let that wait a bit. Come say hi to Morgan. No telling how long he'll be able to sit outside." He held out his hand and helped her out of the truck.

By the time they reached the porch, Peaches had brought Morgan out. Cherie kissed him on the cheek and helped Peaches ease him into a chair.

Jack opened the screen door and stuck his head out. "Anyone seen Abigail? I can't find her in the house."

"I saw her going out to the privy," Peaches said.

Jack spotted Morgan. "Good to see you up and around. You need anything?"

"No, thanks."

"How about a nice cup of coffee?"

Morgan smiled. "That sounds really good."

Jack left, and Morgan looked at the others. "Everyone, sit down, please. You're hovering like a bunch of vultures."

"That's not a very nice image," Peaches said.

Morgan laughed. "Well, that's the last thing the corpse sees."

"Glad you haven't lost your sense of humor," Bryce said. "But don't let Jack hear you talk like that. He'd chew you out for saying a lamp was dying."

Morgan shrugged. "He's got to face it sooner or later."

"Face what?" Jack returned, carrying a cup of coffee. His unsteady hand had slopped coffee into the saucer. He gripped the cup, poured the contents of the saucer back into it and wiped the saucer against his elbow to dry it.

Morgan accepted the coffee from Jack and sniffed it. "Smells good."

"So do you," Cherie said. "You shaved, too."

Morgan grinned. "With Bryce's help."

"Hey, I held the mirror," Peaches said.

"Oh, good," Jack said. "Here's Cyrus with your medicine."

"No, thanks," said Morgan, "I'm barely upright from the last batch."

"Don't worry, buddy," Jack said. "Abigail got the doctor to put you back on the old stuff."

"Well, I'm all right for now. I don't need anything, yet."

"Good," Jack said as Cyrus reached them. "Wow, Cyrus, that was quick. You must have run there and back."

"Carlos Lopez gave me a ride home." Cyrus handed Morgan a paper bag, and whispered to Cherie, "We need to talk."

They did. She took his hand and led him down the porch steps. "Bryce, do you mind if we use your studio?"

"Not my studio, ask Morgan."

Morgan waved them away. "*Mi casa, es tu casa.*"

Cyrus closed the studio door behind them, took Cherie in his arms, and kissed her passionately. "During my walk into town I had time to think."

She pushed them apart. "So have I. Your mother's right. It's time for me to go."

He pulled her against him and said into her neck. "I agree. But we can't leave before Morgan dies. He's been like a second father to me."

Wait. *We?* Cherie took his head in her hands and lifted it so she could see his eyes. "You want to come with me?"

"Back up. My mother? What does she have to do with this?"

"We . . . had a talk earlier."

"I don't know what she said, but what I realized is that I am safer with you than without you. And if you have to have Paris, then I will give it a try."

"That's not what your mother had in mind. She thinks if we get any deeper involved, you'll get hurt, and that I should leave you before then."

Cyrus's body tensed, and his face turned scarlet. He stormed from the building, leaving Cherie alone. Well, that pretty much confirmed her decision. Now if one of these men would just get her trunk, she could still catch the afternoon train.

Cherie returned to the house, pausing on the porch just long enough to tell Bryce she'd be in her room, and now that Cyrus was back would the two of them please bring her trunk upstairs. Peaches, busy fussing over Morgan's hair with a comb, apparently wasn't listening.

In her room, Cherie threw open the door of the wardrobe and began removing dresses from hangers, neatly folding them and putting them in a pile on the chair. When the men brought her luggage, she'd have everything ready to pack.

She reached for the next hanger and started to take off a long, black dress with a high neckline. Wait. This belonged to Peaches, undoubtedly brought for Morgan's funeral. Never say Peaches didn't plan ahead.

Cherie bit her lip. She'd come all this way because Morgan was dying, and hadn't even packed an appropriate dress. Of course, when she left Paris for the States how could she have known she'd wind up here. It didn't matter. Now that she was leaving, she wouldn't need a dress for the funeral.

She hung it back in the wardrobe, thinking she hadn't worn anything this dour since . . .

Buried memories of Marcel rushed up and slammed her against the bureau. She stumbled to the bed, fell on it, and covered her face with both hands.

She hadn't thought about him in four years. Why today of all days?

# CHAPTER 33

The beginning of summer 1914, Cherie was twenty-five, sitting in a café sipping a citron pressé, and listening to Parisians around her complain about the heat. Having grown up in New Mexico, she didn't mind warm weather, though she preferred her heat a little drier. Her refreshing lemonade was on the tart side, just the way she liked it. The French had the right idea. The waiter brought a tall glass of ice, squeezed an entire lemon into it, and left behind a pitcher of water and a bowl of sugar. The customer could then mix in as much or as little sugar and water as desired.

Sitting at the next table was a handsome man about her age. He had a slim build, dark eyes, and dark hair. He smiled at her, and she experienced a quiver, as if a harp string in her core had been plucked.

His eyes danced toward hers, as if he'd felt the same note resonate in him. "Marcel" He extended his hand. *"Comment allez-vous?"*

By this point, Cherie had lived in France almost seven years spending her days and nights with artists and writers. She was fluent in French, albeit with a trace of American accent the locals always detected. But French wasn't called the language of romance for nothing. Marcel could say "May I butter your dinner roll?" and make it sound completely seductive. She took him back to her tiny apartment that very night.

The rest of June and July, she and Marcel hardly ever spent a day apart. Then, some Serbian madman assassinated some Archduke touring Sarajevo, and the world began to take sides and make threats. By August, Germany invaded Belgium and declared war on France.

Marcel's father was a General or Colonel, she couldn't remember which, but as soon as the war started, Marcel enlisted. He didn't have much choice. The first weeks of his training, they wrote letters back and forth every day, and she saved them all, tied with a little ribbon, like a schoolgirl. But once the battles started, his letters stopped coming.

She feared he'd been killed but couldn't get anyone in the military to give her any information. There was too much going on and the French command didn't have time for some American girl who wanted to know where her lover went and if he were he still alive. Fine, she'd do it herself. But they refused to provide a list of which soldiers were on the front. She'd have gone over their heads to his father, but they wouldn't tell her where he was, either. It was hopeless. With no one to turn to except Peaches, she packed up and returned to the States.

Four years later, treaties were signed, the dead were buried, and she returned to Paris. Not for Marcel—he was long forgotten. No, simply because Paris was the place she'd chosen long ago, a city she loved.

Nothing was the same, of course. Paris was untouched, but everything north of the city was in absolute ruin. Pockmarked from artillery bombardments and gashed with trenches, the fields grew no wheat, and there were shortages of everything. But Cherie had lived frugally for years and didn't require much, so she scraped along.

While northern France was plastered with white crosses marking soldiers' graves, the streets of Paris were strewn with walking corpses—shell-shocked men disgorged back into society without a clue how to cope. While standing in line one day outside the boulangerie, hoping they hadn't run out of baguettes, she saw one such wretch huddled in the doorway of a closed shop.

Fortune smiled, and she was able to buy not one, but two baguettes. Leaving the bakery, she decided to share her bounty with the poor man. His gaunt, almost skeletal figure reminded her of a starved puppy who'd been kicked so many times that he hid in the corner. She approached him that way—the way she would a feral animal, with soft gentling words, holding out the bread. He had been chewing nervously on his fingers. Now, he took his hand out of his mouth and reached for the baguette. She noticed his nails were bitten almost down to the quick.

He spoke softly, but clearly. "Shall I butter your roll?"

"What? Marcel?"

He nodded.

"Marcel!" She dropped the baguettes and lunged to embrace him.

He shrank back.

"Sorry," he said, picking them up and handing them to her.

"No, I'm sorry. I startled you. When your letters stopped, I thought you'd been killed. I tried to find out, but no one would tell me anything." She brushed a speck of dirt off the bread and handed it to him. "Here. Please."

She squeezed into the doorway next to him and they sat on the sidewalk eating warm bread, not minding that they didn't have any butter.

"Where are you living?" Cherie asked.

He gestured to the doorway. "Here. Or places like it."

She took him home with her, and he never left. Literally, never. Marcel wouldn't go out. He didn't mind if she did, but he didn't want to be around people. It was like being trapped in a monk's cell. The rare occasions she managed to drag him to a café, he'd cower in a corner where he could watch all the sides of the room at once. He was no fun at all.

She put up with it, mostly for old time's sake. But being stuck in the apartment started making her crazy. She found a job dressing mannequins at Printemps. It provided a little extra money, but more importantly, it gave her a reason to be gone for long stretches of the day. She wanted to love him, to help him heal, but she couldn't seem to do anything that made any difference. Finally, she located his father, who agreed to visit Marcel the next day while she was at work.

That was a mistake. When she returned home that evening, Marcel was worse than ever. The old man had told him to stop malingering and ordered him to join the Foreign Legion in Algeria.

She made supper, but he wouldn't eat. They argued. He said she never should have sent for his father. The row continued. Then he grabbed his pistol from under his pillow and waved it around. At that point, she stormed out and didn't come back. She spent the night with a friend and went straight to work the next morning.

When she came home from work that night, she found him.

# CHAPTER 34

Cherie sat up on the bed with a jerk. There it was, hiding in plain sight all these years. Buster Keaton could have hit her in the face with a cream pie and she wouldn't have recognized it, but there it was. The reason she'd harbored such a low opinion of men wearing bow ties.

Marcel wore bow ties. Hell, Marcel died and was buried in a bow tie. From somewhere deep inside her the abhorrent image of finding him dead broke free. His face, the color of eggplant, had swelled to the size of a pumpkin. She hadn't been able to stomach either vegetable since. And that stupid bow tie, cinching his neck like a knot on a balloon. The doctor explained that tumidity was an effect of the poison he'd taken. An explanation that gave her no comfort.

She'd buried Marcel, and with him, that whole part of her life. Buried it deep enough to stay forgotten and replaced it by becoming a flapper. But she'd harbored this intense hatred of bow ties all these years the way Cyrus was still afraid of thunderstorms. She wasn't quite as wounded as he was, but her hurt at last had a name.

Now it had all resurfaced because of that damned dress of Peaches. A scab had been torn off and it was bleeding.

Cyrus had Marcel-like mood changes, nightmares and tremors. But there their similarities ended. Cyrus abhorred guns. Marcel slept with one under his pillow. It frightened her, but she stuck with him because . . . Well, because she'd run away from the war, and he'd run into it. She felt an obligation to help those unfortunate souls who'd sacrificed their sanity so Parisians could return to a life of croissants and champagne.

Another key difference between the men was that after the war, Marcel couldn't have sex. Now that he'd started, Cyrus couldn't stop.

Not that she objected. Abstinence was never her forte.

But the most significant distinction was that Cherie hadn't been in love with Marcel, not like she was with Cyrus. Maybe before the war they had a spark, but afterwards her role was more nurse or caretaker.

So what now? What was best for Cyrus? Was Abigail right? She fell back into the embracing feather mattress, rolled over into her pillow, and had a long cry.


A tap of fingernails on the door, the sound of a woman clearing her throat, Cherie lifted her head. Abigail entered. Cherie buried her face in the pillow and resumed weeping.

Abigail sat on the edge of the bed and rubbed her back. Cherie turned over, and tried to sit up, but Abigail was in the way. Abigail stood and Cherie got up.

Abigail pulled a lace handkerchief from her pocket and handed it to Cherie. "You're wrong if you think I want you to go."

Cherie dabbed her eyes with the hankie. "But you said—"

"I was trying to give you advice, not as Cyrus's mother, but as yours. It's odd, because in some sense I feel you and Peaches are like my daughters."

"Well, we're not."

"No, you couldn't be. I'm only ten years older than you. But that's nearly the same age difference as between you and Cyrus. I guess I got my feelings all mixed up, thinking if you felt as I do, Cyrus would seem like your son."

"No, I don't see Cyrus that way. Believe me. Besides, I'm not maternal enough to treat someone like a child." That was only partially true. Marcel hadn't been younger than her, but she'd definitely treated him like a child. And failed.

She shook her head to clear away thoughts of Marcel. "To me, Cyrus is a grown man, same as other young men I know. He's been through a terrible war, but so have most of the men in France." Damn, Marcel's ghost again.

No! Cyrus wasn't Marcel. He wasn't going to end up like Marcel.

Abigail suddenly clasped her in a warm embrace. "Cyrus needs you, Morgan needs you, I need you. Here. Please stay."

Cherie started to cry, again. "You mean it?"

"Of course I do. You and Peaches, and even Bryce being here have made the unbearable bearable. Don't even think about leaving."

"You talked with Cyrus?"

"He was . . . not pleased. Said things a son should not say to his mother."

"I'm sorry."

"No, I was glad to see the passion. We've cleared the air. He loves you. I love you. All one happy family again."

"Did he tell you he decided to try Paris?"

Abigail forced a grimace into a smile. "If that happens, I'll wish you bon voyage. But please, put the idea of leaving out of your mind until after Morgan passes. You have worked a miracle with Cyrus, but there's only so much loss I can juggle at one time."

Cherie kissed her. "I love you, too. I'll stay. Just don't mother me. My first mother didn't work out so well."

Abigail glanced at the pile of dresses. "Would you like me to help hang those back up? As a friend."

"Thanks, but no. I'll do it. I need a few minutes alone to pull myself together."

Abigail nodded and left.

She wasn't gone long before Cyrus rushed in and threw his arms around Cherie, crushing the white, fringed, Chanel dress she'd just put on the hanger. She wiggled loose, shook the dress free of wrinkles, and hung it in the wardrobe.

"We need to talk," she said.

Cyrus nodded. "Absolutely. Mom says you've made up, and we're staying until after the funeral."

Cherie gently took Cyrus's hands in hers and looked into his eyes. "I have to tell you something . . ." She swallowed a lump in her throat that seemed the size of a boiled egg. "There was another man."

He laughed. "You've never hidden that there were many others before me."

"No, another soldier. His name was Marcel. We met a few months before the war. I wasn't a flapper then, just a young American living in Paris. When Marcel and I met, there was an instant attraction between us. We became lovers. Then, war came. He volunteered, like you did. But he never came back."

"I'm sorry," Cyrus said.

"I thought he died. But after the war, I found him living on the street—the worst case of shell shock I've ever seen. I tried to help him, but what did I know about shell shock? And he wasn't strong like you. There was something weak, almost cowardly, about him."

Cyrus let go of her hands and jumped away. "Don't say that. Ever! That's the kinds of things captains would say to make us go back into battle after we'd had more war than a man can endure. No one who ever stood in a muddy trench with bullets flying at them was weak."

Cherie broke down and wept.

"Hey, hey, hey, I'm sorry I yelled."

When she regained control, she finished her story. "Maybe he was hurt more badly than you or saw worse things. Maybe he had a less understanding father, I don't know. But he . . . he couldn't stand to go on living."

"I'm so sorry. But don't think he was weak. I've considered that solution myself a couple of times."

"You never took it."

"That may not be strength. I could have just been laziness. Why didn't you tell me sooner?"

"Believe it or not, I didn't know myself. Did your teachers ever make you read Edgar Allan Poe's 'The Cask of Amontillado?'"

He nodded. "Horrifying way to die. I don't know why they make children read it."

"Well, I'd walled off Marcel's memory as surely as Poe's victim. Until today, I had no recollection of anything beyond him leaving for war and presumed dead. I tell you, unearthing it shook me to my core."

Cyrus looked worried. "Does this change things between us?"

"It doesn't change how I feel about you, but I have to consider whether it's right to take you away from here."

"I'm ready. I'm volunteering to go with you."

"You say that now, but . . ."

"I'll say it forever. I love you and never want us to be apart."

Deep in her heart she loved Cyrus like no one before, but didn't love mean considering what was best for the beloved? "I don't think I should stay in your room tonight."

Cyrus looked crestfallen. "Is this the end of us?"

"I'm not saying that. But you know how when you're troubled you need to be alone? Well, that's what I need tonight, a little time to figure everything out."

Cyrus stuck out his lip in a pout.

Cherie kissed it. "You sleep in your room. I'll sleep in mine. We'll see what tomorrow brings."

Cyrus clutched her to him. "Cherie, I love you—I mean, really love you."

The sincerity with which he spoke those words struck her heart like a fist to the chest. Her breath stopped, and it was a moment before she could speak again. "I love you, too. But please, just give me tonight."

* * *

Katydids had long since quieted, and the household had been asleep for hours. Cyrus turned the knob on Cherie's door and edged it open a few inches. "Cherie?"

"Yes."

"Are you alone?"

"Peaches is out in the studio."

He opened the door further. "Can I . . . ?"

"Yes, of course."

He closed the door behind him and walked over to her bed. She flipped the covers back and made room. He shucked his robe and crawled in beside her. The bed springs squeaked. He put his arms around her, and she kissed him.

He scooted closer. "Trying to keep us apart is like pushing the positive poles of two magnets together—as soon as you let go, one of them will switch and they'll clamp together tight."

"Did Jack teach you that?"

"He did. We used to do a lot of experiments with magnets."

"Sounds like he was a good father."

"Morgan, too."

"I'm sure that's true."

"Did you tell Mother about Marcel?"

"No. Do you think I should?"

"Not unless you want to. Your past is nobody's business but your own."

"Cyrus, you're very understanding."

"I have my demons. You can have yours. Did I give you long enough to make peace with yours?"

"I think so."

They fell silent. The rustle made by the breeze on the leaves of the cottonwood drifted in through the open window. He'd gotten off track. This really wasn't what he'd come to say.

"Cherie, do you really love me?"

"You know I do."

"Then please take me with you. The last six hours have been the worst night of my entire life."

"You mean that?"

"Truly the worst."

She tickled his ribs. "Good."

"Good?"

"It means you're fretting about something besides the battles at Meuse-Argonne."

He smiled. "Listen, memories of getting shot at by Huns is nothing compared to the fear of losing you."

# CHAPTER 35

Jack drove to the cabin and siphoned the fresh beer into casks. He came alone this time as Cherie and Cyrus, bless 'em, couldn't bear to be apart. He didn't really need her help, anyway. He'd been doing this on his own for nearly five years. He also wasn't as worried about leaving Morgan's side anymore. The last few days, Morgan's resurgence had been nothing short of a miracle. Surely, he was on the path to recovery.

As he scrubbed the residue from his fermentation crocks, he had time to wonder. Maybe the Heroin he'd thought so bad for Morgan had really done the trick. True, it laid him out for three days, but he'd risen like Lazarus and been walking around ever since. Could be all Morgan needed all along was the deep rest the Heroin had given him. Now, Morgan took meals with them, not that he ate much, but he sat at the table and joined in the conversation, laughing at Bryce's wisecracks and even making a few of his own. Yes, it looked like Morgan was on the mend.

With the crocks clean, ready for the next time he'd make beer, and two casks of fresh brew loaded in the back of the truck, Jack covered his tracks and drove home. When he pulled in, he saw Morgan leaving his studio. "Been painting today?"

Morgan shook his head.

Jack took off his hat and wiped his sweaty forehead with his sleeve. "Am I late for dinner?"

"Not yet."

He carried the casks to the springhouse, and Morgan came with him. It took two trips. Jack didn't want Morgan carrying anything just yet, but God, Morgan's color looked good—better than it'd been in a year. That was something to celebrate. He filled his stein with fresh beer. "You want one?"

Morgan declined and the two friends walked to the porch where everyone except Abigail was gathered. Cherie and Cyrus were sitting close enough to touch, but not actually touching, a rare enough occurrence as of late. Peaches stood and offered Morgan her chair.

Morgan smiled. "It's the other way around. The gentleman offers the lady his seat."

"A gentleman already has." Peaches moved over onto Bryce's lap.

So everyone's relationships were now finally out in the open. Jack raised his stein. "Got fresh beer. Can I get any of you a drink?"

"Is that the batch we made?" Cherie said.

"It is."

"I'll have one."

"What about you, Peaches?"

She hesitated. "Let me taste yours."

Jack handed her the heavy beer stein. She gripped it with both hands, and took a sip, getting foam on her lip. "Okay." She turned to Cherie. "You made this?"

"Jack did. I mostly carried buckets of water."

Cyrus squeezed Cherie's knee. "I'll get the ladies' beers."

"Don't forget your mother," Jack said.

Cyrus called through the screen door, "Mom, Jack's brought new beer. You want some?"

Abigail came to the door. "No, thanks, I forgot Jack had gone to get the beer. I already poured myself a glass of wine. Bring your drinks with you. Dinner's ready."

There was a bottle of wine on the table and glasses at each setting, but only Abigail's had been poured. Cyrus brought Peaches' and Cherie's beers and one for himself. Abigail fixed Morgan a plate and passed serving bowls and platters among the others.

Seating had been rearranged so that now Abigail sat at the head of the table with Morgan and Jack on either side of her. Cherie sat between Jack and Cyrus, and across from her, Peaches was between Morgan and Bryce. As Jack had observed earlier, all relationship secrets were now out.

The seat at the foot of the table was empty. Morgan filled a wine glass and passed it to Bryce.

"I told you, I don't drink anymore," Bryce said.

Morgan gestured to the seat at the end of the table. "Set it there."

"It's not Passover, you know."

"You never know; Elijah might come tonight."

The others gave Bryce and Morgan a puzzled look.

Morgan explained, "At Pesah, we always pour a cup of wine for the prophet Elijah."

* * *

When the meal was ended, much of the food on Morgan's plate remained. The women cleared the dishes and brought out slices of pie. Abigail made fresh coffee and poured for all who wanted it.

Morgan poked his dessert fork into the flaky crust and broke off a bite. He tasted it and smiled. "Abigail, you've outdone yourself. This is delicious!"

"Cherie made it."

"Really? And here I thought you couldn't cook."

Cherie blushed. "I've asked Abigail to teach me."

Morgan ate another forkful of pie. "Well it's working. Try it, everyone. Cherie did really well."

While everyone sampled their dessert and complimented Cherie, Morgan continued to work on his slice of pie until it was gone. He scraped a last bit of filling from the plate with his fork and licked the tines. "I'm glad we've had this meal together." He laid his fork on his plate and looked at those seated around the table. "There's one more thing I'd like to ask of you all."

Jack sat upright. Morgan had been doing so well, but this sounded . . . ominous.

"There is a place in the Taos Mountains where I have always found a special connection. Well, several places, actually, but one in particular. Cherie, you might call it a Thin Place, for something ephemeral is definitely going on there. It's a place where heaven feels so near that if you stood on tiptoes, you might poke your head through into the next realm. I don't think I have much longer, and I'd dearly love to visit there one last time with all of you."

"Oh, don't talk like that," Jack said. "You're looking better than you have in ages."

Morgan turned to Abigail. "I'm thinking we might have a picnic there, tomorrow, if you're not too busy."

"Of course, we can do that," Jack said.  "But let's wait until you're a little stronger. You told me last week your insides can't take too much bouncing."

"That was about your truck.  If we can take Abigail's car, drive slowly, and avoid potholes and washouts, I'll be fine."

Abigail touched his hand. "Of course. Whatever you want."

Morgan covered her hand with his. "Can we go in the morning?"

"God, yes," she said.

He glanced around the table. "Everyone?"

They all nodded.

"I'll help Abigail make the food," Cherie said. "I need the practice."

Morgan stood slowly. "Good. I'm going to bed now, so I'll be rested.  Don't let me sleep in.  Wake me, so we can leave early."  Morgan made his way behind Peaches and Bryce's chairs.  He stopped at the foot of the table, picked up Elijah's glass and drank it.

# CHAPTER 36

Abigail's Pierce-Arrow could carry seven people. She hadn't really needed that big of a car when she bought it. The company made smaller coupe and roadster versions, but at the time the Vestibule Suburban was the only model the dealer had on hand, so she took it. Today she was glad she had. Peaches and Cherie had Cyrus between them in the large backseat while Jack and Bryce sat across from them on two fold-down jump seats. Morgan rode in front; cushioned in a nest of feather pillows Abigail had robbed from the beds and packed around him.

Abigail was behind the wheel. She didn't trust Jack or Cyrus to drive as gently as Morgan would require, so, as they packed the car, she informed them she would do the driving. Jack, who had been trained almost a score of years ago to submit when she had that determined look in her eye, capitulated. Soon, the whole party was aboard, and they set off.

The forty-eight horsepower engine and four-speed transmission easily climbed the mountain roads around Taos, while inside, the passengers enjoyed unequaled comfort of quality upholstery and a smooth ride. The car could easily do sixty, but Abigail was only going a fifth of that, often less, as she threaded her way around ruts and washouts. Jack would have gotten them there in half the time, but she didn't care, as long as Morgan wasn't unduly jarred.

No one in the backseat objected. Jack voiced optimism about Morgan's improvements while Bryce entertained everyone with old stories. In the front seat, Morgan gave Abigail directions.

The mountain road was a twisty incline that had never been improved for automobiles and remained better suited to horse carriages or mules. Fortunately, they met no oncoming traffic, so Abigail had the entire road to work with, but steep ravines appeared alternately on one side of them and then the other.

When they came to an expanse of grass overlooking an arroyo, Morgan said, "We'd better park and walk from here."

Abigail stopped, shifted into the lowest gear, and eased the front wheels into the grass. Once the rear of the car was clear of the road, she turned off the ignition and set the handbrake. Conversations in the backseat stopped. Jack and Bryce opened their doors, stepped out and offered assistance to Cherie and Peaches. Jack opened the driver's door and held out his hand to Abigail. "Very smooth driving."

"Thanks." She stepped on the running board and Jack lifted her by the waist, swinging her to the ground, kissing her as he did so.

"My, we're in a good mood," she said.

Jack grinned. "This was a really good idea."

Meanwhile, on the other side of the car, Bryce and Peaches were untangling Morgan from the cradle of padding. "Abigail packed you in here like a canned sardine," Bryce said, tossing two pillows onto the driver's seat.

Jack looked past Abigail into the car, "You all right there, Morgan?"

Morgan waved a hand at him. "Easy as sleeping in my own bed." He swung his legs out the door and set his heels on the running board. Bryce and Peaches each took a hand and steadied him as he stepped into the foot-tall grass.

Cyrus retrieved blankets from the trunk. "Mom, where do you want the picnic?"

Abigail pointed to where a row of tall conifers cast long shadows. "In the shade, please."

Cherie followed him and helped spread out two large blankets. When she was around, Cyrus looked happier than Abigail had seen him in years. They returned to the car for the picnic baskets and a gallon jug Abigail had filled with lemonade and ice. A light breeze stirred the blankets, threatening to blow them away. Jack carried over a pail of beer and set in on one corner. Cyrus set picnic baskets on two other corners and pointed toward where Cherie should set the lemonade jug.

Jack watched the blankets ripple. "I should have brought more beer."

"It'll be fine," Abigail said. "Once we sit down, the grass will flatten and the blankets will be fine."

Peaches called out from the car, "Morgan, do you want a pillow?"

"Not now," he said. "Maybe later, I can get it then. Let's go for a walk. I want to show all of you something."

With Bryce on one side of him and Jack on the other to keep him steady, Morgan led the party up a slope. A white-tailed kite flew out of the canyon with a chipmunk in its talons.

Bryce nodded toward it. "Lunchtime."

"Not for the chipmunk," Morgan said.

"Hey, don't knock him. Kites have to eat, too."

Peaches and Abigail caught up to them.

"Could be a *her*," Abigail said.

Bryce laughed. "You can tell that from here?"

"No, just making a point. Males aren't always the gender who accomplishes things."

Cyrus and Cherie, holding hands, ambled behind the others.

Morgan paused atop a butte, inhaled deeply and gazed at the vista before them. Abigail followed his eye. And years of studying his paintings let her see things as he saw them. In the high altitude, distant mountain ranges west of them were little more than variegated bands of ochre and smoky blue. Nearer to them, verdant forest carpeted the Taos Mountains. Cumulus clouds dotted the sky, their shadows racing across the woodland below created patches of darker green. It was active, living, and deeply peaceful at the same time. And she wouldn't have seen it if Morgan hadn't opened her eyes.

And for the first time, she began to understand why Jack felt so strongly about Morgan's death. It wasn't just friendship. The world would be a poorer place without his viewpoint in it.

"You know I was born in Taos," Peaches said, "but I don't think I've ever been to this place."

Morgan smiled serenely. "Beautiful, isn't it?"

"Yes. I recognize it from many of your paintings."

Morgan turned to Cherie who was staring out over the landscape as well. "What do you think? Does this stand up to the Thin Places you and Rebecca visited in Ireland and Scotland?"

"Oh, yes. The light here seems softer, gravity bent somehow."

Morgan nodded. "As if we could drift upward, like birds on a thermal."

"Don't fly away yet," Jack said.

"Soon," Morgan said.

"Didn't we bring Rebecca here one time?" Abigail said.

"Sure we did," Jack said. "Cyrus, too."

Cyrus turned away from the view and cocked his head. "Really? I don't remember that." He slipped his arm around Cherie's waist. She snuggled closer.

"I expect not," Jack said. "You were a just a little shaver. It was before your mother and I got married."

Cherie looked at Morgan. "What did Rebecca say when you showed this place to her?"

"About what you might expect. She thought it was magical."

Abigail agreed with her now more than ever. "I believe she said the separation between planes felt as diaphanous as a bride's veil."

Bryce chuckled. "That sounds like her."

Abigail threw up her hands. "She was an educated woman. Why should she hide it?"

"Hey, hey, hey, I know. It was one of the things I liked most about her. But you can be educated and not talk like a preacher."

"She couldn't help it," Morgan said. "What I do with paint, she tried to do with words. After you do it for a while, you can't really stop. Occupational hazard."

# CHAPTER 37

Jack, Bryce, and Morgan became absorbed in reminiscing about their boyhood, shutting the others out. Cherie and Cyrus decided without words to drift away somewhere on their own.

Abigail caught up with them before they could disappear. "Don't be gone too long. We're going to put out lunch in a while."

"How soon do you want us back?" Cherie said.

Abigail lifted her watch brooch and glanced at the time. "Would an hour be all right?"

Cherie nodded, and the two lovers strolled into the forest hand in hand.

They followed a trail made by deer, or maybe elk, until they came to a wide patch of grass. Cyrus took off his jacket and laid it out for her. They stretched out and gazed at puffy clouds in the cerulean sky.

Cyrus pointed upward. "That one looks like an old woman, and those two smaller ones joined at the top could be an elephant walking away."

Cherie laughed. "You mean his butt? No, to me that's the Arc de Triomphe. See how the top is flat?"

Cyrus turned on his side and looked at her. "What are we going to do, my love?"

"I thought we settled all that. As soon as it's feasible, after the funeral, we entrain for New York and find a ship bound for France. We'll avoid battlefields and war cemeteries and stay only in Paris or the southern provinces."

Cyrus pressed his lips together.

"Are you having second thoughts?"

"About us? Oh, hell, no. Just about what demons might be waiting for me. I assume everyone there still speaks French?"

"It will be completely different this time. Paris is alive with art and jazz, and you have me. I'm better than your old sergeant, aren't I?"

"You're certainly better at this." He leaned toward her and kissed her.

She kissed him back. "When we get there, we're going to buy you some new clothes, too; baggy plus-fours in lighter colors, some V-neck sweaters. And a new hat."

"Not a beret."

"No, a smart motoring cap, I think."

"Will we have a car?"

"God, no, not in Paris. But maybe we'll hire one and drive south next winter instead of riding the train." She began to unbutton his shirt. "Don't be afraid. I'll only take you places where you feel safe."

He pushed up her skirt. "Have you ever made love in a field?"

She thought a minute. "In a hay mow, a livery stable, a bed of straw. But no, never in a field."

"Me, either." He unfastened his pants and pulled her closer. "I think it's time we try something neither of us has done before, don't you?"

# CHAPTER 38

Abigail watched Cyrus and Cherie disappear. She knew what they would be up to, but did it matter? Cyrus just seemed so happy.

Peaches caught up with her. "Those three New Yorkers forgot they brought us."

"Seems that way."

The two women walked to the blankets, smoothed out wrinkles where the breeze had rumpled them, and sat down. Peaches opened one of the hampers and started unpacking plates and silverware. Abigail shook her head. "We're in no hurry. Your sister and my son won't be back for at least an hour."

"You're all right with that?"

"In one way, she's lessened my load by a third."

Peaches set aside the silverware and took hold of Abigail's hands. "Oh, you wonderful woman, Atlas couldn't have shouldered what you have."

Abigail cast her eyes down. Having Cherie, Peaches, and Bryce take on her burden didn't feel particularly heroic.

She studied the design woven into the blanket. Navajo, she recalled. Jack had bought it from a trading post in northwest New Mexico five or six years ago. It wasn't colorful, merely black and gray on white. But the design, mirrored at both ends, consisted of what she interpreted to be a female stick figure ensconced in a stepped triangle. The figure's arms extended downward in what she imagined as a gesture of offering solace. But a second, smaller triangle hovered above the figure's head like a suspended weight. To her, it represented all the pressure she'd been under.

What had she done that was so special? What mother wouldn't hold out welcoming arms to her war-ravaged son? What lover wouldn't extend an embrace to a beloved dying of cancer? What wife wouldn't offer consolation to her distraught husband?

What sane woman read meaning into the geometric shapes on a picnic blanket?

"I know you and Bryce have been sleeping together in Morgan's studio," she said. "You may as well move him into your room. Cherie's not using it anymore."

Peaches cheeks turned pink. "I hadn't because I thought you resented Bryce."

"I did. There was no reason for Cyrus to enlist—his birthdate missed all three drafts. But when he was a kid, Bryce was constantly filling his head with the glorious adventures of the Rough Riders. And it was all bullshit. It turned out Bryce never went to Cuba. He just made up stories all the time."

"Cyrus told Cherie that Bryce's stories had nothing to do with it. He hardly remembered them. There was rampant patriotic fever, and he succumbed to it."

"He told me that, too. But what happens in childhood often stays with you, whether you remember it or not."

"I think you have to give Cyrus more credit than that. And believe me, Bryce is no longer a fan of war."

"Oh, I'm all right with Bryce now. I told you, he can move into the house."

Peaches, who had yet to let go of Abigail's hands, gave them a little squeeze. "You know Bryce and I were lovers once, before he left Taos."

"I heard that back then. I can't remember who told me, Morgan or Jack. I suppose you're aware that Bryce and I were once lovers, too."

"No. Really?"

"I swore him to secrecy at the time, but I thought he'd mentioned it after you two reunited. Things have a way of coming out in pillow talk."

"Oh, Bryce doesn't discuss past lovers, and I'm not naming mine. We're all very genteel about it."

"Wise woman." Abigail pulled her hands free of Peaches' and tucked a loose curl of hair behind her ear.

Peaches smiled. "If I'm anything today, it is all because of you, you know."

"Nonsense. You have real business acumen. Morgan kept me up to date on your progress as you turned that gallery into a serious enterprise."

"Morgan helped. It was his suggestion that I open a gallery. But you are my inspiration. Every time I visit Taos, I learn from you how to succeed in a business world run by men."

"Trials in business are nothing compared to my family life these last few years. Morgan's diagnosis and surgery, and my poor sweet Jack, Mr. Fixit who refuses to accept that Morgan's body is beyond repair. I worry every day about what's going to happen to Jack when Morgan finally passes."

"You're a tower of strength."

"No, I'm a facade of plaster and straw that will fall in at the next strong wind. And the worst of it has been that since Penelope died, I haven't had another woman to confide in." Abigail looked away. "I meant what I said the night you and Cherie arrived. You being here saved me."

"I've been meditating with Bryce and Morgan. You should try it. Bryce learned from these swamis."

Abigail smiled. "Thanks, but I'm old enough to remember when Bryce lived with the Indians and got Jack and Morgan to take peyote with him."

"No, this is just breathing and watching your breath and stuff. It's very calming. Morgan says it helps him. It could help you, too."

"I'm glad if it helps Morgan. But you should be careful. Bryce has always been something of a Svengali."

"I thought you didn't have anything against Bryce."

"I don't. Perhaps Svengali was the wrong word. I only meant he's a smooth talker."

Peaches smiled. "That he is."

# CHAPTER 39

"Enough talk about the lost days of our youth." Morgan said to Jack and Bryce. He spread his arms, embracing the vista. "Here is where I want you to remember me. Why don't we sit for a while and enjoy this place?"

Morgan walked to the edge of the gorge, sat down, and dangled his feet off the ledge as Rebecca had done the first time he brought her here. He'd been afraid of heights then, she wasn't.

He peeked over the rim at the depths below and found his old fear. Curious. He was going to die this day, he was sure of it. Yet some survival instinct made him afraid of falling. Did that continue to the end? Would his last breath be a clawing grab for one more grain of sand through the egg timer? He hoped not. Yet, what man knew how he would comport himself at his finale?

Jack and Bryce joined him. Bryce sat Indian-style. Fearless Jack not only sat on the rim, but extended his legs over the nothingness and banged his heels together. Dust flew, and Jack let his feet drop.

Morgan made one long AUM sound and then listened for an echo.

"The echo won't be out there," Bryce said. "It's inside."

Morgan nodded. "I know, but in a place like this, where you feel you can almost touch eternity, why not offer a good AUM?"

Bryce met his eyes. "Do you want to chant?"

"No," Jack said.

Morgan shook his head. "We don't need to. Listen, you can hear the mountains hum their own chant."

Jack took off his shirt, rolled it into a pillow, lay back, and tucked it behind his head.

They sat in silence, letting the peace of the landscape sink into them.

A while later, Bryce said, "When I lived in Lomaland, Katherine Tingley used to say, 'Consciousness uncovered from the enshrouding veil of matter, bathes the soul in radiant light of pure truth.'"

"Radiant light of truth? Is that what you see in this place, Bryce?"

"Not just here, but wherever and whenever something draws us inward and upward. As Christ put it, 'Seek not your treasures upon earth . . . For the kingdom is within you.'"

"You keep forgetting I'm not Christian."

"Of course, but that doesn't mean the kingdom *isn't* within you. Have you studied the Kabbalah?"

"That wasn't something my synagogue taught young boys."

Bryce shrugged. "We haven't seen each other in a while. I thought maybe you'd come across it. Anyway, the idea is the same. You find the heavenly realm by following your own consciousness upward. It's all within us."

They fell quiet again, into a deep stillness. Morgan entered a point of oneness whose beauty surpassed even this, his favorite thin place. Perhaps the moment of death he felt building inside of him for the last few days had finally arrived. It would be fitting, to take his leave from this, his beloved Thin Place.

The sun reached its apex and any trace of morning mist had long ago evaporated. Cumulus clouds hung in the sky, casting shadows on distant forests below. An eagle vaulted from its aerie and soared in large lazy circles. Morgan floated above it all, seeing as if through her eyes the three men sitting on the rim of a canyon. They were of no consequence to her as she rode the thermals searching for small prey. But Morgan's eyes were not her eyes, able to sight a rabbit two miles away. His perception was broader, softer, an impressionist's eye. He felt the colors more than saw them.

The hum of Taos Mountains became louder—an electric whine—the spinning rotor of earth's motor. The planet rotated incredibly fast, yet they experienced no sense of motion. Jack could probably explain why. But he didn't ask. The answer didn't matter as much as enjoying the stillness.

After a time, the sun made the hair on top of his head hot. Icarus flown too high? The eagle was gone. He dug his fingers into the dirt, closing them around fistfuls of gravel. There it was, the primal instinct: hold on to something. Starts the moment the midwife slaps the newborn and sticks with us until our last breath.

Morgan threw the pebbles over the edge of the cliff and dusted the dirt from his hands, the sensation of grittiness proof he wasn't dead. So close, but not maybe today.

Jack stirred and sat up. "Morgan, thank you for reminding me about this place. Whitman and those old transcendentalists would have loved it."

Morgan nodded. "And Bryce, you were right, we didn't need peyote, we never did. The three of us and the hum of the mountain and the ethereal quality of this space are high enough."

"I understand what you mean," Jack said. "We should come here more often. Soon as you get a little stronger, of course."

It was a shame to introduce hard truths into this soft, welcoming moment, but it had to be done. "Jack, we're never going to be together in this place again."

"Oh, what are you talking about?"

"I'm spent. I'm at the end."

Jack jumped up. "Morgan, old buddy, that kind of talk doesn't do you any good."

"Jack, you're preaching to a dead man."

"Stop it!" Jack picked up his shirt and put it back on.

Morgan struggled to rise. Bryce stood and gave him a hand. Morgan locked Jack in a bear hug—a weak one. "I wanted this trip today for more than one reason. I wanted to see this place, to see it with you two. But I also wanted to heal the rift between your denial and reality. Everybody here, except you, accepts that I am dying. I don't understand—"

Jack covered his ears like a child. "I'm not going to listen to that."

Morgan removed Jack's hands. "Look, you're scared. That's okay. Let Bryce and me help you."

"But the surgeon cut out the cancer," Jack said quietly.

"It came back. My cancer begot cancer."

"Well, by golly, we'll just beat it again. I'll help you."

"Jack, the surgeon already took most of my liver. I don't have anything left to beat it with. All I ask is that you don't let my death put you in a dark place."

"Death? Oh, come on, Morgan, enough with the maudlin talk."

"Loss can lead people into depression. We saw that with Cyrus, his life clogged up with too much grief. Where did that get him?"

"Well, killing and dying are different. War's not something he can forget."

"I'm sure no one can. But he's getting better."

Jack smiled. "So will you. That's my point."

"I won't. That's mine."

Jack frowned. "Not with that kind of thinking."

"Jack, I can't kill the cancer with happy thoughts. But don't let my demise get you down. What Cherie did for Cyrus was to get him focused on someone else's happiness."

Bryce jumped in. "It's impossible to stay in the Big Weep when you're being useful to others."

"I try," Jack said.

"I don't think you even have to try," Bryce said. "Empathy just sort of leaks out of you."

"He's right, Jack," Morgan said. "One of the things that Bryce and I have always seen in you is how you spontaneously do things for others."

Bryce nodded. "You've been like that since we were kids."

Jack waved his hand dismissively.

Morgan's voice cracked. "I just don't want my death to make you wind up like Cyrus was the last four years."

"Death? Not that again!"

Morgan gripped Jack's shoulders. "Yes, Jack, death. And soon. If not today, then tomorrow. We're not leaving this mountain until you accept that my time is up."

Jack broke down and wept.

Bryce reached out to comfort him, but Jack shook him off. Turning his back on his friends, he howled at the sky like a wounded mountain lion.

When Jack settled down, Morgan wrapped an arm around him and squeezed. "You know, death is a once in a lifetime experience. Soon I'm going to know stuff people have wondered about for a million years."

Jack pulled away, eyes red and sad. He wiped his nose on his sleeve. "I wish it wasn't so."

Morgan patted him on the shoulder. "If wishes were fishes, we'd be up to our shins in fins."

"Up to our ass in bass," Bryce added.

Morgan laughed. "Up to our belt in smelt."

"Up to our gullet in mullet," Bryce said, grinning.

Morgan tweaked Jack's nose. "Up to our snout in trout."

Jack cracked up and then sobered. "If wishin' were fishin' I'd empty the seas with my pleas."

* * *

In the distance Abigail saw Cyrus and Cherie coming out of the woods. "Is it that time already? We better set out lunch." She opened the basket and began handing things to Peaches: loaves of bread, jars of beets and pickled green beans, butter, cold fried chicken, sliced ham, and potato salad. "There's wine and a blueberry pie still in the car. Would you get it?" Abigail waved at Cyrus. "Go tell Jack and the others that lunch is served."

Cyrus nodded, and he and Cherie walked hand-in-hand toward where they'd last seen the men. In a few moments they returned with Jack, Morgan, and Bryce.

After all had eaten and were lazing about on the blankets, paired off in natural couples, Abigail saw that whatever had happened on the mountain had transformed them all. Jack's manner with Morgan showed he had finally accepted the impending loss, and Cyrus seemed secure with Cherie. Abigail looked at the female figure woven into the Navajo blanket and felt the heavy triangle hanging over her head lift.

When the day waned and they began to pack up the dirty dishes, Morgan said, "It's starting to look like this isn't where I'm going to die."

"Don't rush it," Jack said.

"Oh, I'm not," Morgan said. "It's just that I really expected I would die up here today, in this holy place. It seemed fitting. I guess we don't always get what's fitting."

Jack kicked Morgan's foot. "What, you selfish mug, and leave us to haul your corpse back down?"

"I don't care what happens after I'm gone. Just leave my body wherever it falls."

"As if Abigail would ever allow that," Jack said.

"Seriously, when I'm gone, I wouldn't mind if my body were laid out up here on some Indian rack. Just let the elements take me."

Jack chuckled. "That Indian talk sounds like Bryce."

"You mean the old me," Bryce said. "And you're thinking of some other tribe. The Pueblo bury their dead same as white people. Their cemetery is out near the San Gerónimo Church."

"Yes, but that's a Catholic cemetery," Morgan said, "and the Protestant cemetery is no alternative. Where are you going to find a burial plot for a Jew?" Morgan stood up and stepped off the blanket. Abigail and Peaches picked it up and shook off the crumbs. "No, you may need to do something more creative."

# CHAPTER 40

The morning after the picnic, Morgan's strength abandoned him, but he woke up early and couldn't bear to be confined to his bedroom another minute. What he desired most was to lie in his studio among his paintings. He slowly shuffled to the doorway and leaned against the doorjamb.

The studio was too far to make it alone. "Jack! Jack, are you up?"

Abigail rushed down the hall, tying the sash of her dressing gown. "What is it?"

"I'd like to go out to my studio, but it seems I require some assistance."

"Now?"

"Yes."

"Why don't I help you back into bed, you can go there a little later."

"No, I'm done lying in that bed. I'll be better off on the chaise lounge." Morgan began to work his way down the hall, using the wall for support.

"All right, all right, let me get Jack. We'll help you."

With Jack on one side of him and Abigail on his other, he made his way to his studio, where the lovely scent of turpentine and linseed oil greeted him. He lay back on the chaise.

"Jack, stay with him, and I'll bring you both some breakfast."

Abigail returned shortly, carrying a tray of food and a pot of coffee. She unloaded the tray and poured everyone coffee. Morgan sat up and accepted the proffered cup. He sniffed the aromatic steam. "Thank you."

"You're welcome. Do you feel better out here?"

"I do." Morgan blew on the cup and took a sip. "I've spent an awful lot of days in this place. I'd like to spend my last here, too."

Jack choked on his coffee. Abigail rapped him on the back.

"Stay out here as long as you want," she said. "One of us will be here. We'll take turns." She handed Jack his science magazine. "The others aren't up yet, so you're first watch. I thought you'd like something to read."

"Read?" Jack said in a scratchy voice. "No, Morgan and I will just talk."

"Well, later, when Morgan falls asleep." Abigail measured morphine into a spoon and poured it into Morgan's mouth. She set the bottle on the table beside the daybed. "I'm going to leave this here. When you need more, it'll be at hand." She swept dried flower petals off the table into her hand and took the vase of naked stems. "These need to be thrown out. I'll bring fresh flowers when I come back."

Abigail left.

Jack picked up his plate and poked a corner of toast into the yolk of a fried egg. "You're not hungry, Morgan?"

Morgan shook his head.

"Well, you shouldn't take medicine on an empty stomach. Have a bite of this." He held out the triangle of toast and a drop of yolk fell on Morgan's pants. Morgan wiped it with his finger which he licked.

Morgan accepted Jack's toast, ate a couple of bites, and handed it back to Jack.

"You need more than that."

"No, I don't think I do. Eat yours before it gets cold."

Jack pulled a chair over near Morgan and ate the breakfast Abigail had prepared. When he finished, he set his plate on the tray and refilled his coffee. "I feel guilty about taking you on the picnic yesterday."

"It was my idea, remember?"

"Yeah, but I shouldn't have let you talk me into it. You weren't strong enough. It was too much."

"It wasn't, though. I felt good yesterday."

"Look at you today, though, barely able to walk, even with two people for support."

"That's not your fault. It would have happened anyway. And we would have missed yesterday. Besides, it was entirely my decision."

"Yeah, but you were on drugs. I shouldn't have let you decide."

"You think you could have talked me out of it? My thin place called to me and I responded."

"You and that damned mountain."

Morgan leaned back, rested the cup on his stomach, closed his eyes, and began breathing slowly. "Yeah, that damned lovely mountain."


Jack slipped the cup from Morgan's fingers and set it on the tray. He paced the room for a while and convinced himself it wasn't too early to start drinking. If Morgan were right, they had a long hard day ahead for all of them. At least Morgan had the peace morphine brought him. Jack opened a cabinet and found Morgan's prescription whiskey. He added two fingers worth to his coffee, took a sip, and added two more. He carried the bottle back to his chair and picked up the magazine.

After twenty pages about Heyrovsky's new method of chemical analysis and a Canadian doctor's miraculous results using insulin for treating diabetes—and several more Irish coffees—Jack threw the magazine against the wall, knocking over several canvases. "Screw science!"

"What's the matter?"

Damn, he'd woken Morgan. "I'm pissed that scientists are making all these discoveries, but can't save you."

Morgan struggled to lean up on one elbow. "I know. I've been through what you're going through."

"What do you mean?"

"When I first heard my diagnosis, I thought, 'That can't be true. I won't let it.'"

"I deserve a swift kick in the ass."

"Why is that?"

"I know you better than anyone. I should have seen something was wrong. If I hadn't been so stupid, we could have gotten you treatment sooner."

"How could you know? I live in this body, and even I wasn't aware of it."

"Well . . . I just should have."

"Why? You're no doctor."

"But I read a lot of science magazines, and they all have articles about cancer."

"Your science magazines aren't medical journals. Stop blaming yourself."

But he did blame himself. What could he do to make up for it except provide a friendly ear? "You know better than anybody that I'm no Freud, but if you want to talk about it, I've got something Freud didn't offer. Beer."

"Thanks, Jack, but you know I can't drink."

"Why the hell not? It isn't going to kill you."

Morgan chuckled. "You're right about that, but I'll pass."

"Whatever you decide. Just remember I'm here for you right up until you breathe your last."

"I know that. I love you too, man."

"If it was me, though, and I saw death was certain, I'd want a cold beer."

Morgan laughed. "And I'd give you one."

Beer was a good idea. He couldn't keep drinking Irish coffee—he wouldn't make it through his shift. When Morgan dozed off again, Jack slipped out to the springhouse and brought back a pail of beer. He thought that best. He didn't want to leave Morgan every time his glass went empty, as it was bound to be.

Morgan woke briefly, took another teaspoon of morphine, and dozed off again. Jack stuck with beer. By the time Peaches arrived to relieve him he had formulated a plan.

"Peaches, I made a decision. Tell everybody to get ready. We're going to your mother's church and pray for Morgan."

"Pray? Jack, you're not religious."

"Just because I don't frequent churches doesn't mean I don't believe in God."

"But you're also not Catholic, and Morgan is Jewish."

"Both of those things are true, but any God in a storm."

"We can pray right here."

"No, we need to take our case to God's house. All of us—the more petitioners the better. We'll outnumber Him."

"Oh, Jack, that's a nice idea, but priests can be a little . . . intractable. Maybe you should consider the protestant church. It's more likely to be empty on a weekday."

"Nah, the Presbyterians don't have all those little colored glass candles, no statues of Mary or saints. Why, except for Sunday, the place is as empty as a spinster's bed."

Peaches laughed.

"We'll light every candle the Catholic Church has. You and Cherie teach us a prayer to invoke whatever saint can give Morgan a little more time. Now go find the others and tell them to dress for church."

"We can't all go. Someone has to stay with Morgan."

"Bryce will do it. While we're pleading to the Catholic saints, he can be here saying some Hindu chant. We'll get everybody's god into it."

# CHAPTER 41

Abigail entered their bedroom and found Jack untying and retying his tie. He had on the suit he saved for weddings and funerals.

"Help me get this. My fingers seem all confused."

She came over and reached for the tie ends, and her eyes began to water. "Oh my, Jack!"

"What?"

"It's only nine-thirty and you smell like a brewery."

"I'm celebrating."

"What are you celebrating?"

"Any saint who will come to Mo's rescue."

Abigail finished the knot and pulled it extra tight against Jack's throat.

He inserted his finger in his collar and wiggled it looser. "You're not dressed."

"I am so."

"Not for church. Better get changed, time's wasting."

"Yes, Peaches told us. What's this all about?"

"Last hope doesn't mean no hope. It's time to get the Big Guy involved. We all go. We all plead our case for a few more days with Morgan."

She'd thought he had come to terms with all this. But this might just be the last gasp of Mr. Fixit. And the beer didn't help. "I don't think that's the way it works."

"It can't hurt. That's the best deal we're offered when the cards are stacked against us. Now, please dress. I'll get the car out of the garage."

"Wait! You're not planning to drive?"

"Well, there's no point in all of us walking. We don't want to be gone that long." Jack crossed the hall and rapped on Cyrus's door. "Cherie, you decent?"

"She's getting dressed in Peaches' room," Cyrus said.

"Good." Jack opened the door. "How about you, ready yet?"

"Oh, I don't want to go."

"Everybody's going, son. You know that saying, there's no atheist in the trenches. Well, it's time to demand Heaven send aid. Suit up. We're about to storm headquarters."

As Jack headed for Peaches' room, Abigail poked her head into Cyrus's doorway. "He's drunk. You're driving. Put on your navy-blue suit and shine your shoes."

Abigail heard Jack knock at Peaches' door. "How are you girls doing?"

"Almost finished," Cherie said.

"Ready to do a little horse trading with the priest?"

Cherie opened the door. "What's that mean?"

"Put some money in the coffer and stake claim to all the saints he's got."

She and Peaches came out wearing conservative dresses with matching hats. Their dresses were calf-length—short for Taos, but long for them. They'd do for church. Abigail joined them, and Cherie left to check on Cyrus.

"Morgan can't really walk to the privy," Peaches said. "Bryce asked if we could bring a chamber pot to the studio before we leave. In case Morgan needs it."

"He won't," Abigail said. "Morgan hasn't passed anything the last seven days. But I'll stop and explain that to Bryce on my way to the car."

* * *

In an alcove of the sanctuary, a rack held votive candles. Jack began lighting them one after the other. Peaches put a hand on his arm. "You're supposed to just light one."

"Not this time. We're going all in."

"And you're supposed to say a prayer when you light it."

"I'll set the fires. You and Cherie say the words."

"We need to put an offering in the box, too," Cherie said.

Jack pulled out a handful of coins, selected a twenty-dollar gold piece, and deposited it in the slot of a black metal box. "No reason to cheap-out, but twenty ought to buy the whole lot, wouldn't you say?"

Peaches laughed. "Yes, Jack, most people give a penny or a nickel."

"Well, desperate times, and all that. Tell me the words."

The prayer was in Latin and Jack stumbled through the first few tries. But the first rule of inebriated elocution is, if the words don't come out right, say them louder. Not that Jack was slurring, he was merely full of beer and shed of inhibitions.

The church, devoid of people since morning mass, now resounded with sweet prayers from the women and Jack's boisterous endeavor to imitate them. The priest entered from a door behind the altar.

Peaches stopped praying and put her hand over Jack's mouth. "Good morning, Padre." She genuflected, as did Cherie. Jack stood his ground.

The priest cocked his head, inviting further explanation.

Jack stepped forward. "How much for a service?"

"Mass," Peaches whispered.

"Mass, I mean. We've come for a mass."

"Morning mass has ended, but there is another this evening.  You're welcome to—"

"He may not be alive this evening.  We're looking for a more immediate intercession."

"We're speaking of your artist friend, yes?  Are you asking me to come to his house to conduct Last Rites?"

"We came more or less seeking intervention to keep him alive."

"What is the parishioner's full name?"

"Mordecai Silverstein," Jack said.

"It is?" Cyrus said.

Jack nodded his head.

The priest shook his head. "Silverstein? That sounds Jewish."

Jack leaned into the priest's face. "What of it?  Didn't Jesus worship the same God as Moses?"

"Well, a convert normally has to take catechism first, but if he's dying, I suppose I could give him the holy rites of baptism, first communion, and last rites—in that order, of course."

"Look, we're not here to try to get him into heaven. We think he's got that covered. We just want God to give him extra time."

Abigail put her hand on Jack's arm and pulled him away. "Father, we're not here to make trouble. We just came to pray. If you'd like to join us, that would be appreciated."

"Of course," said the priest. "What is the dying man's name, again?"

"Morgan Silver," Abigail said.

The priest said his prayer, made the sign of the cross and told them to go in peace.

"Wait a second," Jack said. "We haven't lit all the candles."

"What are you talking about?" the priest said.

"I want to light every one you got."

"Only one vigil light per person in need. Others may want to light a candle for their loved ones."

Jack eyed the rack of candles. "Hey, I dropped twenty dollars in there. Even if we raise the ante to twenty cents apiece, I reckon we've another eighty to go."

The priest took the box of matches from Jack. "It's time to take your leave."

Jack reached for the box, but Abigail hooked her arm in his and steered him toward the exit. "Thank you for your prayer, Father."

Peaches and Cherie genuflected before the altar and left with Cyrus.

Cyrus drove while Jack snoozed against Abigail's shoulder. When they arrived home, Bryce came out to greet them. "How'd it go?"

Peaches kissed him. "We went, we prayed, we came home. How's Morgan?"

"Still sleeping."

"Jack's passed out. Abigail could use your help to get him out of the car. I'll watch Morgan."

Bryce walked to the rear passenger door, reached in, drew Jack's arm across his shoulder, and pulled him out the car door. "Cyrus get on Jack's other side."

"Take him in the house, and let him sleep it off," Abigail said.

Jack tried to shake them off. "No, I want to see Morgan."

"He's asleep," Bryce said. "Just do as Abigail says. I'll come and get you when Morgan wakes."

"You promise?"

"Cross my heart."

Jack mumbled, "Morgan did wake us awful early. I *could* use a nap. Just a short one though."

When they reached Jack's room, Cyrus and Bryce sat him on the edge of the bed and worked his suit coat off him. He fell back onto the mattress and Abigail pulled off his shoes.

"Abigail, lie down with me," Jack said.

"Maybe after a bit," she said. "You sleep now."

# CHAPTER 42

Jack was still sleeping off his church debacle, so Abigail took the next turn to sit with Morgan. When she entered his studio, he was awake, talking quietly with Peaches and Bryce. Abigail kissed him on the forehead and took measure of the remaining morphine. "I'll be right back. I'm going to send Cyrus into town for another bottle. We don't want to run out in the middle of the night."

"I'll tell him," Peaches said. "I need to pick up something for myself, and I can ride along." She kissed Morgan and hurried out the door.

Bryce started to follow her, but Morgan said, "Wait, Bryce, don't go yet."

"You need something?"

"Yes. Abigail, look in my secretary. There's an envelope marked 'Will.' I want you two to witness it."

She opened the desk and found it next to his bank book. Her hand trembled a bit when she picked it up. She had so often gotten frustrated with Jack over his fear of Morgan's death. But now that it was growing closer, the reality of it was beginning to hit her. "When did you write this?"

"The day before the picnic. I was going to have it witnessed before we went up there, but it slipped my mind."

"Good thing you didn't die there like you planned," Bryce said.

Abigail rebuked him with a sharp glance.

"Good thing," Morgan said. With an effort, he scooted up higher on the chaise lounge so he was almost sitting up. "Abigail, sit here. Bryce, bring your chair closer. I want to make sure you're both all right with what I've decided."

"We will be," Bryce said.

Abigail perched on the edge of the chaise and squeezed Morgan's hand. "That goes without saying."

He smiled. "When we were young, I pushed you into the arms of Bryce because I was afraid you were thinking of remarrying, and I wasn't ready."

She stroked Morgan's cheek with her fingers. "You weren't deciding anything. I always chose my own men."

"And I didn't object," Bryce said.

Abigail slapped Bryce playfully.

Morgan reached for his water. Abigail helped him. He took a sip and handed her the glass. "But after you and Jack married, you brought me back into your life, and in these past decades we've been a family of sorts. A life for each other—"

A tear slipped down her left cheek. "And you for us."

"I know you're financially sound, and you'll take care of Jack."

"I will."

"My parents are dead. I don't have any close relatives. Maybe there are some distant cousins, but the family cut me off for not being orthodox enough, and I wouldn't know these hypothetical cousins if I met them on the street. My friends are my real family."

Abigail furrowed her brow. "Where is all this going?"

"All I leave behind are these paintings stacked around the room. I could give them to a museum if one wanted them."

"We could open a small museum here, a legacy to you," Bryce said.

"Who would administer it? You? Abigail? I can't ask her to take on more work than she already has. No, I decided their best use is to provide for the next generation—if that's all right with you. I mean Abigail and Jack are solvent, and Bryce, you have your trust fund."

Bryce nodded.

"But everyone should get something. I figure that each of my family—you, Abigail, Jack, Cyrus, Peaches, and Cherie—can choose one painting that inspires you, that tickles your fancy, that you wish to hold as a memory of me. The remainder I'm going to entrust to Peaches to sell in her gallery and divide the proceeds equally between Cherie, Cyrus, and herself."

Abigail began to cry. She couldn't help herself.

Morgan patted her hand. "When you stop crying, I need you to witness the will. Bryce, you too." He patted his pockets. "It seems I haven't anything to sign with. Bryce, there's a fountain pen and a bottle of ink in the desk."

Bryce found the pen, filled it, and removed the dishes from the breakfast tray to give Morgan something to write on. He set the tray across Morgan's legs.

Morgan pried the envelope from Abigail's hand. "Pull yourself together. We'll have this business finished in two shakes of a lamb's tail." He opened the envelope flap, removed the will, turned to the last page and signed his name—twice—Morgan Silver and Mordecai Silverstein. He handed the pen to Bryce. "Your turn."

Bryce signed and offered Abigail the pen. She hesitated.

Morgan squeezed her hand. "You'll be all right. Sign and we're done."

She pressed her finger to her upper lip, sniffed, then took the pen from Bryce and added her name to the document.

Bryce lifted the tray off Morgan's lap and re-stacked the dishes on it.

Morgan folded the pages, put them back in the envelope, and gave it to Abigail. "You hold on to this until . . . you know, after."

A sob burst from her, and she fell across Morgan, in a tight embrace. Bryce picked up the breakfast tray and headed out the door. "I'll give you two some privacy."

* * *

Jack sat up and shook the cobwebs from his mind. How could something so mule-headed seem like a good idea at the time? He made his way to the kitchen, lit a burner on the kerosene stove, and reheated some cold coffee.

Bryce came in, "I thought I smelled coffee."

"It's old."

Bryce poured a cup and tasted it. "It'll do."

"Kind of like the old days. Remember that little kitchen in the back of our store?"

Bryce nodded. "Never wasted leftover coffee—always warmed it up again."

"Who's with Morgan?"

"Abigail."

"Where are the girls?"

"They drove into Taos with Cyrus to get more drugs for Morgan but haven't come back."

"We should have stopped at the apothecary on our way home from church."

Bryce chuckled. "You were in no condition for side trips. Cyrus and I had to carry you from the car."

Jack set his cup in the sink. "Well, I'm up now, more or less. I better go spell Abigail." He rinsed his mouth out with water and spit in the sink, then plucked two mint leaves from a flowerpot on the sideboard and chewed them.

"I'll come with you," Bryce said.

When he and Bryce entered the studio, Jack saw Abigail lying next to Morgan with her eyes open. Morgan had his eyes closed, snoring softly, with one arm draped across Abigail. She gently slipped it aside and stood.

Jack took her in his arms and kissed her. "I'll take the next shift."

Abigail turned back to Morgan and ran her fingers across his forehead. "Okay, I'm going to start dinner. It could be a long night, and we'll all need to eat."

"I'll stay with Jack," Bryce said.

She kissed Jack again, hugged Bryce, and left.

A few moments later Morgan's eyes fluttered open. He tried to stand, but couldn't.

"You need to use the privy?" Bryce said. "I told them to bring you a chamber pot."

"Not what I was going for. I need to finish that." He pointed at the canvas that had sat unfinished for weeks. "But I can't make it over there. Maybe if you scoot the easel next to me and bring my palette, I can paint it from here."

Jack moved the easel as near to Morgan's couch as the legs would allow while Bryce got the paint and brushes. Morgan made several attempts, but even holding the brush by the end of its handle he could barely reach and had no control over his strokes.

"Wait, a minute." Jack pushed the easel out of the way. "Bryce, you and I will hold the canvas over Morgan's bed so he can reach."

Jack's scheme worked. Morgan scooted further up the back of the chaise which made it easier to move his brush across the canvas. But he kept nodding off. After fifteen minutes he'd only added a few ragged strokes. With a heavy sigh, he said, "That will have to do." He scrawled an illegible signature in the lower corner and waved for them to take it away.

They set the painting on the easel, and Bryce took the brush and palette from Morgan. He dropped the brush in a jar of turpentine and dragged the easel out of the way.

Jack moved the chair close to Morgan's bed and sat down. Morgan reached over and patted his friend. "Jack, I have something to tell you. I wrote a will."

Jack frowned.

"Now, don't start. Bryce and Abigail witnessed it while you were sleeping. I gave it to her for safekeeping, but I didn't let her read it. She only knows half of what it says."

Bryce cleared his throat.

"I want to be cremated. I didn't have the courage to tell Abigail because she kept weeping the whole time we were signing it."

Jack blanched. "What?"

Morgan nodded. "Then take my ashes to the mountain where we were yesterday and scatter them off the cliff."

"Doesn't Jewish law forbid cremation?" Bryce said.

Morgan shrugged. "I haven't been a practicing Jew for twenty years. There's no reason to start when I'm dead."

Jack knitted his brow. "I don't think New Mexico has a crematory. At least I've never heard of one."

"I trust you guys. You'll figure something out."

# CHAPTER 43

Cherie rapped on Abigail and Jack's bedroom door, and said in a hoarse whisper, "Abigail, can I come in?"

"What is it?" Abigail said.

Cherie opened the door a crack. "Will you come and check on Morgan?"

In the evening hours, Morgan had been brought into the house and helped into his bed. The household had continued to take turns sitting with him, and it was currently Cherie's watch.

Abigail rubbed her eyes. "What time is it?"

"Near to dawn—about five-thirty, I'd guess."

"Is Morgan all right?"

"That's what I want you to tell me. He hasn't stirred in a while."

Abigail slid out of bed and fumbled for her dressing gown. "I'm not surprised. He's been drinking his morphine like sarsaparilla."

Jack sat up. "What's going on?"

Abigail patted his shoulder. "I'm going to check on Morgan."

Jack got out of bed. He was naked and didn't even seem to notice. Cherie turned away and started back toward Morgan's room.

Abigail followed her. "Is Cyrus with him?"

"No, just me. Cyrus went to bed around three." Cherie walked to Morgan's side and stooped over, afraid to touch him. "He's the same. I can't see any breathing."

Abigail put her hand on his forehead. "He's cool, but not cold. It could be the drug."

Jack came in. He was shirtless, but had at least put on pants. He scratched the hairs on his chest. "Is he all right?"

Abigail straightened up. "I don't know. I've never seen anyone die before."

Marcel's memory intruded. But Cherie hadn't seen him die, just later when his face was the color of eggplant. Morgan looked like . . . he was sleeping. She turned to Jack. "You took care of my mother. Surely you knew when she was dead."

"No, the doctor did that. My only part in it was calling the undertaker."

"Then we should call the doctor," Cherie said.

Abigail hesitated. "I hate to call him at this hour. What if Morgan's just deeply drugged?"

"Even more reason to call the doctor."

"But if it's the drugs, shouldn't we try to revive him?" Jack said.

Abigail shook her head. "Not if it's keeping his pain at bay. He doesn't need to suffer unnecessarily."

"Let me get Bryce," Jack said. "He knows more about drugs than the rest of us."

Jack left and returned with Bryce. Peaches came too. "Is Morgan . . . ?" she said.

Cherie choked, ready to burst into tears. "We can't tell." She turned to Bryce. "What do you think?"

He studied Morgan from a distance. "Not sure."

Jack paced the room. "If it's morphine, Bryce, what can counteract it?"

"I only ever took peyote. We better ask the doctor."

"I'll make the call," Abigail said, and left to use the telephone.

Cherie saw Cyrus watching from the doorway and went to him for comfort. She picked up his arm and pulled it around her shoulder, nestling under his arm.

Cyrus gave her a squeeze and then stepped forward. "I'll check him out."

"Are you all right with this?" Cherie asked.

"Yeah. It's different with someone you know, someone who goes quietly, surrounded by friends. And I guess I'm the only one who's actually seen a dead person outside of a coffin. I'll do it."

Not exactly true. She'd told Cyrus about Marcel, but not that she'd been the one to find him. Her shoulders began to convulse, and then unexplainably, she got the hiccups.


Cyrus pounded Cherie on her back, but it did nothing to stop her hiccups. Morgan was waiting. He kissed Cherie's forehead and started toward Morgan's bed. With each step forward the distance doubled. Handling a dead body was the last thing he wanted to do. He forced himself to take another step and then hesitated. His friend, mentor, second father lay immobile on the feather mattress—a shallow depression in a cloud of white linen. He glanced back at Cherie. Her lips quivered as she met his eyes and nodded encouragement. This was the first time he'd faced death since returning from France. He could never have gotten this far without her. Cyrus took the final step.

He placed his fingers beneath Morgan's nose and sensed no movement of air. On the battlefield, corpses stared wide-eyed at the gray sky. Morgan's eyes were closed.

Reluctantly he sniffed the body. Stale sweat, slightly sweet, not the stink of shit he remembered with horror. Of course, not having ate or drunk for days, maybe Morgan had nothing to let go of.

Only one test left. He lifted Morgan's eyelids and peered into the sightless black pupils. When he let go, the eyes stayed open.

Cyrus drew the sheet over Morgan's face. "Someone tell Mom not to bother the doctor."

Jack's voice cracked. "I'll go." He left the room and descended the stairs two at a time.

Cherie ran to Cyrus and embraced him. Peaches, weeping, hugged them both. Bryce patted Cyrus's back soothingly. "You did a hard thing. Well done."

# CHAPTER 44

Everyone milled around the kitchen stove waiting for the coffee. It was crowded, but no one wanted to leave the others' company.

"It's too early to call the undertaker," Abigail said. "We ought to wait until at least eight."

"I agree," Jack said. "Besides, we've got Morgan's will to read first."

Abigail frowned. "Oh, let's wait until after the funeral."

Bryce cleared his throat. "It would be better not to."

Tears ran down Peaches' cheeks. "Do we have to?"

Bryce nodded. "Yeah. He left instructions."

Jack picked up the coffeepot. "Let's do it in the dining room. Cherie, set out cups and saucers. Abigail, where did you put Morgan's will?"

They took their seats and Jack poured while Abigail fetched the envelope. Jack's hands were shaking, and he spilled coffee in a couple of their saucers. Abigail returned and took her seat next to Jack. "I'm sorry. I didn't bake anything to go with the coffee."

Peaches patted her hand. "No one expects it. I'll help you make breakfast in a few minutes."

Abigail opened the envelope and removed its contents. She skimmed the pages and threw them on the table. "Oh, hell no!"

"It's what he wanted," Bryce said.

Peaches swiveled the pages toward her and read them. "Cremated?"

"What?" Cherie said. "Let me see." Peaches handed her Morgan's will. She held it so Cyrus could read along with her.

Abigail pulled her long hair into a ponytail, wrapped it around her fingers, and threaded the end through, forming a loose chignon. "I don't care what this will says. He wasn't right when he wrote it."

"You know that's not true," Bryce said. "I was there, too. He was perfectly lucid when he described how he wanted his affairs settled. There was no fault in his reasoning. You can't say he was of a sound mind in one part, and not in the other. In fact, his mental state was so clear, that he had the presence of mind not to tell you at that time."

Jack wrapped his arms around her. "It's true. Morgan told Bryce and me that he hadn't shared this part of his will with you to protect your feelings."

"It doesn't matter. Taos hasn't got a crematory. In fact, I don't think there's one in all of New Mexico or an undertaker who would do such a deed."

"We told him that," Jack said. "But he said we would figure it out."

"Besides," Bryce said. "Where are you going to bury him? The Catholics aren't going to plant a Jew in their cemetery. The Protestants wouldn't be much happier with it."

Abigail burst into tears. "We'll bury him here."

Jack held her, and rocked her, and rubbed her back.

Cherie looked at the will again. "He seems determined to have his remains taken to his thin place."

"Cherie!" Peaches said.

"He says right here, we are his only family. If this is what he wanted . . ."

"But he never said how." Peaches turned to Bryce. "What do you think?"

"I believe Mark Twain can answer that." Bryce went to Jack's library and returned with the voluminous *Following the Equator*. He consulted the table of contents and located the section he was looking for. "Twain observed many Hindu cremations in Banaras and wrote about them." He turned the page. "Look here's even a photo of how the pyre's constructed."

"That's disgusting," Abigail said.

"No, it's information we need. Give me a minute to learn what else we need to do." Bryce scanned the pages.

Peaches stood up and gently pulled Abigail from Jack's arms. "Let's go make breakfast."

Abigail frowned. "I doubt anyone will have the stomach for it after this conversation."

Jack and Bryce huddled over Twain's book. Cherie and Cyrus stood behind them, looking over their shoulders.

"It says to wrap him in a white sheet," Jack said.

"That won't be a problem," Bryce said. "We'll tell the undertaker it's a Jewish custom. He won't know the difference."

Jack nodded. "I'll tell him we want a plain wood box—something that burns well."

Bryce shook his head. "I'd leave out the burn part. But plain is good, you can even tell him we want pine."

"Are you going to talk to him?" Cherie said.

Jack shrugged. "I'll have to. Abigail's too distraught."

"She's not alone," Cherie said. "If she wasn't a hair's breadth from going topsy-turvy, another of us would have."

Bryce continued reading. "Twain says the son of the deceased lights the pyre."

"Morgan didn't have a son," Jack said.

Bryce grinned. "That you know of—"

"I'm sure."

Bryce looked over his shoulder at Cyrus. "I guess you would be the nearest thing to a son, then."

Cyrus trembled. "I . . . can't. I'm sorry"

Cherie drew him close to her.

"Have either of you smelled men burning after a flame-thrower?  I have, and I . . . just . . . No.  It would set me back too far and undo whatever good Cherie has done me."

Bryce grimaced. "I'm sorry, Cyrus.  I hadn't thought about that.  It would be unfair to ask you."

"Oh, hell," Jack said. "I'll do it."

# CHAPTER 45

Abigail had been right about breakfast. Hardly anyone touched their food. While Peaches cleared the table, she met with Jack and Bryce in the parlor. "He has to have a funeral service."

Jack frowned. "At what church? Who will we get to officiate? That Catholic priest we met the other day? I think he's more likely to have us arrested. Or maybe we call Mrs. Wentworth and ask if her Protestant minister will do it? I don't think so."

Abigail dabbed her eyes and blew her nose. "We have to do something. He had a lot of friends in Taos who will want to pay their respects."

"We'll have a home funeral," Bryce said. "Lay him out in the parlor for viewing, then let everyone think his body is being shipped back east afterwards."

Abigail slumped into the armchair. Bryce hadn't changed, still quick to make up plausible lies. The people in town were their friends. It felt wrong to deceive them, but they couldn't tell them, either. Finally, she looked up and nodded. "We'll hold the funeral here."

Cyrus appeared in the doorway. "Cherie sat up with Morgan until he—well, she never slept. So, we're going to lie down for a bit before people start pouring in. Jack, you and Bryce wake me when you're ready to . . ."

"Yes," Abigail said. "You two need some rest."

Cyrus started to leave and turned back. "Oh, and the undertaker's outside."

She wrung her hands. "Jack, you and Bryce deal with him. I'll start making telephone calls."

Jack invited the undertaker in, told him they planned a home service. "We just want you to wash the body, put it in a white shroud, and a plain box."

The old vulture looked sorely disappointed.

"We're not being cheap," Bryce said. "It's a Jewish custom."

"If this is truly what you want, it might be wise to keep him iced. I can provide ice for a small additional fee."

"No, thanks," Jack said. "We'll take care of that."

The undertaker turned his nose up and left, promising to return later in the morning with a rough pine coffin, a white shroud, and a bill for his services.

* * *

Cherie was already in bed by the time Cyrus returned to his room. He fell in beside her. They kissed briefly, embraced, and both fell asleep almost immediately.

Cyrus wasn't sure how long he'd slept. The sun outside was higher now, but he couldn't guess the time. He'd been vaguely aware of the phone ringing throughout the morning, not quite enough to wake him. Cherie, apparently not bothered by any of it, kept snoring. He didn't know women did that.

He heard the undertaker's wagon return, and men's footsteps on the stairway and in the hall. He doubled up his pillow behind his head and waited for someone to knock. No one did. The footsteps passed his door again, back down the way they'd come. He turned on his side and kissed Cherie's ear. This is where he wanted to be. No reason to leap into that business downstairs until Jack needed him.

He stared at the ceiling until the undertaker's wagon left, then eased away from Cherie and sat up on the edge of the bed. Jack'd come for him soon now. May as well get shaved and dressed. He poured water into the basin and splashed his face. He unfolded his razor and began stropping it. A few long strokes usually did the job.

Glancing in the mirror, he rubbed the stubble on his chin and caught the reflection of Cherie standing behind him. He laid the razor on the bureau and turned to take her in his arms. "Did I wake you? I'm sorry. Go back to bed."

"No, I'm rested enough." She kissed him on the mouth. When they parted she ran her fingers along his cheek.

"I know. It feels rough," he said. "I was just about to shave."

She smiled. "Let me."

"What?"

"Shave you. I've shaved a man before. You'll enjoy it."

He wasn't sure about that.

She pushed him down onto the chair. "Trust me?"

He nodded, but his heart raced and his leg jittered. Having somebody put a blade to his neck . . . his worst nightmare.

Cherie picked up his shaving mug. A round piece of soap lay in the bottom. She wet the shaving brush and swirled it in the mug until a froth of white foam filled the cup. Cherie painted him with shaving soap, easily twice as much as he would have used. He must look like Santa Claus.

She picked up the open razor. Light from the window glinted off its freshly honed edge.

Cyrus swallowed a lump in his throat.

Cherie steadied his head with her left hand, and turned the hand holding the razor different angles, as if undecided where to start. Her hand moved toward his neck.

He saw a Hun's hand. He grabbed her wrist and bent it away from him.

"Ouch!"

He let her go and hid his face, getting shaving soap on his hands.

Cherie laid the razor on the dresser and pulled his hands down. "I'm sorry. This was a poor idea on my part."

Cyrus felt tears collect at the brink of spilling out. He swiped his arm across his eyes, getting lather on that, too.

Cherie laughed. "You're a mess. It's my fault. Let me." She pulled the sleeve of her nightgown over her hand and wiped the shaving soap off his arm.

He grasped her wrists, this time with a gentler hold. "What are you doing?"

"I slathered you pretty good. I'm clearing it off."

"You'll get it all over your gown. There's a towel right there next to the basin."

"Oh. I hadn't noticed. Doesn't matter, this gown needs to be washed anyhow."

He let go of her, retrieved the towel, and wiped soap off his hands. He took her hands in his again and looked into her eyes. Deep brown eyes he loved so much. Words he needed to say choked him. "You asked me to trust you. I do . . . But I failed. I'm so sorry. We've come so far, but I couldn't let you put a blade near my throat without going berserk." He hung his head.

Cherie put her fingers beneath his chin and lifted his face to meet her eyes. "No. It's my fault. I was only thinking it'd be intimate. I didn't consider how frightening it could be." She picked up the razor and handed it to him. "Here. You shave and I'll watch. It'll be just as much fun."

He doubted that was true. He'd spoiled the moment. But hell, Morgan's death had started the day on the wrong foot. Here he was worrying about himself when everyone around him was ass-deep in their own grief. He put his arm around Cherie and pulled her to him. "Okay. I'll handle the razor and you watch how." He kissed her, leaving a mustache of shaving cream above her lip.

Cyrus gripped the razor with a sure, steady hand and made the first stroke, removing the whiskers on his right cheek. He swished the blade in the basin of water and said to Cherie's watchful eyes. "I don't know about you, but as soon as this cremation is over, I'm ready to leave for Paris."

She threw her arms around him and squeezed.

"Careful, I've got a razor in my hand."

She laughed. "Better in your hand than mine."

When he finished shaving, they started to dress. "I'm just going to put on yesterday's clothes," he said. "I promised Jack I'd help him and Bryce find some dead trees we could cut up for . . ." His voice cracked.

Cherie kissed him and stripped off her nightgown. "Makes sense. I'm sure Abigail and Peaches will need my help in the kitchen. I'll just put on my clothes from last night and change later—into what I don't know. I didn't bring anything suitable for a funeral."

"Mom has black dresses. I'm sure she'll lend you one."

Cyrus waited for her. Jack hadn't called him yet, and he was in no hurry to go downstairs where the coffin with Morgan's shrouded body had been set up in the parlor.

Cherie buttoned her dress, ran a comb through her bobbed hair, and opened the bedroom door. He guessed it was time.

They went down together. He avoided the parlor and found Jack and Bryce. "Ready to go?"

Jack nodded and started the truck. Bryce was already in the front seat. Three of them together would be a squeeze. "I'll ride in back."

"You sure?" Jack said. "With no load to weigh it down, it could get rough."

Cyrus nodded and climbed up on the bed of the truck.

"Hold on tight," Jack yelled as he put the Ford in gear. They drove along a forest road searching for dried, fallen trees. It wasn't hard—dead trees were plentiful.

While they were cutting wood, Cyrus had an idea. "Why don't we build the pyre on the edge of the cliff?"

"I like it," Bryce said. "Morgan believed it was a sacred space, so why not cremate him there? Plus, when the fire is out, we can just scoop his ashes over the ledge."

Jack shook his head. "The entire valley can see a fire on the mountain. Besides, there are too many trees there. We might set the whole forest ablaze."

Bryce smiled. "Morgan might like that."

"No, he wouldn't. I know a safer place."

When the back of Jack's truck was nearly full, Bryce said they had enough wood. Jack drove them to a deserted area of rocks and sand well off the road. Bryce studied the photograph of the Banaras pyre in Twain's book and directed them as they wove a rectangular nest of interlocking logs. Once Bryce seemed satisfied, he laid the book on the passenger seat and helped scavenge tumbleweeds and other dry brush for kindling. These, they tucked beneath and between the logs.

By the time he, Jack, and Bryce returned home, the women had bathed and put on black dresses. While they'd been gone, Cherie and Peaches had busied themselves in the kitchen preparing food for the wake. His mother had telephoned everyone in town who needed to be notified, asking those she spoke with to call others. Word spread, and she said soon so many sympathy calls were coming in that it tied up her line.

Cyrus found Cherie in the parlor but didn't go in. Morgan was there. He watched from the doorway as she nailed a length of black cotton fabric around lip of the coffin with tiny brads.

Cherie spotted him. "You're back!"

Cyrus did his best to smile, but it was weak and he knew it. Cherie melted his heart, but the corpse beside her had meant more to him than his father. He'd be missed in ways Cyrus couldn't explain, not even to himself.

"How was it? Are you okay?"

He shrugged. "I will be. What are you doing?"

"The esthetics of that undertaker's crude pine box offended me. I'm skirting it with this material I found in Abigail's sewing room."

"You know we're going to burn that box as soon as the funeral is over."

"That doesn't mean it has to look like a packing crate until then." The hammer struck her thumb. "Damn it!"

For a split second he hesitated, then crossed to her and reached for the hammer. "Let me."

She held it away from him. "I can do this. You guys need to take your baths. People will be arriving soon."

# CHAPTER 46

Abigail's brother-in-law, Walter, and his sons were the first to arrive. "Abigail, I'm so sorry for your loss," Walter said. Walter, Jr. and Jimmy each kissed her and said, "Sorry, Auntie."

She introduced her nephews to Peaches and Cherie. "You may not remember the Romero girls; they were ahead of you in school."

Cyrus slid between Cherie and his cousins and shook their hands.

Bryce came in. "Jack's almost dressed."

Abigail made introductions.

Walter stuck out his hand. "I remember you."

Bryce shook his hand. "And I you. I was sorry to hear about Penelope."

Walter's lips tightened, and he briefly dipped his head.

Peaches brought a dozen of Morgan's smaller paintings in from the studio and placed them around the room. It took her two trips. Three stood on the credenza, leaning against the wall. Several more balanced on the piano. The rest she set anywhere she could find space.

Bryce wrapped his arms around her waist and whispered, "It looks nice."

Soon the house filled with mourners, and the crowd spilled onto the porch and lawn. It seemed every woman in town brought food. The dining room table was full, and dishes born by latecomers threatened to overflow the kitchen. Jack excused himself, and he and Cyrus carried sawhorses and planks from the garage to create a makeshift table on the lawn. Cherie came outside with tablecloths, and Cyrus helped her spread them over the boards. She turned to nearby guests and sent them to the kitchen to fetch the comestibles they'd contributed.

Jack wanted to have some men help him move Morgan's coffin onto the porch, but Abigail nixed the idea. "We can say some words on the porch, but people who want to pass by the coffin can just do it in here."

When the flow of arrivals seemed to have stopped, Bryce ushered those Morgan considered his family onto the porch and clapped to get the crowd's attention.

"I know some of you, most I don't. My name is Bryce Holloway. Jack and I grew up with Morgan in New York City and we came to Taos together in aught-four. There is a prayer Mo's people say for the dead, Kaddish. Does anyone here speak Hebrew?"

No one volunteered.

"All right, then, I'm going to read it in English. When I finish, anyone who wants to say a kind word about Morgan, or share a memory can do so. After everyone's said their piece, we'll have a bite to eat." He looked at Jack. "What's the protocol for Kaddish? Does everyone bow their heads?"

Jack shrugged. "Probably. It's a prayer."

"Let us bow our heads," Bryce said to the crowd. He read from a sheet of paper onto which he'd copied the lines. The prayer wasn't that long, but about every other verse ended with "Amen," and some would look up, thinking it was over. To indicate that he'd finally finished, he cleared throat and asked who wanted to speak next.

Quite a few did—Morgan had been well liked. After those who wanted to say something had their turn, and everyone ate a plate or two of food,

Jack got itchy. He thanked everyone for coming but said they needed to get going, as it was time for the family to take Morgan's body onward. A few friends wanted a final moment with Morgan, but the rest of the crowd left in an orderly fashion, except four ladies who helped Abigail put away the leftovers. There was too much food for the icebox, so Cyrus and Cherie carried perishables to the springhouse. The women offered to help, but Cyrus knew Jack didn't want anyone to see his beer, so he politely declined.

Walter and his sons held back, waiting to help carry the coffin to Jack's truck. Cherie tore the skirting material from the brads, and the men set the lid on. She followed them to the truck. The men pushed the box as close to the cab as it would go. Cherie handed Jack the black material. "Here, cover it with this."

Walter offered to follow them to the depot.

"No, point in that," Jack said. "We'll manage fine." He shook Walter's hand. "But thanks for coming. I know it meant a lot to Abigail." He tugged Cyrus's sleeve, and they walked Walter and his boys to their wagon.

Walter climbed up and picked up the reins. Walter, Jr. and Jimmy got in. "You need anything, just send word."

Jack waved. "Thanks. And don't be a stranger."

Walter unset the brake and snapped the reins.

Jack waited until they were out of sight, then got shovels and a washtub from the garage. "Cyrus, drive the ladies in your mom's car. Cherie, tell Peaches and Abigail we're ready to go. And bring some blankets and whiskey, we could be out there a while. I've never cremated anyone before. Don't know how long it will take."

In one final act, Jack walked into the studio and returned with Morgan's final painting. He opened the driver's door of the truck and wedged it behind the seat.

# CHAPTER 47

The women of Taos, Abigail foremost among them, did not wilt at the prospect of doing a man's task. So when Cyrus parked the Pierce-Arrow behind Jack's truck and went to help unload Morgan's coffin, Abigail, Peaches, and Cherie joined shoulder-to-shoulder with the men, carrying it over the rocky ground. She drew the line, however, when the cover was pried off to lift the shrouded form from the box and place it on the log pile. Even though Morgan's body was wrapped in a white sheet, the women stepped away and busied themselves folding the black drape that now lay in a heap at the back of the truck.

Bryce took Morgan's head, Jack the feet, and they carried him to the nest they had prepared. Lovingly, they laid him in a swale they had left in the pile. Meanwhile, Cyrus got a hammer from the truck and began knocking apart the pine box. Jack and Bryce laid the long boards over Morgan like a down quilt over a sleeping babe. Cherie and Peaches picked up the shorter pieces and stood them against the side of the pile.

Jack got a can of gasoline from the truck and splashed it over the wood, wetting it from one end to the other. He set the can down a safe distance away and looked at the others. "Ready?"

Bryce began to chant AUM, and Peaches joined in. Jack fished a match from his pocket and struck it against the bottom of his shoe. The match flared, and he tossed it on the pile.

With a *whoosh*, a great conflagration blazed skyward. Jack jumped back.

Cyrus began shaking violently, ran to the car, and curled up in the backseat.

Cherie raced to comfort him. "I was afraid this is what would happen."

Abigail glanced between the car and her husband. Jack came and stood behind her, kneading her shoulders. "Maybe I should have used less gas."

"You think?"

He kissed the back of her head. "I'll be right back."

Jack brought Morgan's final painting from the truck and threw it on the fire. The canvas hissed, warped and charred instantly. The stretchers separated and fell into the flames.

Peaches cried out, "What did you do that for?"

"Because it wasn't anything near what he could do, and if he hadn't been doped, he'd never have wanted it seen. He said we each got one of his paintings. Well, that was mine."

The bonfire continued to roar. Beneath the odor of gasoline fumes and the turpentine smell of burning pine boards emerged the scent of roasting flesh.

Abigail glanced at the car. "I'm going to take Cyrus home." She kissed Jack goodbye. "Come get us when you're ready to take his ashes to the mountain. Peaches, do you want to come with us? If you prefer to stay longer, you can ride back with the guys."

Peaches embraced Bryce, wetting his shirt with her tears. "I'm going with them."

He kissed her forehead. "I understand."

Abigail walked toward the driver's door of the Pierce-Arrow, so Peaches got in the front passenger seat. But Abigail continued to the rear door. She slipped into the backseat next to Cyrus and stroked his hair. "Do you want me to drive?"

Cyrus sat up and wiped his face. "No, I can . . . I'm all right."

She let him out and slid back in next to Cherie, whom she clutched to her bosom, kissing the top of her head.

Cyrus turned on the ignition and the Pierce-Arrow's six cylinders responded. He backed the car in a half-circle, shifted into first gear, and, following the tracks they had made coming in, crept across gravel wasteland out to the highway.

* * *

As they rode back home Cherie allowed Abigail to continue to hold her. "Morgan was a true gentleman."

Abigail smiled. "He was."

"Some lesser monkey would have pleasured himself in my vulnerability."

"What do you mean, dear?"

"After Mother died, I was staying with Reverend Sullivan while Peaches was still contagious. Morgan lived on the other side of the building, in back of his and Jack's store. In the middle of the night, I slipped quietly out of Rebecca's quarters, and headed straight for Morgan's cot."

She wiped her nose. "I didn't want to sleep alone, was all. I missed sharing my bed with Peaches. But I was no virgin, so I was prepared for anything when I got in next to him. What happened was, Morgan shot up like I'd electrocuted him, pushed me off his bed, and said, 'Cherry, you can't sleep here. It's a terrible thing you're going through, but this isn't a solution.'"

Cherie whimpered. "That was the closest I ever came to having relations with Morgan."

Abigail patted her soothingly. "No, Morgan wouldn't have. You were what, sixteen? But he kept your secret. I lived with the man all these years, and he never mentioned your escapade."

Peaches turned in her seat. "Morgan stuck to his own code. All the times I posed for him, all of his trips to New York, I never could get him in my bed —even when I was twenty and thirty. Bryce on the other hand, you just needed to brush up against him and he was ready to go."

Abigail laughed for the first time today. "Yes, those three were quite the phenomenon when they arrived in Taos. I don't know how many women they slept with. I suspect any who wanted."

"But not me," Cherie said.

"Maybe not, but he cared about you girls deeply. It was Morgan who asked me to teach you about birth control. He was so worried one of you would get pregnant and your mother would sell you to that pimp, Sneed."

Cyrus spoke over his shoulder. "Mom, I don't remember Mrs. Romero dying. Where was I?"

"You stayed with Aunt Penelope and Uncle Walter. I didn't want to take you to her funeral for fear that seeing the dead mother of someone you knew would be too frightening."

# CHAPTER 48

The fire evolved according to its nature, converting dross to heat and light. Daylight waned. Jack and Bryce spread out the blankets Abigail had left them and stretched out on their backs. A star emerged, and then another. The darkness deepened until the Milky Way shone like a great swath of confetti strewn across the night.

"Do you think Morgan's up there somewhere?" Jack said.

"No. Do you?"

Jack raised up on his elbows. "No, I think that's just stars and planets so far away they appear as points of light. But I suspect there is a heaven, and I'm sure Morgan's there. It's just invisible to us."

"Is it? What about Thin Places Morgan and Rebecca talked about?"

"Oh, if you're not completely hardened, you sense something mystical when you're standing on the precipice. But I don't think you can step into it. It's more like being able to sense impending rain by something in the air. Nothing you can smell exactly. Some quality you're aware of, but you'd be hard pressed to name."

Bryce nodded. "A mystery that makes itself felt, but defies the five senses."

"That's what I like about this scientist, Einstein. He understands eternal time and space although he cannot physically go to those places."

"That's why I study the great yogis. As boys we were taught heaven was above. The ancient yogis describe a path ascending seven plexuses in the spine and brain to a realm of consciousness above the physical realm. According to them, the real Thin Place is within us."

"Yeah, I can see that."

Jack and Bryce silently watched the constellations move across the heaven.

* * *

After the fire collapsed into a mound of hot coals, Bryce recalled Twain saying the Hindu fire keepers broke up any remaining bones with a large pole.

With a sigh, Jack picked up the shovel, and walked over to the fire. He poked and prodded it, scooping shovelfuls of embers and turning them over until he came to the skull. Jack threw Bryce the shovel. "You'll have to do it. I loved Morgan, and I'd do anything for him, but I can't bring myself to cave in his skull."

Bryce approached the fire, shovel in hand, and stared into it for a time. Then he dropped the shovel and wiped the sweat from his forehead with his arm. "Me, neither."

"Well, it's not much better to send it bouncing down the ravine."

"You could always bring it home and put it on the mantle. Morgan might have liked that."

"Cyrus wouldn't."

"Oh, of course not. Sorry. Maybe we can heat it up further."

"What? No, wait—"

Bryce picked up the gasoline can and emptied the contents over the bone cage that once held Morgan's brain.

An intense flash burst forth, engulfing Bryce.

Jack grabbed the blanket and threw it over him, pushing him to the ground.

Bryce uttered a muffled, "I'm all right, let me up."

Jack uncovered him and studied his face. "Well, your skin appears no worse than a sunburn, but your eyebrows are gone, and your hair is singed."

Bryce sat up. "Let's not mention this to the women."

"Bryce, they're going to know as soon as they see you."

"We'll stop somewhere on the way home, and I'll wash up."

"That's not going to grow your eyebrows back."

# CHAPTER 49

It was daybreak before the fire was out.  Jack dug through the ashes and found no signs of a skull.  Bryce's gasoline trick must have worked.

He brought the washtub from the truck and he and Bryce scooped the ashes into it with shovels.

"Careful, Bryce, you're getting the sand, too."

"It won't hurt. Morgan always had grit."

Jack scraped the last bits of gray and black from the ground.  "Not that much of a man remains. I'd imagined there'd be more."

"Yes, a small pail would have been sufficient.  But how could we know? We'd never done this before."

Jack set the washtub in back of the truck. "Bryce, gather those blankets and wrap the tub with them so the ashes won't blow out as we drive.  Morgan never asked to be scattered along the roads of Taos County."

Jack started the Model T, and they headed back to the house to pick up the women so they could all ride up to Morgan's thin place together.  A pink flare of sunrise glared on the windshield, making Jack squint.

The incoming morning air was cool, so Bryce closed the window. "When's the last time you and Abigail took a trip together?"

"Does the dance at the Grange Hall last week count?"

"No, I mean away from Taos, overnight."

"Probably our honeymoon in Santa Fe?"

"That was what, seventeen years ago?"

Jack shrugged. "Life has its way of living itself for you. Next thing you know, decades slip past."

"Yes, but grief has a way of pulling people down as well. You don't want that to happen to Abigail."

No, he certainly did not. His poor sweet Abigail. He'd been so obsessed with pretending Morgan wasn't dying, he'd failed to realize what it must have been like for her. Now, he saw it. Abigail, beautiful as one of those goddess sculptures architects use for pillars on building entrances. But keeping the ceiling from falling in on everyone else is too much to ask of anyone. Jack shook his head.

Bryce was still talking. "Cyrus and Cherie are going to New York with Peaches. I'm traveling with them and then heading to Boston to meet this Swami Yogananda. That leaves you and Abigail kicking around this huge empty place, bumping into memories of Morgan at every turn. That's no good for either of you."

Nothing about Morgan's absence would be good. Abigail wasn't a widow, but losing Morgan would certainly seem like it to her. And Bryce was right. There wasn't a corner of their property, or a place in Taos, that wouldn't remind him of something Morgan did or said.

"Come east with us. Call it a well-deserved vacation or a second honeymoon. Get a little reprieve from this place, and you'll both come back happier."

"Abigail will never go for it. She's got her business to run."

"It can't hurt to ask."

Jack didn't respond and Bryce didn't say anymore. In the silence, Jack drummed his fingers on the steering wheel. The last few years, Abigail had constantly dealt with three men in crisis. Yes, him, too. With Morgan and Cyrus both gone, there was going to be a sudden void. Everything she'd done every day wouldn't need doing.

He glanced at Bryce. Going to Boston to meet a swami wouldn't appeal to Abigail, but getting out of Taos for a while might be a smart idea.

Jack pulled in the driveway. He and Bryce wiped their feet on the mat and entered the house. Though the hour was early, the women were up, dressed and drinking coffee at the dining table. When they saw Bryce's condition, all three women began to fuss over him. Peaches undid his scorched shirt to check him for additional burns. Abigail wiped his face and arms with a cool cloth then proceeded to slather cocoa butter on him until he smelled like a Hershey's bar. Cherie clipped burnt ends from his hair. "I'm not very good at this. You're going to need to see a barber."

"You're also going to need a story," Jack said. "We can't tell anyone how this really happened."

"No, they'd think I was an idiot."

"Only because you were." Jack took Abigail in his arms and kissed her. "Haven't you slept?"

"No, we didn't know what time you'd get here."

"We'd have woken you."

"I know, but we couldn't sleep. We had things to talk about."

"Like what?"

"Mostly Morgan. We women do things differently than men. We need to talk our feelings out, it's our way."

"Cyrus, too?"

"No," Cherie said. "I put him to bed as soon as we got home. He gets over things by not talking."

Bryce brushed bits of hair from his shoulders. "Men talk. Didn't we Jack?"

"About yoga or constellations by any chance?" Peaches said.

"How did you—?" Jack said.

Abigail yawned. "She knows you guys pretty well."

"As a matter of fact," Bryce said, "we talked about you and Jack coming east with us."

"Oh, we couldn't do that," Abigail said.

"Not a reason in the world not to," Bryce said. "Get away for a vacation. Give yourselves time to heal someplace where every bend in the path doesn't remind you of Morgan."

"You can stay with me," Peaches said. "You've never seen my place. It's right in the heart of Greenwich Village."

Abigail shook her head. "We have things to take care of here."

Cherie clasped Abigail's hands. "Cyrus and I are leaving. You and Jack will be all alone here. Come to New York and see our ship off. Wait, better yet, sail with us. I'll show you Paris."

"Impossible. We've never been out of the country. We don't even have passports."

"You can get them in New York."

Abigail bit her lip and rocked back and forth.

Jack kept his mouth shut and watched the dynamics. It was going to have to be up to her.

Cherie gave Abigail's hands a squeeze. "I need to wake Cyrus, anyway. Should we ask him? I'll bet he'd like a few more months with you."

"We can talk about this in the car," Bryce said. "We should go now."

"Don't you want baths?" Peaches said.

"When we get back."

"At least let me get you a clean shirt." Peaches left to get Bryce a shirt.

Cherie went to wake Cyrus.

Jack took a sip of Abigail's coffee. "There's not much of Morgan left. We can all go in your car. I'll meet everyone outside." Jack left to strap the blanket-wrapped washtub onto the back of the Pierce-Arrow.

* * *

Cyrus drove them and parked the car in the place they'd come to with Morgan a few days before.

Jack carried the washtub to the edge of the cliff and set it down. "The other day Morgan said, 'We shall never be together in this place again.'" Jack peered into the tub of ashes. "Well, old friend, as it turns out, you were wrong. Here we all are, back at your thin place."

"How should we do this?" Bryce said. "Have everyone throw some of him off the cliff?"

Cyrus took a step back. "You and Jack do it."

Bryce looked at the women. "Anyone else?"

They shook their heads.

"Is it all right if I read a little poem first?" Bryce opened a book he had with him. "It's by a Hindu poet named Rabindranath Tagore."

I stand under the golden canopy of thine evening sky and I lift my eager eyes to thy face.

I have come to the brink of eternity from which nothing can vanish—no hope, no happiness, no vision of a face seen through tears.

Oh, dip my emptied life into that ocean, plunge it into the deepest fullness.  Let me for once feel that lost sweet touch in the all-ness of the universe.

"Nice," Jack said.

Cherie and Peaches fell into Abigail's arms, all three of them weeping.

Jack grabbed one handle of the washtub and motioned for Bryce to pick up the other side.  They tipped the lip of the tub over the ledge and gave it a firm shake.

An updraft blew the ashes back on Jack, but somehow they missed Bryce.

Jack brushed himself off.  "Morgan, when you asked me to do this, you didn't tell me you were going to fly back to haunt me."

# CHAPTER 50

Back at the house, Abigail filled two copper kettles to heat Jack's bathwater. While she waited for the water to boil, she went into the bathroom to fill the tub for him. But when she turned on the faucet less than a half-gallon sputtered out.

"Jack, cistern's empty."

"Understandable, there's been a lot more people taking baths. Nothing to do about that but carry in water from outside until it rains again."

Jack went outside and returned a few minutes later with a bucket of water he emptied into the tub. "Pump is squeaking. Remind me to oil the handle."

Abigail nodded. Jack kissed her and left to get another bucket of water. She took a spoon from the silverware drawer, got a water glass, and opened the icebox to see if there was any lemonade left. If not, she'd have to make more. Morgan preferred his medicine mixed in something rather than straight out of the bottle.

Wait. Morgan was . . .

Her legs felt weak. She held onto the icebox door and stared into the logjam of leftovers crammed into every nook and cranny.

Abigail shut the door and leaned against it. Well, she wouldn't have to cook for a week at least. She picked up Morgan's prescription and tossed it in the trash can. Done with that, too. A sob wracked her body, and she started to bawl.

The bucket banged against the backdoor as Jack opened it.

She covered her face with a dishtowel, choked down her emotions, and wiped her eyes. Jack didn't need to see her falling apart. One of them would be enough.

She heard water pour into the tub and Jack passed behind her as he returned to the pump. She kept her back to him and busied herself, checking to see if the kettles were near boiling. Jack! What would become of him now that Morgan was finally dead? They'd been closer than brothers since they were schoolboys, sharing everything, even her. Now it felt like they'd lost a limb. No, more, a part of their selves. How would Jack handle that? Fall to the bottom of the beer barrel?

She didn't think so. Jack would definitely drink. Jack always drank. But he'd never get lost in it.

Then she had a terrible thought, what if he crawled into himself, like Cyrus had been before Cherie came?

It was all on her to prevent that. No one else could do it.

Suddenly bone tired, she wished she could go to bed and sleep for a week. It was nice that everyone had come for Morgan, but now, if they would just leave . . .

Then again, she and Jack could never eat all this food.

The kettles boiled. Jack reached around her and turned off the burners. He picked up one, and she the other. They carried them into the bathroom and poured them into the tub, raising clouds of steam. Jack set his kettle on the floor and stripped off his shirt. Abigail reached down into the tub and swirled her hand to mix the water. "Just right."

Jack took her kettle from her and set it next to his. She stood up. He closed the bathroom door and began unbuttoning her dress.

"Jack!"

"Ssshhh . . ." He nuzzled her neck.

"I already had my bath. While you and Bryce were—you know, before we took Morgan's ashes." Her shoulders began to quake, and she let out a sob.

His arms enveloped her and he squeezed her tightly against him. Swaddled in his embrace, she calmed.

"So what if you've bathed," he said. "The water is hot, and tub is big enough for two. It'll relax you."

She kissed him and wiggled free. "Jack, we're not twenty anymore."

He grinned. "You can wash my back."

She gave him a wry smile. "I know where this is going. I've taken baths with you before." Her smile turned into a frown. "It's too soon. I'm not ready."

"Ready for what? We'll just have a soothing bath together. That's all. I need an hour in the tub with my wife to soak away the last few days' events. And so do you."

Maybe. Maybe if she listened carefully, he was telling her how to help him get over Morgan. She let her dress drop to her feet and shucked her undergarments. Jack finished undressing and stepped into the tub. Abigail took a bottle of lavender scented bubble bath from the shelf and stirred some into the water.

"You're going to make me smell like a girl."

"That would be a step up."

"You're right. Get in."

She settled between his legs with her back against his chest. A sense of warmth and peace enveloped her. She leaned her head back into the hollow below his collar bone and closed her eyes.

He turned his head and kissed her temple, letting his lips linger. She smiled. He tipped his head back against the wall and they sat, immersed in silence, for a long while.

Abigail lifted her hand from the water and noticed the skin on her fingers had pruned. She had no idea how long they'd been in here. The bubbles were gone and the water cool. It must be past time for breakfast. Yet they hadn't heard anyone come into the kitchen—probably still asleep. It'd been a hell of a night. A hell of a week, now that she thought about it. "We should get out."

Jack cupped his hands and raised them above her thighs, making tiny waterfalls trickle over her legs. "Why?"

"I don't know. Start breakfast, I guess." Actually, she couldn't eat a thing.

Jack wrapped his arms around her waist and squeezed her. "We're the only ones up."

She put her hands over his arms and hugged him back. "I think you're right."

"Let's let them sleep in."

She snuggled into his embrace and felt her muscles relax. She had a good man in Jack.

Jack dipped his hands in the water and, when he lifted them out, began gently washing her arms. "I saw that you put Morgan's morphine bottle in the wastebasket."

Abigail stiffened. "This morning I started to prepare his medicine out of habit, and realized I'll never do that again." A stray tear made its way down her cheek. She scooped up water and splashed her face.

Jack kissed her wet cheek. "Bryce is right. We're going to find memories of Morgan in every corner of this place for a long time to come."

She made a half turn so she could see his face. "Can you handle that?"

"Sure, I'm tough."

*Not about this, and neither am I.*

Jack wet a washcloth and began washing her back. "But . . ."

"But?"

"We ought to take some time. Go east when the others do."

"Oh, Jack, I don't think so."

"You've never seen New York. I could show you the sights, the Statue of Liberty, and take you to the place I grew up."

"Is that one of the sights?"

"Probably have a statue of me there by now."

She laughed and flicked water in his face with her fingertips.

"From there, we'll do like Cherie suggested, and sail with them. I've never seen Paris. She could show us the sights."

"Now you're going too far." But was he? She'd realized earlier that he might tell her in his own way what he needed to cope with losing Morgan.

"Money's not a problem, and you're going to miss Cyrus, just like you did when he went to war."

"No, this time I'm not worried about him getting killed."

"True." Jack soaped the rag and began washing her all over.

"Hey, I thought it was your back you wanted washed."

He handed her the soap and washcloth. "Well, get to it."

The water was cold now, but neither of them cared. Abigail took a pitcher from a shelf, scooped up bathwater, and emptied it over his head. She reached for the bottle of Watkins Mulsified Cocoanut Oil Shampoo, poured some in her palm, and washed his hair. When she'd rinsed it twice, he said, "So, let's go."

"Not yet, I haven't rinsed the rest of you."

"I mean go with the kids. Go east, young woman."

"We can't just pack up and take off, Jack. What about your delivery business? You wouldn't leave the merchants hanging."

"I'm thinking Billy could drive in my place while I'm gone."

"Billy?"

"The pharmacist's son. He's dogged about finishing a delivery, very reliable."

"He's only a kid."

"He's sixteen, old enough."

"I couldn't possibly go before I made arrangements for my business interests."

"You've got plenty of time for that, and you've got good managers in place already. Billy needs more driving lessons, and I'll have to show him the way to Santa Fe. Besides, the others aren't leaving until Bryce and I build crates and pack all those paintings."

Morgan's artwork. Yes, after seventeen years together, he was everywhere. She stood up, grabbed a towel and dried off.

Jack looked up. "Does that mean bath time is over? Promise me you'll consider it."

She stepped out of the tub, wrapping the towel around her. It seemed unlikely she'd be able to think about anything else.

# CHAPTER 51

Jack stood behind Abigail with his arms wrapped around her as they looked out over Paris from the top of the Eiffel Tower. Cherie and Cyrus were nearby, similarly entwined. It was certainly true, Paris was the city of love. He was glad they had come.

This was the second time they'd been atop the Eiffel Tower. The first time was a week ago, their first morning in Paris. He and Abigail were still in bed when a cute little French maid had knocked on their door to deliver breakfast on a tray. "Madame, Monsieur, la petit déjeuner."

"Mercy," he said.

"Jack, it's merci," said Abigail from the bed.

Breakfast in bed consisted of orange juice, a flaky pastry called a croissant served with butter and strawberry jam, and the most delicious coffee he'd ever tasted. A man could get used to this.

Once they'd eaten and dressed, Abigail went to Cherie and Cyrus's room to see if they were ready. They were. Cherie said the Eiffel Tower wasn't far from their hotel, and would be their first stop. They walked a few blocks from the hotel and then down a long promenade called the Champ de Mars to the thousand-foot-tall iron tower. Jack had to crane his neck to see the top.

God, Morgan would have loved this.

"The tower has three levels," Cherie said. "We can climb stairs to the first and second levels or take the lift."

"Let's take the elevator," Abigail said.

Cherie patted Abigail's hand. "May as well. We have to take a lift to reach the third level, anyway."

They rode up, changing cars at the second level. The experience was rewarding in every way. The observation platform at the third level allowed visitors to walk completely around the tower, viewing Paris from every side. At nine hundred feet above ground level, it afforded unobstructed views one could have only seen from a zeppelin. Not that Jack had ever ridden in one. Maybe that would be next.

A man sold champagne, and they sipped glasses of the cold bubby wine while Cherie pointed out sights in the distance. What a pleasure it was to be in a city where he could buy a drink anyplace, anytime. As they circumnavigated the third level, Jack compared what he was seeing to a map he had purchased at a tourist stall below. Cherie pointed out the important structures and the various neighborhood districts.

Seeing Paris from the observation deck on the first day was one of the wisest things they had done. It fixed in his mind the layout of the whole city, and since then, whenever he was confused about where he was, he only had to spot the Eiffel Tower and compare its position to his map. Not that he had to do this often. The four of them had usually gone places together, and Cherie knew her way around.

Paris was laid out in twenty arrondissements arranged in a clockwise spiral. It reminded him of a snail shell. Cherie had talked him into eating snails for lunch that first day in the tower—there were restaurants on the first and second levels, and they decided to eat lunch in one of them before they left. The waiter said escargot was a specialty. Abigail declined, but Jack was a good sport. They weren't bad. He'd eaten oysters and clams when he lived in New York. The texture was similar, but unlike shellfish, these critters swam in garlic butter.

A river, the Seine, cut through the city in an L shape. Parisians referred to the arrondissements north of the river as the Right Bank, and those to the south as the Left Bank. He had now been on both sides. That first day Cherie had pointed out Montmartre to the north of them. Situated on the highest point in Paris, the beautiful white-domed Basilica of Sacré-Cœur was easy to spot.

Back in his days at the Saint Louis World's Fair, when he and Bryce and Morgan had met European artists and decided to come to Taos, Montmartre had been home to Monet, Renoir, and Degas. Cherie took them there on their second day.

Morgan would have loved that, too.

Along narrow roads and cobblestone alleyways, a new generation of artists painted en plein-air. Others had studios tucked into century-old buildings. They strolled among the painters and complimented their work. Jack wondered if their friends from Taos, Ernie Blumenschein, Bert Phillips, and Joseph Henry Sharp, had once stood on these streets, painting. Maybe that girl over there leaning against a doorframe, or that couple walking through the garden? Montmartre was lovely, but seeing all the painters couldn't help but bring back memories of Morgan and a feeling of despondency began to overtake their group. They left there and Cherie took Abigail to buy new hats.

Paris had an abundance of wonderful art museums, but Cherie said they'd avoid paintings for the time being. The third day they visited the Musée Rodin—sculpture rather than painting. Jack loved it and rated it one of his best memories. The museum was the master sculptor's house, and inside were several of his great pieces, plus many smaller items he had made while working out the shape of a foot or a hand that he later enlarged when he did the full-size sculpture.

A larger-than-life plaster statue of a man wearing a heavy monk's robe caught Jack's eye. The face was by no means handsome, but the long hair and deep-set eyes carried . . . gravitas. Jack read the plaque. "Look, Abigail, Balzac. He was the first author your ladies' book club read, back when we had the emporium."

Abigail peered into the sculpted face. "Not as I imagined him. He seems aristocratic, even aloof."

"It says here that Rodin claimed the sculpture portrayed the author's persona, not his physical likeness."

"So, Balzac didn't really look so . . . standoffish if you met him in the street?"

"I guess not. But I don't see him as standoffish. I think Rodin gave him an expression of detachment, distancing himself from his critics."

Abigail tweaked his nose. "Well, hasn't Paris turned you into the art connoisseur?"

"Always admired Rodin, ever since I saw *The Thinker* on display at the St. Louis World's Fair."

"The version originale is just here, monsieur," said a nearby docent, "installed in the museum garden only this year." He pointed toward a door at the back.

"Oh, Abigail, you have to see it."

Cherie and Cyrus joined them and he led them outside. The grounds behind Rodin's house had been turned in to a giant sculpture garden, holding pieces too large for the building. Visitors were free to roam among them or stretch out on the grassy lawn beneath one of the master's works. At precisely noon, a cart appeared selling sandwiches and wine. They ate a picnic sitting in the midst of the world's greatest Rodin collection. As far as Jack was concerned, it just didn't get any better.

Every night Cherie took them to jazz clubs where black American musicians commanded great adoration from the French and repaid their audience with rapid tempo songs driven by a driving bass drum and punctuated with clarinets, trumpets, and trombones. It was clear Cherie was at home in Paris, strutting out her best flapper dresses and fitting right in with the crowd.

Men, including Jack and Cyrus, wore evening clothes to the clubs. Abigail had been shopping, and she and Cherie dressed to the nines. Jack didn't mind. It was only money, and the Parisian clubs were fun. Liquor flowed abundantly, and no one had to look over their shoulder for the police.

When a champagne bottle at a nearby table popped its cork with a loud bang, Abigail dug her fingernails into his hand and kept her eyes on Cyrus. But the boy didn't dive under a table or run screaming from the room. Cherie hugged him close, and that seemed to be enough. The dance floor surged with humanity moving wildly in ways that never would have gone over at the Grange hall in Taos. Cherie and Abigail had dragged the men into the melee, and they'd gone back for more every evening they'd been in Paris.

This morning, well before the maid was to bring their breakfast, Abigail had gone to the toilet. Jack, in that netherworld between half-awake and half-asleep, sensed her leave. Moments later, his dream-self heard her splash water.

The bed gave way as she slid back under the covers, wiggled her arm beneath his shoulder, and rolled him over onto her, kissing him fiercely. He felt dewy drops of water clinging to her pubic hair, and the moistness of her loins. Jack was already in that state of readiness he still woke to and so required no further encouragement to firm his resolve. But he took his time, and she repaid him in soft moans—the first time they'd made love since Morgan died.

After breakfast arrived, Cherie knocked on their door. "We're going to the Left Bank today."

A taxi took them to 12 rue de l'Odéon. The sign read, "Shakespeare and Company." Jack pushed open the door and bumped into a lively brunette woman about Peaches' age. "Excuse me. I'm sorry."

She stuck out her hand. "Sylvia Beach, welcome."

"Hi, Jack Diamond. You speak English!"

"I was born in Baltimore."

He shook her hand and stepped aside so the others could enter. "This is my wife Abigail, our son Cyrus, and his amour, Cherie." Jack looked around. Books were stacked haphazardly floor to ceiling. "Now this is a bookstore. Too bad Bryce can't see this."

"Half bookstore, half lending library," Sylvia said. Her brown eyes danced with merriment.

"Jack used to own a bookstore," Cherie said.

"Oh, really? Where?"

"Taos, New Mexico, it's a tiny mountain town."

"You'll be surprised to learn that I've heard of it. Huxley and Lawrence talked about going there. What's the name of your store?"

Jack turned sheepish. "It's not there anymore. We weren't very good businessmen."

"I'm probably not either. I've just pissed away a year's earnings publishing a book nobody will want to read." A plump, fair-haired woman, a little younger than Cherie, came over to them, and Sylvia introduced them. "This is Adrienne Monnier. She owns the bookstore across the street. These are the Diamond family, visiting from America."

"Actually," Cherie said. "Cyrus and I are planning to stay. Do you know of any reasonably priced apartments?"

"Why, yes, there are several notices on the board over there."

"Sylvia," Adrienne said, "we're about to start."

"Oh, of course. Adrienne is hosting a reading, today. Won't you join us?"

They decided they would, and ended up spending the day with Sylvia and Adrienne, also meeting several British and American writers. After the reading, they returned to Sylvia's store and Jack bought a copy of that book she said nobody would read. While Cherie perused apartment advertisements and selected several possibilities, Jack read a page or two from the book. He decided that Sylvia was right.

# CHAPTER 52

The lovers nestled in the sweet afterglow. Through the open window, sounds from the Parisian streets below drifted into their room on the afternoon breeze. They had returned to the hotel to dress for dinner, but Cherie and Cyrus had stolen a few precious minutes to make love.

"Cherie?"

"Yes, Cyrus."

"You know the Canadian man I introduced you to at Adrienne Monnier's reading?"

"Joe?"

"Yes."

"What about him?"

"We were together in the . . ." Cyrus choked.

Cherie stroked his naked chest with her fingers. "Take a few breaths. Don't hurry it."

After a moment Cyrus mumbled, "Meuse-Argonne Offensive."

"Was Joe in your company?"

"He was with the Canadians. But his unit fought alongside ours. Anyway, he said he's been writing for a magazine in Toronto. Says writing stories about what we went through helped him."

"Good for him."

"I think I might try that."

"Writing?"

"Yes."

That was unexpected, but why not? "Only if you want to."

"I think I do. But can we afford it? I doubt the job Miss Beech offered me in her bookstore will pay enough."

"They say two can live as cheaply as one. I managed for years on a minimal stipend from Peaches. And that will still be coming, after all."

"Yes, but you always had men buying your drinks and dinners."

"Good point, but I'm done with that. Not that I'm giving up being a flapper, but I'm yours exclusively from now on."

Cyrus scratched his jaw. "I've never supported anyone before."

"I can contribute, too. I'm sure the manager at Printemps would hire me to dress his mannequins." He'd effusively praised her flair for creating pleasing clothing ensembles when she and Abigail shopped there earlier this week. When she told him she'd worked there before, he offered her a job. The new metro station at Havre-Caumartin was scheduled to open next year. That would make getting to work a snap.

"What about the piano?"

Piano? Cherie stopped her woolgathering. "I'm sorry I was thinking of something else. What were you saying?"

"I said, if we could get a piano, I could give lessons. I'm a little rusty, but I studied for nine years. That's more than enough to teach scales to the American writers' snot-nose kids."

Cherie laughed. "You won't get any students if their parents hear you call their children that. Besides you might be one of those writers with a snot-nose kid."

Cyrus sat up abruptly. "Cherie! You're not—"

"God, no. I'm just pointing out that soon you'll be a writer, and maybe someday we'll start a family."

Cyrus furrowed his brow. "I'm not ready for that."

She kissed him. "Me, neither, so that works out well, then."

A knock on the door, Jack's voice on the other side, "You kids ready to go yet?"

"Go ahead without us. Cyrus and I are going to look at an apartment first. We'll meet you at that café on the Avenue des Champs-Élysées where we had supper the first night we arrived. Do you remember how to find it, or shall I write down directions."

"Nah, I've got a map in my head. What time should we meet?"

"Let's say seven o'clock. Do you think that gives us enough time, Cyrus?"

Cyrus shrugged. "You know Paris better than I do."

"Seven it is," Jack said through the door.

Cherie heard him walk away. She got out of bed, hovered over the bidet, and washed herself. She dampened a washcloth in the sink and wiped her face and underarms. Picking up a tortoise-shell comb, Cherie smoothed her bob as she walked over to the bed. She leaned down, kissing Cyrus on the lips. "We better get a move on."

Cyrus grazed the side of her naked breast with his fingers and rubbed his thumb in a circle over her nipple. "I love you."

She pushed his hand down. "I love you, too, but we're done playing for the moment. The landlady said to meet her at five-thirty." He touched her thigh, and she stepped out of reach. "I'm going to change your name to Randy."

"Aw, you're no fun."

She grabbed his shirt off the chair and threw it to him. "I'm loads of fun, and you know it."

# CHAPTER 53

Summer light in Paris seemed to linger even after city lights came alive. Jack and Abigail were sitting at a small round table outside a café on the Avenue des Champs-Élysées admiring the Arc de Triomphe further up the road. He was drinking a cold beer and she a glass of Bordeaux. They were on the Right Bank awaiting the return of Cherie and Cyrus who had gone to the Left Bank to see about renting a place.

Jack didn't speak much French. Bonjour, oui, merci and s'il vous plaît pretty much capped his list. So far it hadn't been necessary as they relied on Cherie to negotiate their needs. Also, the influx of a million American soldiers, two million British troops, plus armed forces from Canada, Australia, New Zealand, and other parts of the British Empire during the Great War had left a lot of French citizens with more than a smattering of English. But Jack, being Jack, took no chances and had the hotel manager teach him how to say beer. It turned out to be simply "beer" pronounced a little funny and spelled oddly on the menu—bière.

He held up his empty glass and wiggled it toward the waiter. "Bière, s'il vous plaît."

"Un moment," the waiter said.

Jack was getting the hang of French.

Two musicians made their way down the sidewalk toward them. One played the smallest accordion thing Jack had ever seen—not much bigger than the body of a toy poodle. Close on his heels followed a violinist. They were playing what Jack could only assume must be a traditional folk song. The men approached and hovered. They weren't bad performers, but Jack had been spoiled by Bryce's ragtime piano and the Paris jazz clubs. What these men played was neither.

Abigail took a coin from her purse.

"No, Abigail, if we pay them they'll never leave."

She pressed the franc into his palm. He handed it to the accordion player, which at least forced the musician to pause while pocketing it. "Bonsoir, now move along." Jack motioned in the direction of the Arc de Triomphe.

"Merci, beaucoup." The men nodded and moved toward the next couple.

Abigail sat silently swirling the wine in her glass.

"Did you want them to stay?"

She furrowed her brow. "No, I was thinking about the kids. I'm glad to see Cyrus on a path to recovery, but . . ."

"But what?"

"Now Cherie is back in Paris, will she stick with another broken man? Or will she get back in touch with her previous lovers?"

"Oh, I don't think that will happen," Jack said. "She wouldn't do that to him. Besides, they're out right now getting an apartment together."

"Well, a mother worries. What if she takes multiple lovers?"

"We managed, didn't we?"

"That was us. Cyrus couldn't handle it."

"Cherie promised not to abandon Cyrus. You have no choice but to believe her."

Abigail pulled on her lower lip. Jack loved that lip. Loved that woman, but hated the worry lines he saw forming on her forehead.

"And he's taken a job helping Sylvia unpack and shelve books. Admit it, it's pretty amazing, Cyrus with a job and a girlfriend. Aren't those the miracles you've spent the last four years praying for?"

She gave a reluctant nod and took a sip of her wine.

Jack tapped his glass to hers, making a pleasant chime. "Two miracles—and all Cherie's doing." He grinned at his wife. "I understand two is enough to qualify a candidate for sainthood."

Abigail laughed. "Cherie's no saint."

"She'd agree with you about that, but I'm glad I could make you laugh. Still, don't you find there's a nice symmetry that Cyrus is getting his first job at a bookstore about the same age as when Morgan and I started our bookstore?"

Abigail looked at her watch and drummed her fingers on the table. "But Paris is so far from Taos."

"Maybe it's what's right for them. We liked Taos because we chose it. Morgan, Bryce, and I moved there on purpose, and so did you. But we all left the places we were born because we felt stifled by them. The Taos we think is paradise probably feels to the kids like somewhere to get away from."

"I know you're right."

"I always am."

She clasped his face with her hands and kissed him on the mouth. When she released him, he put his hand behind her head and kissed her right back.

The waiter caught his eye and winked. "Oui, oui, viva l'amour."

That wasn't the reaction you'd hear in America. But viva la France.

Abigail intertwined her fingers between his and they held hands.

Jack smiled. "I remember when Bryce and Morgan and I first decided to come to Taos back in aught-four. The century just born seemed on the cusp of all that was new and exhilarating. Paris feels very much like that to me now."

Abigail squeezed his hand. "Paris is certainly an exciting place."

"Cyrus and Cherie will be happy here. Paris is the hotbed for their generation."

*fini*

# ACKNOWLEDGMENTS

Thank you to fellow members of Writers Alliance of Gainesville who critiqued the book as I was writing it: Pat Caren, Joy Southwell, Bonnie Ogle, Ken Campbell, Jane Camerlengo, Jolaine Jones-Porkney; my editor: Dave King; my proofreaders: Pat Caren and Cindy Elder; and my beta readers: Sharyl Beal, Scott Camil, Dick Gartee, and Dennis Shuman.

Special thanks to Joyce Orr and Scott Camil for describing to me the too-real symptoms and effects of post- traumatic stress on war veterans. Thanks also to the Taos Public Library for access to their historical archives. Let me also acknowledge use of the following print resources whose copyrights have all expired. "Sheik of Araby" lyrics by Harry B. Smith and Francis Wheeler, published by Waterson, Berlin and Snyder, © 1921; "Toot, Toot, Tootsie (Goo'bye)" written by Gus Kahn, Ernie Erdman, and Danny Russo, published by Leo Fiest, Inc. 1922. Brief portions of Bryce's dialog are paraphrased from *Raja Yoga* by Swami Vivekananda, *Mandukya Upanishad* translated by Swami Premananda, select writings of Katherine Tingley, and *Gitanjali* by Rabindranath Tagor, published by MacMillan Publishing Company © 1916; The flapper on the front cover is by Ellen Pyle, published by *Saturday Evening Post*, February 4, 1922.

Fact: Bayer, a pharmaceutical company, trademarked the name Heroin in 1898. The opiate was sold in the US over-the-counter until 1914 and then continued to be sold by prescription until 1924.

Richard Gartee is an award-winning novelist who has also authored seven college textbooks, five collections of poetry and a biography, *Skating on Skim Ice*. His previous novels include *Lancelot's Grail*, *Lancelot's Disciple* and *Ragtime Dudes in a Thin Place* which won the Royal Palm Literary Award First Place. *Ragtime Dudes Meet a Paris Flapper* also won a Royal Palm Literary Award under its pre-publication title: *A Paris Flapper and the Ragtime Dudes*. Watch for his forthcoming prequel: *Ragtime Dudes at the World's Fair*.

A complete list of available titles, upcoming events, and coming books is available at www.gartee.com where you can also sign up to receive updates on his newest publications as they become available.

If you enjoyed this book, please take a moment to leave a short review on Amazon and/or other booksellers' websites. Reviews help to sell books, and sales help an author to keep writing. You can readily find links to online booksellers' websites by visiting www.gartee.com and clicking on the book cover image.